Diamonds in the Mud

Jill Sanders

GRAYTON

Printed in the United States of America

DIGITAL ISBN: 978-1-945100-97-0

Paperback 5x8 PRINT ISBN: 979-8-326581-30-3

PRINT ISBN: 978-1-945100-98-7

Copyeditor: Erica Ellis—inkdeepediting.com

Summary

When Rayne becomes the lead detective in a high-profile murder case, she's thrown into a world of danger and deception. With the killer on the loose and all eyes on her, she's forced to navigate treacherous waters and stay one step ahead of the game. But when a mysterious stranger comes to town, she finds herself drawn to him despite her better judgment.

Jameson is a seasoned undercover cop who's seen it all, or so he thought. When he's assigned to a small town to take down a major drug ring, he never expects to get caught up in a deadly game of cat and mouse. And he certainly didn't expect to fall for Rayne, the tough-as-nails detective who's leading the charge.

As they work together to bring down the criminals who threaten their town, Rayne and Jameson can't deny the sparks that fly between them. But with danger lurking around every corner, can they risk opening their hearts to each other? Find out in this thrilling mystery romance about two people who find love in the midst of chaos and danger.

Dedication of my 100th book

"Make new friends, keep the old,
one is silver and the other is gold."
–Joseph Parry

My addition to this timeless verse.

"To find a true friend and not another dud,
is like finding a perfect diamond in the mud."
–Jill Sanders

To all of my diamonds in the mud
Thank you for seeing me through some great times and
being there to help pick me up during the not-so-great ones.

To my sisters
Is there anything better than diamonds?
Cuz that's what you all are to me.

To my husband

Thank you for standing by my side through every wild idea and adventure and walking the path with me every step of the way.

To my editor, Erica
We've journeyed through 100 babies and countless words together! Thank you for your unwavering support.

To every single reader who has enjoyed any of my books. Thank you for allowing me to fill your head with my stories. Without you, I would have never reached 100 books.

An important message from the author

As some of my loyal readers may know, right before I started writing this book, I underwent a double mastectomy, and I was awaiting my last reconstructive surgery while I wrote this book.

Unfortunately, I wasn't alone in this battle. Not only was my cousin undergoing the same surgeries at the very same time, but a couple of my school friends had to fight the same battle.

I'm grateful my cousin and I both caught our cancer early enough to avoid the more agonizing treatments like chemotherapy or radiation. Neither of my close school friends was so lucky. Within the same year, the four of us were all fighting a battle that millions of women and men face in their lifetimes.

Invasive breast cancer affects approximately 13%, or one in eight, of US women within their lifetime. These statistics are alarmingly high.

I urge you to take a moment to schedule your yearly

mammogram and/or doctor's appointment while reading this book.

Thank you, and I hope you enjoy *Diamonds in the Mud*.

Prologue

From the case files of the local police department in Avoyelles Parish, Louisiana, dated November 3rd:

"Today at approximately 06:15 a.m. CST, Officers James Lee and Randy Cordova were out on patrol on County Road 56 near mile marker 38 when they pulled onto the highway's shoulder to remove some tree debris in the road from last night's storm.

Officer Cordova claims that roughly five minutes after pulling over, he heard a sound like that of a dying animal emanating from the eastern marsh. The officers worked their way approximately thirty feet into the wetlands and then called for immediate backup when they spotted a child. They were unable to reach the exact spot without sinking into the marsh themselves.

When Chief Roswell arrived, it took the three of them almost half an hour to pull the young girl, estimated to be about five years old, out of the soggy marsh. She had been buried chest-deep in the mud and was covered with bug bites and what appeared to be burns and lacerations.

The child was rushed to the medical center where it

was estimated that she had been stuck in the marsh for more than twenty-four hours. The girl, who couldn't remember her name, was severely dehydrated and..."

The rest of the words in the handwritten report were smudged and no longer legible.

Chapter One

"A real diamond is never perfect."
−Anthony Doerr

Rayne

I finished typing my single-page report and immediately fought the urge to wad it up and chuck it at someone's head.

Who in the hell would do such a thing?

An entire box of puppies, no older than a few hours old, had been tossed into the dumpster behind the Piggly Wiggly on O'Riley Street. Their little bodies were stuck in place due to the tar-like substance that someone had poured all over their fur.

I'd seen a lot in the five years since I'd taken the job as investigations lieutenant at the PD in my hometown of Gemsville, Louisiana, but this was the worst thing I'd ever laid eyes on. The worst kinds of criminals were those who harmed the innocent and weak.

Gemsville was built like a lot of small towns scattered all over the South. The city and county buildings and the old town center were in the heart of the town, which was circled by a large highway. Most of the businesses, schools, and homes were in the inner circle. The Red River ran smack through the middle of the town and was the unofficial separation between classes.

The larger, higher-class homes sat to the east side of the river while the smaller ones were on the west. These rules were set long before I'd been born, and most of the businesses followed them too, except for the businesses directly downtown, which had been renovated in the past ten years or so. Most of them catered to younger crowds in an effort to drive money into the revived location.

Since taking this job in the town I'd been raised in, home of some forty-thousand people, I'd witnessed drug overdoses, spousal and child abuse, and straight-up murders. Still, I knew that the box of dead puppies would be the thing to keep me up at night.

It wasn't even seven o'clock in the morning and my gut was rolling. I doubted I could eat the kolache I'd picked up before getting the call about the dogs.

"Rayne?" Someone knocked on my door, and I jerked my head up from my messy desk. "We got a call." Sherry Ericson, the PD's version of an office assistant, stuck her head in my door. The woman's perfect mocha-colored skin always reminded me that I should take better care of my own skin.

"A call?" I asked, waiting. I knew Sherry did things on her own time. If she was ever in a hurry, that's when I knew I'd better start to worry.

She leaned on my doorway and sighed. "You know the two Bobbys?"

I rolled my eyes. "What'd they do now?"

"Nothing." She shook her head back, sending her beautiful afro swaying. Which reminded me that I was probably due for a hair appointment. How long had it been? A year? I reached up as I waited for Sherry to finish the story and played with the split ends in my muddy brown, straight-as-a-nail hair. "They called in to complain about loud noises coming from the Taylor's last night around one."

This surprised me. The two Bobbys, as everyone in the precinct called them, were Robert Elwood Sr. and Robert Elwood Jr. Over the course of the last ten years or so, the father and son duo had spent more time in the drunk tank than they'd spent in their own beds. What surprised me wasn't the fact that the Bobbys had called the cops, but that they'd called about a noise problem at Henry and Sharon Taylor's residence. The Taylors were Gemsville's very own "It" family. Sharon Taylor had recently been re-elected as the town's mayor, while her husband sat on almost every single board in town, including the school board, the city council, and the boards responsible for planning and building, parks and recreation, and historical preservation. He even sometimes sat in on the police and fire district meetings. The family had their hands in everything that was Gemsville.

The Bobbys' single-wide trailer sat less than five hundred yards from the Taylor's old ten-thousand-square-foot mansion and its pristine ten-acre, perfectly manicured yard. The historic plantation, complete with white marble columns, had been in Henry Taylor's family since the slave trading days. It was a historic gem and also one of the largest homes in the parish.

There were a lot of rumors around town about the Taylor plantation. Some were good and some, like the fact that it was haunted, not so good.

It was a well-known fact that the Taylors never let

common people, such as they considered me to be, into the massive place. Every year during the holidays, they held an elite ball with a very exclusive guest list that included ten other couples either from very wealthy families or of high political station. They never allowed anyone single into the mix, or so the rumors said. There were a few exceptions for coworkers who held power or money, but that was it.

The fact that the two Bobbys had heard a loud noise coming from the place didn't sit well with me.

"So, have a couple uniforms stop by and—"

Sherry sighed and shook her head. "Can't, everyone is out on morning calls already. It's you and the rookie."

I held in a groan. Owen Morrison wasn't really a rookie. He'd been there almost two years. It had taken almost three years of working behind this desk before they stopped calling me a rookie.

"I'll make a call to the Taylors." I reached for my phone only to have Sherry make a tsking sound. "What?" I set my phone back down.

"I tried that. No one answered," she responded.

I frowned. "Okay," I said slowly.

Sherry sighed. "Rayne, I don't want to tell you how to do your job—"

She stopped when I laughed, a dry burst that I hoped would show Sherry just how humorous I thought her statement was. It must have done the job because her eyes narrowed at me and her lips twitched slightly. "Okay, so that's how it is," she said with a nod, sending her hair flying again. "Girl, get your skinny white-as-a-ghost butt out of that chair and drive out to that god-ugly plantation, which is a high-and-mighty symbol of all the Taylor family took from my people decades ago, and check it out in person. I know you're not a beat cop, but you're still a cop. And take the rookie with you."

Before I could respond, she turned on her heels and strolled out of my office.

Damn it. She was right.

I held in a groan and grabbed the paper bag with my now very cold bacon kolache in it and headed out the door.

"Where you off to, boss?" Owen Morrison asked as I walked by. He was one of the Strategic Intel Analysis Officers, or SIAs, under me.

I stopped a few feet from him and narrowed my eyes at the blond man. He was roughly my age, tall and blond. He looked like a Greek god and was sexy enough that there was a line of women hoping to hang on his arm each weekend. Even though he ticked a few of my must-have marks, such as his many tattoos and general bad-boy vibe, I hadn't fallen for his tricks. Mainly because I knew that there was only half a brain under that gorgeous blond head of hair.

"What have you got going right now?" I asked begrudgingly. I didn't want to drag the man with me, but if he drove I might have enough time to eat my cold food.

Owen shrugged. "Nothing."

I nodded for him to follow me. "We're heading out to the Taylor plantation for a Code 415," I threw over my shoulder at him. "You're driving."

While Owen drove, I downed my cold breakfast and scanned through the day's headlines on my phone. By the time we pulled into the long drive to the plantation, which was lined with hundred-year-old oak trees, I was feeling more myself, but the image of the puppies' bodies was still seared in my brain as I climbed out of the patrol car and headed up the long stone pathway to the massive wood and glass doors.

"Jesus, look at this place," Owen said beside me.

"Watch your language, officer," I mumbled just as I rang the doorbell. I knew how stuffy the Taylors were. The family was easily one of the most influential in town, not to mention in the largest church in the county.

I watched Owen straighten his shoulders and quickly cracked my fingers as I waited.

When no one answered, I took a step closer to the door to peer through the etched-glass windows.

"Shit," I groaned. I closed my eyes at the horror I'd gotten a glimpse of just inside the massive entryway of the home. The image of the dead puppies was no longer the most gruesome thing in my mind.

"What?" Owen said from behind me.

Reaching out, I nudged the door with my elbow. I wasn't surprised when the heavy door slid open smoothly.

"Boss?" Owen cautioned.

"Get me a wagon here stat," I said, before stepping inside. "And call the captain," I tossed over my shoulder. "Scratch that, call the Chief," I said upon seeing Mayor Sharon Taylor lying on the gray-and-white Italian marble floor with half of her face missing.

"Shit," Owen groaned behind me. I glanced back just in time to see my officer lose his breakfast outside the front door.

"Clean that up," I barked at him. "After you make those calls."

We both turned when we heard a car pull up behind the patrol car.

Seeing the pink Cadillac, I groaned. It was the same one that Sharon and Henry Taylor drove all over town. In her younger years, long before she or her husband had dipped their toes into politics, Sharon Taylor had sold Mary Kay products.

"Is that the husband?" Owen asked, wiping his mouth with his sleeve.

"Yup. Go make yourself useful and play offensive lineman. Don't let him inside," I added when he narrowed his eyes at me. Then I nudged Owen towards the older man, who was storming up the drive with a very angry look on his face.

Stepping into the home again, I pulled out my cell phone and made the call to the chief of police myself. Instantly, I noticed the temperature change inside. The air must have been turned up high. How much did it cost to cool the massive place? Too much, I thought as the phone rang.

Chief Randy Cordova picked up on the second ring.

"Hey, sweetie." Just hearing his voice made me smile.

"Hey," I said, then I dropped the smile as I turned to the mess that used to be the mayor of the town. "I have a Code 187 at the Taylor residence." I paused. "It's Sharon." I walked over and knelt beside what I assumed was her neck area and felt for a pulse. "DOA," I added.

"Shit." Randy sighed. "Have you secured the scene?"

"Yes," I said just as Henry Taylor burst through the door, pushing Owen into what looked like an antique table, knocking over a massive vase that held more than two dozen long-stem white roses.

I closed my eyes at the sound of the loud crash as Randy screamed in my ear, "What was that?"

"I'll call you back. Just get the crew out here." I hung up the phone in time to catch Henry Taylor from throwing up and passing out all over his dead wife.

"Damn it, officer!" I screamed. "Get this man out of my crime scene."

Owen jumped up and then stumbled forward, keeping his eyes far from the scene behind my shoulder as I pushed the now almost unconscious Henry Taylor into his arms.

"I swear to god, this is the last time I take you on a call," I mumbled towards Owen.

"I'm good with that," Owen shot back as he half pulled, half carried the man back out of the door.

Now there was water from the vase, flowers, and bits of broken vase all over my crime scene. Shit.

Turning around, I crushed one of the white flowers under my boot and sent a silent curse up to the heavens. What in the fuck did I do to deserve this?

Taking several calm breaths, I straightened my shoulders, pulled out my phone, and snapped a few photos of the scene before the spilled water could reach the body. Then I turned on the recording app on my phone and started taking notes. No detail was too small.

I pretty much had photographic memory, but the recordings helped to remind me of small details.

I noted the temperature of the home. The position of the body. What she was wearing. The fact that the front door hadn't been locked or shut all the way.

I glanced around and rattled off a few key notes about items found near her, such as rugs, furniture, and a slipper that had fallen off her foot and was lying almost two feet away.

Then I knelt next to the body and started listing off things about her.

There was black soot on her left index finger, and a small sample of blood under her nails. She might have fought back at one point or it could be her blood. The forensic pathologist would determine that.

There were more than two dozen stab wounds to the chest, face, hands, arms, and legs that I could see. Part of her face was hamburger meat. Could a knife cause such damage?

I glanced around the room for the weapon.

Stepping over more white roses, I knelt beside the body again.

From what I could remember of Sharon Taylor, she'd been a woman roughly sixty years old. She had sandy blonde hair that was always in style and perfectly highlighted, and she dressed in the most expensive fashions.

I glanced down at the simple gray pants, dark black hiking boots, and black button-up shirt that I normally wore. It wasn't that I didn't have style, I just didn't wear it to work. Not when there was a possibility of getting vomit, piss, or blood on me.

Just then, the front door opened. I jerked my head up and was instantly blinded by the flash from a camera. Not the small flashes you have on a cell phone, the real deal. The kind attached to cameras that made a noise when they snapped a picture.

For less than a second, I was blinded completely.

"Owen!" I screamed as I started blinking frantically.

"Shit!" I heard Owen say and then I focused my eyes just in time to see him struggling to pull back a dark-haired woman. I didn't get a look at her face as a mass of long wavy dark hair blocked my view. Still, I knew exactly who it was and held in a groan.

"Detain her," I called out, shaking my head and blinking a few dozen times. "Handcuff her if you have to," I yelled as I rubbed my eyes to force them to focus again. When I could see more than a few inches in front of my face again, I turned back to my job.

Sharon was dressed in a bathrobe. The sexy kind, not your average stay-at-home-and-watch-a-movie-on-the-week-night kind. The kind that said, "You'll like what's underneath."

I pulled the pen out of my pocket and nudged the silk aside. Yup, more silk in hot pink underneath.

I glanced up at the door when I heard shouting, which brought a few questions to mind. Where were their twin boys, Beau and Wyatt. Did they still live at home? I'd gone to school with them. They'd been stars in every sport and members of every club in school, while I'd been a shy kid who had enjoyed dissecting lab animals and working hard for both of my black belts, but I still knew almost everything there was to know about the two most popular boys in my class. Maybe that was the reason that Owen, a blond clean-cut super-jock, wasn't my type? The brothers fit that mold and were, well, spoiled brats.

Why in the hell was the husband just getting home? Were they separated? I hadn't heard any rumors about it. Then again, I wasn't the gossiping type.

I jotted down a few questions in my notepad as I glanced around the room. I stood up and started to head further into the room but stopped when I heard a car door slam outside. I moved towards the door, trying not to slip in the water from the flowers or crush any more roses under my boots.

"Damn it, Owen," I barked when I saw a dark sedan peel out of the driveway.

"She's a slippery one," Owen said with a smirk. I narrowed my eyes at him. "Shit, boss, Sabrina's not going anywhere." He held up a camera.

"Sabrina?" I asked. "Since when are you and DeRouen on a first-name basis?" I narrowed my eyes as Owen looked guiltily at me.

Sabrina DeRouen was the town's hottest on-scene reporter. I'd known the woman for as long as I could remember. She was by far the nosiest person in town. Well, right behind me. At any rate, she had a reputation for not letting up on anything she sank her teeth into. I was the same way, which is why I made a damned good investigations lieutenant.

"How in the hell did she know what's going on here?" I asked.

Owen shrugged. "She said she got a tip that she should head out here from an anonymous caller. I took her camera so we should be good."

I reached up and flipped open the back of the Canon camera. "Yeah, she played you." I pointed out that the SD card slot was empty.

"Shit." Owen ran his hands through his hair. "Sorry, boss."

"Was that Sharon?" Henry Taylor asked from where he sat on one of the cushioned lounge chairs on the massive porch. "Who would have done such a thing to her?" The man ran his hands through his hair.

Henry Taylor was a lot like his sons. Fit, blonde, and for a man his age, very good-looking. Both the Taylors had been fit to my recollection. The rumors were they were looking to buy the twenty-four-hour gym that sat on the outskirts of town.

"Bag that," I told Owen, motioning towards the camera. "You're batting zero, buddy," I warned him. "I'll have your badge if you don't..." Owen's eyebrows shot up and I sighed. "Just because your daddy is the damned deputy chief of police doesn't mean I can't send you to the hole and have you filing papers for the rest of your life," I hissed, and then I walked over and sat next to Henry.

"Mr. Taylor, do you know who I am?" I asked firmly.

The man wiped his eyes with his hands and then nodded. "Detective Rayne."

I nodded. "Then you know my reputation around town." It was meant as a warning, but I could see by the way the man was looking at me that he'd taken it as a promise that I'd catch whoever did this to his wife. "Want to tell me exactly where you were?" He frowned as he looked down into his hands. "Where did you just come from?" I switched tactics.

"The Bayou," Henry mumbled.

Bayou Brews and Blues was one of the many dive bars in town. I knew for a fact that it closed down at one each morning.

I made a show of glancing at my watch slowly. It was a quarter past eight, which meant that the man had been MIA for more than seven hours.

"I..." Henry jerked his gaze up and then added, "Stayed late."

"With?" I asked, understanding his meaning. The handful of waitresses that worked at Bayou's did more than flirt. And since I'd noticed his disheveled appearance when he'd barged into the house, it was very obvious that the man had spent the night in someone's bed.

Henry's eyes jerked up towards mine. "You don't need..." He stopped when my eyebrows arched, then he glanced towards the front door. "This can't get out. It will ruin..." He dropped off, his eyes still on the door. "Shit."

I could see that he'd realized that his marriage had come to a crashing end already. Not because of a scandal stemming from an affair, but because his wife was lying in pieces just inside the front door of their home.

"Yeah, shit," I agreed. "Who?" I asked again.

"Faye," he said finally with a sigh. "Faye Baker. She and I... Well, Sharon and I... we had an understanding." He broke off as a tear slid down his cheek. It wasn't the fake kind either. I'd seen plenty over the years and could tell.

"Right. Do you happen to know who your wife was with last night, for her end of the understanding?" I asked.

Henry shook his head. "There are several possibilities. She didn't tell me who she was with each time. I didn't want to know." He ran his hands through his hair again.

"I'll need names," I said, pulling out my notepad and pen, and handing them to him. "Phone numbers if you have them."

He took the pad and pen and, as he wrote, I noticed how badly his hands shook. This was a man who was either seriously emotionally affected by his wife's death or scared. I hadn't made up my mind yet which.

"We'll need you down at the station," I started just as several cars pulled into the long drive. "You can ride with Owen." I stood up, tucking the pad and pen back into my pocket.

Henry stood and watched the cars park beside his. "When can I..." He motioned back towards the front door.

"I'd suggest you get a room down at the Cypress Inn for a few days." I turned away from him and nodded at the chief of police as he strolled up the stairs on the porch. "You didn't have to come all the way down here, Chief," I pointed out as he stopped in front of me.

Randy Cordova stood for a moment and smiled at me. The man's silver hair had always been cut short. His silver-blue eyes shone with kindness and most of the time with humor. His smile was addictive to everyone who knew him. The man had a way of making everyone, especially me, relax.

"Hi, sweetie," he said finally and wrapped his arm around my shoulders as he nudged me aside so Owen and Mr. Taylor could pass by. "Henry," he said to the man with a nod. Henry, for his part, nodded his respect and kept following Owen. We both stood in silence for a moment. Then he turned back towards me. "I figured I'd better make an appearance with a case this big." He shook his head while he watched Owen helping Henry into the back of his patrol car. The man was pale and shaken. "He doesn't look to be holding up well. Was he here?"

"Nope, arrived less than five minutes after we did." I motioned as we stepped up on the porch. "That's Officer Morrison's mess there." I pointed to the pile of vomit outside the door. "And that's Mr. Taylor's," I said, stepping over the other man's mess just inside the door. "This mess" —I waved towards the water, broken vase, and crushed flowers—"is thanks to the son of the man you made your deputy."

Randy sighed. "Shit."

"Yeah." I shook my head.

"He sure did make a mess," Randy said, stepping over the flowers. "Shit," he said when he saw Sharon.

"Yeah," I said again, moving beside him.

"Well, detective, where do you want me to start?" he asked me.

"Dad," I groaned as I rolled my eyes. "Get the hell out of my crime scene," I begged.

Randy smiled. "There's my girl." He patted me on the shoulder and walked towards the door. "I expect you to keep me updated," he called as he stepped out the door.

Chapter Two

"Let us not be too particular; it is better to have old secondhand diamonds than none at all."
—Mark Twain

Rayne

For the next few hours after returning to my office, I interviewed everyone in the Taylor family. Henry Taylor was the perfect picture of a grieving husband. Even though he had been with another woman the last night of his wife's life, he played the part perfectly.

I knew there were people out there that had open marriages and, even though it was extremely difficult for me, I had to let that slide. What I saw was a man who was in complete shock that his wife was gone.

The way he'd been when he'd seen her lying on their entryway floor... there was no faking the horror in his eyes.

The two Taylor boys, Beau and Wyatt, came into the station for their interviews at different times. Beau had been in Lafayette for a week for a job and had rushed home hours after finding out about his mother. His alibi checked out, and I was fairly sure the guy was more pissed at whoever had dared to do this than he was grief-stricken at the loss of his mother. But I knew anger was a step in the recovery from losing someone so violently.

Wyatt had spent the night with his on again, off again girlfriend Clara Mangrum. Clara worked at the station in the Standards and Accountability office. I didn't know where exactly, either Internal Affairs or records.

Before I even had a chance to contact Wyatt to have him come in for an interview, Clara knocked on my office door. The woman's short brown hair was cut in that new style all the newly graduated girls wore.

I didn't know much about her other than she was roughly nineteen or twenty. The Taylor boys were my age, which meant there was easily a ten-year difference.

"Got a sec?" Clara asked.

I motioned to the chair across from my desk. "Shut the door," I said and waited until she settled in the seat.

"Wyatt was with me last night. The whole night," she blurted out.

"Okay." I waited.

"I saw you meeting with Beau, and the whole town is talking about his mother's death, so I figured you'd be calling Wyatt next," she added.

I nodded. "I was just about to call him in."

She smiled. "Now you don't have to." She started to get up, but I held my hand up, stopping her.

"I'll still need to talk to him personally," I said and motioned for her to sit back down. "Plus, I'll need more details from you." I flipped open my notepad while she sank back in the chair.

"I'll need your address," I asked.

Clara rattled off an address on the east side of town.

The Taylor's plantation sat directly outside the highway circling Gemsville, to the northeast. Not a long drive from Clara's house.

I'd pegged her from the first day as having been raised with money. The clothes she wore, her hairstyle, and the fact that she always had diamonds in her ears weren't the only clues. She walked and talked like someone who had done everything she could to avoid letting anyone know she was from a small town in Louisiana.

"Do you live there alone?" I asked.

"Yes," she answered. I raised my eyebrows at her. "My parents summer in Maine."

I narrowed my eyes at her. "And they live in Gemsville the rest of the time?"

She sighed. "No, they bought a winter home in Florida last year after I graduated."

I nodded. "They left you the house?"

She shrugged. "They haven't sold it out from under me, if that's what you're asking."

"Are you going to college?" I asked.

She shrugged again. "I was going to community college, but after getting this job and..." She dropped off.

I waited. "Go on," I said when she didn't continue.

She sighed. "After I started seeing Wyatt, I dropped out."

"Any reason?" I asked.

"Wyatt is important to me," she said, and once more I waited for more details. "He doesn't like to date women smarter than he is."

I chuckled and then balked when I realized she meant it.

"Seriously?" I asked.

She nodded. I rolled my eyes and could tell that she was embarrassed at her admission.

"What time did you and he meet up yesterday?" I asked, trying to focus on the questions.

"After I got off work. We went to Louie's for dinner."

Louie's was an upscale restaurant that sat on the banks of the river. Most nights there was music on the patio and deck area that hung over the water's edge. Still, the place charged more for a burger than I wanted to pay, so I didn't normally frequent the joint.

"How long did you stay?" I asked.

"Until the band stopped playing, around midnight. Then we headed to my place. I tried to convince Wyatt to move back in with me..." She shook her head, sending her spiky hair to sway. "He was there until he got the call from his dad this morning about what had happened."

I had a few more questions for her but my phone rang and she motioned that she had to get back to work.

When Wyatt came in half an hour later, he corroborated Clara's story down to every last detail. He had the appearance of a grieving son, emotions that I was sure his brother would eventually reach. The fact that Wyatt was further along in the healing process didn't surprise me. Wyatt had always been a few steps ahead of Beau in life.

After I had the immediate family interviews done, I knew there was one major loose end I had to tie up, so I took a stroll down the street to Sabrina DeRouen's office at the local newspaper building.

"Got a sec?" I asked her when I knocked on her office door.

Her eyes narrowed and she nodded slowly at me.

"Good." I smiled and moved to stand next to her.

"Stand up, hands behind your back." I pulled out my handcuffs.

"You are not doing this." She groaned.

My smile grew. "Sure I am." I waited.

She took a deep breath and then shook her head. "Why? For taking a picture?"

"You were on my crime scene moments after I arrived. I'd like to know why. For now, let's call it trespassing. Oh, and bring the drive from that fancy camera you carry around."

"You have my camera," she pointed out.

"And you have the drive." I held up the cuffs. "Coming?" I tilted my head and remained silent.

"Rayne," she groaned.

"We can do this the hard way?" I wiggled the cuffs. "Or we can just take a little stroll. I seem to remember outdoing you on the mats last time we sparred. You're still a brown belt?"

She narrowed her eyes. "I quit karate when we were thirteen."

"Still." I motioned for her to stand up and turn around.

"This is stupid." She threw her hands up and stood, motioning for me to lead the way.

"Everything okay, Sabrina?" Larry, the editor of the paper, asked from the doorway.

"Just taking Sabrina in for a few questions," I said cheerfully as I put my cuffs back in my pocket.

"You girls really should learn to get along again," Larry said, shaking his head.

"This isn't necessary," Sabrina said as we walked down the sidewalk together.

"Sure it is. Do you know why?" I asked as I held the door to the station open for her.

"Why?" Sabrina asked.

"Because you embarrassed me by sneaking onto my crime scene," I answered as I ushered her towards one of the interview rooms. "I'd like to know how you knew to be there."

I motioned for her to get comfortable. When she sat down in the chair, I smiled and said, "I'll be back."

I walked out of the room, making sure the door was locked behind me, and grabbed a cup of coffee. I enjoyed every sip of the foul-tasting mug before walking back into the room half an hour later.

"You're a child," Sabrina said when I finally sat across from her.

"I need that camera drive," I said in return.

"What drive?" Sabrina smiled.

I laughed.

Sabrina DeRouen was my best and worst enemy. I think we butted heads because we were so much alike. I appreciated her smarts, her wit, and her strength. I'm sure she felt the same about me.

We had been close friends when we were younger. I liked to think we still were. Only, the friendship we had was nothing like the one I had with anyone else in town. We seemed to feed off one another. Yin and yang. The connection of complementary forces connected by the common goal of doing right in the world.

I had become a cop while Sabrina had turned to telling the world the hidden truths.

"Why were you at the Taylor's this morning?" I asked.

"I followed you and Owen," she answered quickly. My eyebrows rose slightly. "Officer Morrison."

"Why?" I asked.

"You don't go out on many calls. When you do, it tends

to be... newsworthy. I've followed you on a few other calls that ended up helping me build my career." She leaned on the table. "I followed a hunch and it paid off."

Yeah, I knew Sabrina often followed me around town. This morning, however, since I hadn't been driving, I hadn't noticed or even looked out for her bright blue Honda in the rear mirror.

"Where were you last night up until you walked into my crime scene?" I asked.

Sabrina leaned back in the chair and took a moment to answer.

"Nowhere near the Taylor's place. I worked at the office until around nine. Went home, alone, and was back at my office around six. When I knew it was going to be a slow workday, I headed across the street for coffee and a muffin. I spotted you and Owen heading out and took a chance." She tilted her head. "How many suspects do you have?"

"You don't get to ask questions," I pointed out. "You were seeing Beau Taylor at one point," I said, looking down at my file.

Sabrina laughed. "In junior high school. Up until I found out he is a narcissist."

"What about Wyatt?" I asked.

She shook her head. "He has a whole different set of issues that I didn't want to try fixing."

"The drive?" I said, holding out my hand.

It was another half an hour before she finally coughed over the drive and I released her to go back to work. It was obvious that she had nothing to do with Sharon's murder. Still, I admired her strength and persistence as she peppered me with questions.

At this moment, I had to keep my cards close to my chest. A murderer was lurking in the shadows of this town, fully convinced they had just evaded justice. Any misstep on my part could unravel the entire investigation just as it was getting started. The thought of not catching Sharon's murderer weighed heavily on me for the rest of the day.

First thing the following morning, as I was scanning over the autopsy reports, Sherry tossed a newspaper on my desk. The image of me kneeling over the mayor's mutilated body was front and center on the cover.

"Son of a..." I dropped off as I scanned the headline and article. "I should have used the cuffs on Sabrina DeRouen." I groaned as I tossed the paper down on my desk.

Sherry chuckled. "You two either need to fight or fuck," she said as she turned and walked out of my office.

I thought of paying the local newspaper office another visit, but my day was stacked as it was. I had more than a dozen interviews lined up. Every single employee in the mayor's office was scheduled to come in and sit with me.

The day after that, the story broke nationwide, and the image of me hovering over Sharon Taylor flashed on every television screen in the world. Some of them blurred the gruesome details out. Others didn't even bother.

In the next few days, I finished interviewing everyone who had ever worked in the mayor's office. The woman's secretary was the one coordinating the funeral arrangements, since she was an old family friend.

In the mayor's absence, Jackson Pennington, the city council president, filled her shoes. I had tried several times to get in to interview him, but I had only been able to talk to his secretary so far.

Everyone else in the city building cooperated with me. Not only because I'd known every one of them my entire life but because they were good people who cared about what had happened.

I had yet to interview anyone down at Bayou Brews and Blues, where Henry Taylor had spent the night his wife was killed.

I had never met Faye Baker before. She, like Clara, was almost ten years younger than I was. I didn't know her from school and I doubted I could pick her out of the handful of other waitresses that worked at the bar. Even though I'd frequented the place, she wasn't one of the waitresses that I knew personally. Yet.

Even though it was too early for most of the staff to be in the bar, I headed down to Bayou Brews and Blues just before lunch.

Kenya Jackson, the manager of the bar, unlocked the door for me.

"Morning, officer." The woman ran her eyes up and down me. "We don't open for another half hour."

"Is Faye Baker around?" I asked, glancing inside. I could see Evelyn Hart, Zoey Thompson, and Autumn Carter, all waitresses, setting up for the day.

"No, she's out for the week." Kenya leaned on the door. "Can I help you?"

"Kenya, we both know why I need to talk to Faye. When will she be working?" I asked. "Better yet, why don't you tell me where she's staying?"

Kenya's smile flashed. "Get a warrant."

"Better yet, how about I get an inspection?" I warned, nodding towards the bar.

"My place is clean," Kenya countered, her eyes narrowing.

"Then you have nothing to fear from an inspection." I waited.

"She lives upstairs." She motioned above her with her

chin. "Third floor." My eyebrows arched in surprise. "But I know for a fact that she's not there today."

Without waiting, I headed towards the iron stairs on the side of the alleyway that led up to the third floor.

I knocked on the door for almost five minutes.

After slipping one of my cards into the door handle with a quick note on the back, I headed back down and stopped when I saw Evelyn leaning against the back door, smoking.

"You have rats," Evelyn said firmly. My eyes narrowed slightly. "The kind that scurry around in the middle of the night. The kind that talk and tell stories they shouldn't," she added.

I understood her meaning instantly. She was saying someone in the precinct was dirty.

"Have any names for me?" I asked.

She tilted her head slightly, then shook it. "No. But I'm sure you can find out how many there are yourself. After all, you're the famous detective that's all over the news right now." She smiled, dropped her cigarette, toed it into the pavement, and walked back inside.

I turned to go and then stopped and flashed a smile.

"Drinking already?" Aria Hartwell, my best friend since, well, as long as I could remember, said as she walked toward me on the sidewalk.

"No, just work," I answered.

Aria was pretty much my opposite in looks. I was a very firm five foot eight inches tall while Aria was a petite five foot even. My long dark brown hair looked dull next to her short spiky platinum blonde style, even with the caramel highlights she'd given me. Then there were my brown eyes, which were dull compared to her shiny sky-blue ones.

Still, our friendship was probably one of the most solid

things in my life. Shortly after graduating, Aria attended cosmetology school and then opened up her own hair salon business, Jazzed Up, which was the sole reason I always had caramel highlights in my hair.

"You didn't respond to my text." She wiggled her bright teal phone in my face.

"I'm working," I replied as I fell in step with her while we headed towards her salon.

"Are you on for this weekend?" she asked, wrapping her arm in mine.

"Maybe," I answered and got an immediate groan from Aria.

"Rayne," she whined.

"What time? Where?" I asked.

"We were thinking of heading to Alexandria. There's this little bar—"

"Nope." I stopped. "What about..." I motioned with my head back towards Bayou Brews.

Aria sighed. "Do you want to stick close to home or is it a work thing?"

"Both," I answered.

Aria rolled her eyes. "Fine, we'll see you there at eight?"

I nodded.

Then she reached up and touched my hair. "You're due for a trim. When you bring your mom in, I'll carve out time."

"I don't know if Edith wants to come in yet," I answered.

Aria's blue eyes turned sad. "I have everything set for her when she's ready. It has to be her decision though." She leaned in and hugged me. "Go, be a detective. Catch a bad guy or girl," she added with a smile.

"See you this weekend," I called out as she let herself into her building.

I glanced around the town and watched people come and go.

The older part of downtown had morphed into a very nice place to be. When I'd been in high school, I could scarcely remember ever wanting to be down here let alone walk on the sidewalk alone.

Back then, most of the old buildings had sat empty or had dusty antique stores in them. There had been a handful of old smoky bars that only the hardest drunks frequented.

Now we had four popular restaurants, more than a dozen little shops like Aria's place, clothing stores, and a home goods store. Two very popular bars had live music and packed out each weekend.

"Hey, Rayne," someone called out as they passed by in a car.

I waved and then walked back to the station. I unlocked my office door and tossed my keys down on the desk. I sat down and glanced around my office. It was a little messy, but I had gotten so caught up in the case that I hadn't taken the time to clean. There were files scattered everywhere, along with several cups of coffee.

I picked up a cup of cold coffee, hoping it was the one from this morning, and quickly chugged down the cold liquid.

I was not even close to solving this case. Usually, I was one of the first people at the station in the morning and the last one to leave.

I took my work very seriously and wanted to do whatever it took to make my fellow officers and my community feel safe.

The murderer had either been very smart and had

covered their tracks or had gotten lucky and left very few clues. My guess was the first one. We were dealing with someone who planned this out. They wanted Sharon dead for a reason.

One thing was clear at this point—this wasn't a crime of passion. Even the gruesome way she'd died, there was an art to it. Each slice was meticulous. Calculated. Precise.

We were still going through all of the fingerprints lifted from the home, but thus far, there weren't any that didn't belong to the family, close friends, or coworkers. Any of them could be the murderer.

The murder weapon hadn't been found anywhere in the home or on the grounds. Since the driveway was part gravel and part asphalt, there weren't any tire tracks to look out for either.

Hell, there wasn't even a muddy boot print to go off.

I scoured the reports until my eyes blurred. Sherry dropped off a sandwich that I'd ordered along with a cold soda from the machine in the lobby area.

I hadn't realized it had gotten so late until Randy knocked on my door.

"Go home," he said, running his eyes over my messy office. "And clean your room," he added with a wink.

"Night." I waved to him as he left.

Standing up and stretching, I accidentally knocked over a stack of paperwork. When I picked up the folder that had fallen, I noticed something odd in one of the files. Someone had gone through it, taking some of the pages and replacing them with blank ones.

After half an hour of glancing through all the files, I realized that they had all been tampered with in some way. I had no idea who would have done this or why they would have done it. My office was always locked. The files were always kept inside a locked drawer or file cabinet.

Only Randy and I had keys. Not even the cleaning crew that came in after hours to clean the building had keys to my office. I normally left my full trash bin just outside for them to empty each evening.

I sat back down at my desk and went through the files, trying to figure out what had happened. I had files on each of the suspects in this case. Files I had worked very hard on putting together since the murder.

The only file that was missing pages was the one on Jackson Pennington. Why his file?

So far, the man was low on my radar to interview in Sharon's death. Yes, he and Sharon worked together in the county building downtown but, as far as I could tell, that was as far as their relationship went.

His prints hadn't appeared anywhere in the Taylor home. Yet.

Besides the fact that they owned half of the town, Pennington's family was a mystery. The man had come into town more than five years back, reeking of wealth. The first thing he'd done was buy up half of the businesses and properties and raise rents everywhere.

I'd never seen the man without an expensive suit on and at least two secretaries following behind him getting anything he wanted. He oozed wealth and knew how to show it off. He wore arrogance as well as he wore his Armani suit.

I pulled up the digital files and compared them to the physical files to see what was missing.

It seemed to be timelines of the man's schedule that I'd gotten from his secretary. One of the reasons I'd put him lower on the list of suspects was because he'd been out of town when Sharon had been killed, which had been esti-mated as between one fifteen and one forty-five in the morning.

None of the missing papers seemed all that important. Not that I could tell, at any rate.

I printed extra copies of the missing papers and replaced them in the files and then finished cleaning up and organizing my office. Then I took the files home with me.

By that weekend, I was seriously running on fumes. With only a handful of clues, which didn't amount to squat, and a very small list of suspects, I was growing frustrated.

Chapter Three

"Life keeps throwing me stones.
And I keep finding the diamonds."
–Ana Claudia Antunes

Jameson

There was little in this world that I hated more than seeing someone mistreat a person who was weaker than they were. Especially when I couldn't do a damned thing about it.

Sitting on a barstool in Bayou's near the back of the smoky bar, I watched Declan O'Malley twist the arm of his latest lady friend behind her back and laugh as she cried out in pain.

"Why so glum, Jameson?" Felix Woolf slapped me hard on the back as he stepped up beside me to order another round of shots for his crew, which filled the entire back room of the bar. I was pretty sure the moment we stepped foot in the dark place, everyone else left out of fear.

I glanced over at Felix and grunted. "Just horny as fuck," I joked. That did the trick. Felix laughed and slapped me hard on the back again. I knew the man had a twisted sense of humor, and sex always made the guy laugh for some reason.

I'd be trying to worm my way into the organization without spooking Felix Woolf for almost a year now. A very long year in which I'd kept the guy off my scent.

Felix Woolf was one of the leaders of the Swamp Reapers Motorcycle Club. The Swamp Reapers had added me to their official ranks after a very long initiation phase that involved, well, more than I wanted to think about at the moment.

Declan O'Malley was a long-standing member of the Reapers and one I wanted to beat the living shit out of one day. The man was a snake. Hell, most of the Reapers were. But Declan was a special kind of snake, the kind that liked to toss around women. His latest victim, Evelyn, worked at Bayou Brews and Blues.

The pretty brunette didn't deserve to be jerked around like this. No woman did. Still, there wasn't anything I could do without catching the attention of either Felix or his right-hand man, Ben Blackwood.

Both men were my real targets.

The other dozen or so members of the Reapers were just collateral damage, as far as I was concerned. Sure, they did the bidding of Felix or Ben. Anytime either man told them to jump, they did so without question.

"Lay off it," Felix barked at Declan when he'd grabbed Evelyn, causing her to drop a tray of beer that she'd been delivering to the group playing pool in the back. "You can fuck with her later on your own damn time. Right now, she's got a job to do keeping us hydrated."

Declan narrowed his eyes slightly at Felix, but then went and sulked in the corner like a kicked dog. The man had zero backbone when it came to dealing with Felix or Ben but sure as hell knew how to throw his weight around with everyone else.

It was my opinion that Declan was trying to weasel his way up the chain of command. He was nothing more than a kiss-ass and a bully. I was pretty sure that both Felix and Ben knew it.

"So..." Felix leaned against the bar as he downed the shot of whiskey he'd just gotten. "Which one are you thinking of fucking?"

I shrugged, trying to play it cool. "Almost anyone. I mean, it's been"—I pretended to count on my fingers—"hours." Felix laughed again. In truth, the last time I'd been with anyone was three goddamned years ago.

My number-one rule was to never mix business with pleasure. I might play a bad guy but there was no way I'd shack up with anyone while lying about who and what I was.

"You know Izzy has had her eyes on you for a while now." Felix nodded to the pretty blonde woman leaning over the pool table.

As if the woman knew we were talking about her, she glanced up and licked her lips at me. Isabella Sinclair, or Izzy to everyone in the Reapers, was not technically a member of the gang since they didn't allow women to join. But she was a staple, along with Nadia Monroe and a few others who came and went. Most of them stuck close to the men they associated with.

Izzy's bright blonde hair currently had hot pink highlights at the ends of the long tresses and was braided back on one side tight to her head. She was covered in tattoos, like most of the people in the bar, including myself.

To be honest, she wouldn't have been my type even if I

was free to play. For the whole time that I'd been stuck in Gemsville, Louisiana, Izzy had done everything she could to get my attention.

"Not my type," I told Felix.

The man laughed. "If you're as fucking horny as you claim, does it matter?"

"I don't see you fucking Nadia, and everyone knows she's been boning for you," I pointed out.

Felix sighed and then motioned for another shot. He held up two fingers and waited. When the bartender set two shots down on the bar, Felix handed me one and tapped my glass. "I'll stay out of your sex life if you stay the fuck out of mine."

"Agreed," I said before downing the shot.

After that, Felix disappeared into some dark corner while I continued to nurse the warm beer I'd been given moments after entering the bar with the rest of the gang.

What in the hell had I done to deserve to be shoved in some backwater hellhole? Two years ago I'd been in the heart of Las Vegas, and before that, I had been in LA for a year or two. That had been my first DEA gig as an undercover special agent in narcotics. That job had lifted me to the heights that I am now—senior special agent. That first sting in LA, I took down fourteen dealers, seven smugglers and runners, and three mules. Unfortunately, the kingpin coordinating more than two million dollars of cocaine and other narcotics slipping through the country had escaped my grasp. So I followed the money and ended up in Las Vegas.

It had taken me a year to snag three more runners and more than two dozen dealers, most of whom had doubled as pimps, and one smuggler who became a victim of human trafficking in the end.

After that bust, I continued to follow the trail and ended up in a small mud pit in a state I knew shit-all about. Louisiana. From my knowledge of geography, the state was only good for Mardi Gras and hurricanes. Hell, I had never even seen a real-life gator until I'd had to catch three of them as part of my initiation into the gang.

The Louisiana accent wasn't hard for me to slip into just as long as I remembered to talk slowly. Besides, I'd been around this bunch long enough that I swore it was rubbing off on me for real. The slower pace of life was a little harder for me to adjust to. Everything in Vegas and LA had moved at light speed compared to the South.

Now, even my Supervisory Special Agent, Jasmine Thompson, joked with me whenever we connected that the South had rubbed off on me.

Though the last time I'd contacted my SSA was a little over two months before.

Hearing more glasses shatter, I glanced over in time to see a feisty long-haired brunette shove Declan up against the wall. The woman moved like lightning. Fast, hard, and with such efficiency, Declan never stood a chance.

"Try that again and you'll be missing a hand," the woman said smoothly.

The fact that she had the man pinned up against the wall had me smiling and, oddly, hornier than I'd been in a while.

Standing up, I made my way slowly towards the pair as I quickly assessed the woman. Five foot eight, maybe one-hundred-thirty sexy pounds, long straight dark hair with a natural tint of auburn. She was wearing black jeans that fit her firm body perfectly and a white button-up shirt covered by a leather jacket that had seen many years of wear. The worn leather-heeled boots she wore probably gave her a couple extra inches.

Declan was trying to break free of the woman's hold. Trying and, from the looks of it, failing.

Even though Declan had almost half a foot on the woman, they probably weighed the same amount since Declan was a skinny son of a bitch.

"Now, listen up," she continued, her tone deadly serious. "If I catch you laying so much as a finger on any woman in my town again..."—with a calculated shift of her body, she pressed her knee against Declan's groin, and he winced in pain—"it won't just be your ego that's shattered."

I was less than five feet from her when Felix gripped Declan's shoulder and yanked him free of the woman's hold.

To my surprise, instead of berating the woman for harming one of his men, Felix pulled Declan away and hauled him out the back door.

I didn't know why Felix decided to retreat, but I was thankful, as I wanted to get a few moments alone with the woman.

"I'm impressed," I said, getting the brunette's attention.

She jerked her gaze towards me. Her dark eyes scanned me from head to toe before she turned away without a word and headed towards the bar.

Being a stupid, horny fool, I followed.

"Not really into talking?" I joked.

She stopped a few feet from the bar and narrowed her eyes at me. Damn, she was hot. Okay, so maybe the few years of celibacy had finally caught up with me.

"Do I know you?" she asked as she slightly tilted her head. "What's your name?"

I smiled. The smile I knew that women liked. The kind that said, no, but if you wanted to know me...

Less than a heartbeat later, she turned away and continued to march towards the bar. I caught up with her right as she ordered a ginger ale.

Then, for some reason, my brain finally caught up with the rest of me. Shit. She's a cop. I should have sniffed it out first thing. If I hadn't been so damned horny and impressed by her pinning that asshole Declan to the wall, I would have spotted it right away.

Hell. Even just talking to her, I could blow everything.

I glanced around the dark bar. Luckily, every single one of the Reapers had followed Felix and Declan outside in retreat.

Deciding to cut my losses, I turned to join them, only to have her grip my arm. Firmly.

"I didn't say you could go," she said smoothly, her voice laced with the natural rhythm of the South. She turned her right shoulder slightly as her eyes ran over me again. "I asked you a question, Yank."

Shit. Double shit. Okay, she was a damned good cop. She'd seen through my fake accent if she knew I was from somewhere up north.

"You do know the North won that war?" I joked and leaned against the bar as I laid on the accent heavy.

Her eyes narrowed. "Thankfully."

"Don't let too many people in these parts hear you say that," I joked.

"You were about to tell me your name?" she motioned with her chin.

I slowly smiled again, stalling, since I oddly enjoyed the look of annoyance in her eyes. "You have to pay the piper first," I said as I wiggled my eyebrows. "A name for a name," I said when she continued to look at me in question.

I held firm. The woman had a look about her. Damn. Where in the hell had she been hiding?

"You're with them." She motioned with her head slightly behind her towards the back door where all of the Reapers had disappeared.

"I am," I said and, for the first time in years, I wished I could drop all pretenses. Damn.

The bartender set the glass of ginger ale down, and the sexy cop picked it up and took a sip. "Do you know Faye Baker?"

I glanced back to where she'd just pinned Declan up against the wall.

"Does this have to do with you going all Rambo on Declan?" I asked, trying to be charming.

Her eyes narrowed, then she leaned closer to me.

God, she smelled like leather and sin. It was too dark and smoky in the bar to see the proper color of her eyes but I just bet they were like bourbon when the sunlight hit them. Her face was something I could spend hours exploring. Even with the all-business look that she was currently giving me, she was sexy as hell.

"I see right through you, you know," she whispered, then she set her drink down on the bar and walked away.

Damn.

I froze.

What in the hell did that mean?

Did that mean she knew who I was? What I was doing there? No. No fucking way.

Before I knew what I was doing, I stormed after her. When I caught up with her, she was asking a waitress about Faye.

I knew most of the waitresses in the place. After all, it was one of the only places in town that the gang hung out at. Faye Baker was a petite waitress with jet-black hair who stood her ground and had a backbone. She had earned the respect of most of the gang, which meant she made big tips when we were in the bar.

She was also a close friend of Evelyn's.

The girl pointed towards the back corner where Faye had been last. The moment the cop turned to head towards the back, I positioned myself so that she would bump solidly into me. However, she was quick enough on her feet to skirt around me.

"I don't play games." She tossed it over her shoulder. I barely heard it over the loud music that was pumping out of the speakers.

When had the place grown so crowded with people other than the Reapers? I suppose I'd been too preoccupied to notice the switch-out of clientele.

We were a few feet from the back when I grabbed her arm, stopping her from walking out the back door. I wasn't positive the gang had left the premises yet. If they were hanging in the alley and she walked outside, well, I didn't want to think of what might happen.

"You don't want to go out there," I warned.

She broke free of my light hold easily enough and glared at me.

"Rayne!" someone shouted from behind me. Then a mass of blonde hair flew past me and hugged the cop. Rayne. An unusual name. Was that her first name or last?

I watched as the pretty blonde woman hugged the cop. Rayne.

"I didn't think you'd come. Tobias and Charlotte swore that you'd be here, but I reminded them that you didn't do bars." The blonde turned slightly towards me and stilled. Then she shocked me by holding out her hand towards me. "I'm Aria Hartwell, Rayne's BFF. She didn't tell me she was bringing someone tonight."

I watched Rayne's eyes widen a little as she tugged on her friend's hand, no doubt to quiet the woman down. Still, this was my opportunity.

With the gang out of there, I could at least flirt. If Felix or anyone else got wind of the fact that I'd been seen with a cop, I could play dumb and tell them I hadn't known. After all, technically, I still didn't know for sure. But after so many years in the field, I could sniff them out. Besides, I had just made a point to tell Felix I was horny, and Rayne was just what I needed at the moment.

I smiled a full toothy grin as I took Aria's hand in mine. The woman's smile was oddly contagious, but I locked eyes with Rayne as I said, "Jameson Lorenzo. Rayne and I just bumped into one another."

Chapter Four

"Just because it looks and shines like a diamond, doesn't necessarily make it one."
–Edmond Mbiaka

Rayne

I thought I knew every single member of the Reapers. I knew everything there was about each of the men who wreaked havoc whenever they rolled into town. Their loud motorcycles weren't a problem, at least not in my book.

I'd had a boyfriend in high school with a Harley and had taken many wonderful summer rides with him. That was up until I caught the SOB cheating and sent him to the curb.

But the Reapers were a special kind of trouble. Somehow, they had a knack for skirting the law, which pissed me off whenever I saw them harass the townsfolks.

The members had enough money to take good care of their bikes, and they spread it around town like they somehow grew the green paper magically on trees. Anytime one of the members did end up staying in the gray-bar hotel, it was usually the drunk tank and they were released once they sobered up. Only once that I could remember had a member gotten in deep trouble and that was the sleazy little man-weasel that I'd pinned against the wall earlier. Declan O'Malley. The man was bad news. Rumors were he'd spent a full year in county lockup for beating a man half to death at a biker bar that sat just across the county line.

As for the rest of the gang, I knew their names, faces, and every single time they'd been in one of my jail cells.

Yet, somehow, Jameson Lorenzo was not on any of my lists. Was he really a member of the gang? My curiosity ate at me, caused me to want to find out more about him.

I had never even seen the man in my town before tonight. Trust me, I would have remembered if I had.

He was tall, with dark curly hair and a chiseled chin and face like a Greek god. He had the kind of lips that you just couldn't look away from when he spoke. Not to mention that his skin was tan, toned, and, especially to my liking, tattooed.

Plus, under the black pants and T-shirt he was wearing, I just knew there was a rock-hard body to match the dark looks he was giving me.

The part of me that drove me to find all the answers to other's secrets wanted to spend more time with the man in order to dive as deep as I could. Everyone slipped up eventually, allowing me to see the darkness or light they hid at first meeting. What was Jameson hiding?

I knew how to get answers from men like him. Flirting went a long way in getting men to let their guards down.

Besides, what else was I going to do for the night? Boredom often set in on nights like this.

Aria nudged my hip. "Invite him to sit with us for a drink," she hissed into my ear.

Aria and I had been BFFs ever since second grade, when I'd kicked Ricky Jorge's butt for pulling Aria's pigtails and making her cry.

Come to think of it, Aria was pretty much my only friend at the moment. Sure, I had plenty of acquaintances. Like Charlotte Hawthorne, who happened to be standing just behind tall-dark-and-sexy, along with her brother, Tobias, who was Aria's boyfriend of three years and fiancé of half that time. They were a stupidly cute couple and, besides living together for the past two years, had gone into business together. Jazzed Up was by far the best hair salon in town.

Of course, I was biased since Aria always did my hair for free.

"Friends don't charge friends," she always said.

It wasn't as if I went in often. Hell, the last time I'd had a haircut was... too long ago.

I could tell Aria was thinking the same thing. She was currently playing with my split ends, and I could tell she'd continue nagging me if I didn't go in soon.

She'd kept her bright blonde hair short since graduation. The spunky colors she added to her bleached look suited her personality.

Guess I'd better add a haircut to my list of things to do, besides solving a freaking murder.

"My BFF wants me to invite you to sit with us," I said, dryly, since it was obvious that Jameson had heard Aria clearly.

The man smiled and I swear to god, my underpants grew wet. Shifting, I nudged Aria and started pushing her towards a booth.

We all found an empty booth in the back, and Aria sat down after nudging me onto the bench across from her.

"This is Tobias," Aria said, taking her man's hand and pulling him down beside her. "And Charlotte, his sister." She pulled Charlotte next to her brother.

I watched Jameson's reaction. I knew for a fact that most of the Reapers were racist asshats. Tobias had had a few run-ins with a couple of members last month. Nothing that had warranted an arrest, but still, I was keeping a close eye on the situation.

"Hey," Jameson said easily and held out his hand as he took the seat next to me. "Jameson," he said to them both with an easy smile.

Okay, not on the racist asshat list, I thought when I noticed his genuine easy smile around the brother and sister.

"How about we head up to the bar and grab a round?" Tobias said, nudging his sister out of the booth. "Beer?" Tobias asked Jameson.

"Sure, whatever you're having," Jameson said easily.

Tobias nodded. "Come on, Aria." He tugged her arm and, before I could blink, the three of them were weaving their way through the crowd.

"You know what I want," I called after Aria. Then I turned to Jameson. "I should warn you," I said, catching my breath when I got a whiff of his sexy scent.

Was that sandalwood? Shit, the soft scent mixed with the leather did something to my insides.

"Oh?" Jameson smiled and rested his arm behind my shoulders on the back of the booth. "If it's about your friend trying to set us up"—his smile doubled—"I think I'm on to her."

I chuckled, the genuine sound somehow an odd one

coming from me since most men didn't earn such a girlie reaction from me. Shit. Was I going soft?

"No." I straightened my shoulders and somehow ended up brushing them against his arm. It sent mini-shock waves throughout my entire body, so I slouched to avoid the contact again. "Since you're with the Swamp Reapers, I think it's only fair to warn you that I wear a badge."

To my surprise, his smile didn't disappear.

"Yeah, I was clued onto that fact the moment you ordered a ginger ale," he said smoothly.

I narrowed my eyes. "Lots of people order ginger ale."

He laughed. "Who? People with upset stomachs? People over the age of seventy?"

I shifted and narrowed my eyes at him. "Okay, so I don't choose to nurse a hot beer for hours." When I noticed his eyebrows rise slowly, I held in a groan. Shit. Yeah, I'd noticed him at the bar before I'd spotted Declan shove Evelyn around.

"Keen eye. Detective?" he said slowly. I nodded. "How did you know my beer was hot?"

"Everyone else's drinks or bottles sitting on the bar were dripping with condensation, leaving little wet rings on the bar top. Yours was dry." I shrugged. "Very dry."

Suddenly, his dark eyes grew more inquisitive. "What else can you tell about me?"

I smiled. I liked this game. Shifting again, I ran my eyes up and down him slowly.

"You're not a smoker," I said and he nodded. "Not much of a drinker," I added. He rolled his eyes.

"I thought we established that already?" he joked.

I smiled. "You're from up north." I felt him tense beside me. His poker face was good. He could have easily hidden his worry from anyone else. If I hadn't been sitting close to him with his arm pressed against my shoulders, I wouldn't have felt the slightest move. "But it's important to you that people think otherwise," I added. He didn't even blink, so I moved on. "You're packing heat." I smiled. His eyebrows rose slightly. "Then again, I'd wager everyone else in this bar is too."

"You?" he asked.

My smile dipped slightly. "Always," I said seriously.

"Go on." He nodded slightly.

"You can't stand Declan O'Malley," I added, taking a chance.

I felt him tense again. "How do you know that?"

"Because, while everyone else in your little club watched me pin the bastard to the wall, only you looked like you wanted to help me. The rest, if they could, would have taken me out back and…"

"Yeah," he agreed, and I watched him run his hands through his thick curly hair.

Then, for a split second, I saw something else. Something I must be wrong about. There was no way.

"Shots!" Aria said, breaking into the awkward silence as she set a tray of bright yellow drinks in little tubes down in front of us. "Let's get this birthday party started!" she cheered, and I groaned.

"Whose birthday?" Jameson asked after downing the very sweet and very strong shot.

"She thinks it's mine," I answered and took a sip of the beer that Aria had gotten me.

No more ginger ale for me tonight. Damn it. Not with Aria here. She'd want me to party and, well, I wanted to cut loose too.

"Thinks?" Jameson asked after taking a swig of his new

cold beer. "I thought you two were BFFs. If it's not your birthday, then..."

I smiled. "I don't have one," I said as I watched Aria pull Tobias out on the dance floor. Charlotte had disappeared with a man on the dance floor before the drinks had even arrived.

"You... everyone has a birthday," he said.

I shook my head. "Nope, I don't have a last name either."

His eyes narrowed. "Rayne? First and last name?" I nodded. "Now I'm intrigued," he added.

I shook my head. "I don't tell everyone my past." I nudged his shoulder. "Can you dance? Because it's my pretend birthday and I feel like dancing."

He nodded and then slid out of the booth.

When I put my hand in his offered one, a quick jolt raced up my arm and spread throughout my entire body like a bolt of lightning.

How in the hell was I going to not jump this guy's bones tonight?

I didn't do quick in relationships, and I certainly stayed away from one-night stands. Especially, in a town where almost everyone knew everyone else's dirty secrets.

When we hit the dance floor, I was shocked at how well the man moved, and for two entire songs, I put my work world behind me and just enjoyed the moment.

Sweaty, breathless, and thirsty, I pulled Jameson back to our booth.

Charlotte was there, sipping a cocktail while looking at her phone.

"Didn't hit it off with Carl?" I asked as we sat back down.

"Carl is an ass," Charlotte said without looking up.

"Agreed." I laughed.

Charlotte smiled up at me. "What do you do?" she asked Jameson after she set down her phone.

"I'm a fitness trainer," he answered, slightly surprising me.

The hell he was. I narrowed my eyes as I took a sip of my now warm beer.

"Where?" Charlotte asked.

"Red River Iron Gym," Jameson answered. I stiffened, causing him to glance over at me. "Problems?"

I quickly shook my head and took another sip of my drink. "Bathroom break," I said and waited for him to get out of the booth.

I made a beeline to where Aria and Tobias were slow dancing.

"Sorry, stealing your woman for a few," I called out as I yanked Aria with me towards the bathroom.

"Hey, I was just about to get lucky." Aria laughed.

"Not on my watch," I joked back. When we were locked in the bathroom stall together, I took a couple of deep breaths and closed my eyes. "What in the hell am I doing?" I asked her as she yanked up her shiny golden skirt on the sheer dress she'd worn and started to pee.

"Having a good time with an incredibly sexy man." Aria wiggled her blonde eyebrows.

"I think he's a Reaper," I whispered. I didn't know who else was in the bathroom.

Aria stilled. "The hell he is." She narrowed her eyes and then stood and flushed the toilet.

I figured since I was here... I pulled my pants down and went.

"No way." Aria shook her head. "Him?"

I nodded. "Yup." I closed my eyes. "Why? Why do all

the sexy men that cause me to soak my panties have to be so out of reach?"

"Sweetie," Aria said as she leaned against the door to the stall. "Does he know... about you?"

I nodded. "He said he picked up on it right away."

Aria was quiet for a moment while I finished using the bathroom and flushed.

"Why didn't you wear a dress?" she asked suddenly.

"Because then you couldn't be the hottest one here tonight," I teased as we stepped out of the stall to wash our hands.

She stopped me from walking out by laying a hand on my arm. "If he knows about you, then there are two possibilities. One, he's using you, which I just don't see him doing. The way he looks at you makes me think that it's option two."

"Which is?" I asked.

Aria smiled. "Sweetie, he's just as horny as you are and you should strap in and enjoy that ride for as long as you can hold on."

I laughed.

She was right. As we stepped out into the bar again, the moment Jameson spotted me, I saw the spark in his eyes.

Yeah, this was either going to be the best night of my life or I'd hit the ground after being bucked off the sexiest ride in town.

Chapter Five

"Every diamond has the ability to shine when there is someone to recognize its good facets and inhibit its flaws."
—Wes Fesler

Jameson

I didn't know exactly what changed, but after the two friends came back from the bathroom, I could see that the caution that Rayne had before was completely gone.

She easily leaned against my shoulder now as she laughed and joked with her friends.

It wasn't hard for me to drop most of the pretense that I had around them. After all, it had been such a long time that I felt comfortable just listening to a group of people telling stories and hanging out.

I had to keep glancing around the place to ensure that none of the other gang members were there. I had convinced myself that the entire night could be written off as me trying to get laid if I was spotted.

Besides, I'd earned Felix's trust after the last few months. The smaller drug runs weren't the first I'd done while undercover. Over the past few months, Felix had trusted me with more than a dozen. I wasn't in this deep for a few ounces here or there.

I knew the hard-hitting truth. If it wasn't me making the drops, then it was going to be someone else. The fact that I worked at the gym opened doors to the entire operation. Which is why it was picked as my cover from the start.

Also, it was a job that allowed me the freedom to come and go while watching everyone I needed to. Most of the Reapers were members of the gym. Almost every member had a job around town. A few of them were plumbers for the same company, and two brothers worked at a landscape company. Declan worked in an auto parts store. Felix and Ben didn't have full-time jobs. They seemed to spend most of their time watching over the other members.

They had a huge house on the very outskirts of town. The massive six-bedroom place backed a bayou.

I'd staked the place out as much as I could, but Ben had three rottweilers named Larry, Curly, and Moe that alerted him anytime I got too close.

The first time I'd been invited out to the place, I knew I had to play it cool if I wanted to be invited back.

It was three months before I finally had a chance to look around. Ben had hosted a large crawfish boil as a birthday party for Felix.

There were almost a hundred people going in and out of the home, which had given me plenty of time to look around. I'd even dragged a very drunk Izzy with me, knowing if I got caught looking around, I could always pretend we'd been looking for a quiet place.

Maybe that's why Izzy kept trying to get with me. I hated stringing women on.

Damn it. Wasn't that what I was doing now with Rayne?

I knew the truth. There was no way that anything could come out of tonight. I didn't even know why she continued to hang out with me at this point. She knew I was one of the Reapers and from how she was acting earlier, she knew that the Reapers were trouble.

When Aria dragged Tobias to the dance floor again and Charlotte disappeared somewhere, leaving me alone with Rayne, I figured I'd ask her. Only I didn't get a chance to.

"Don't bullshit me," she said the moment we were alone.

"I won't," I said, figuring to play along with whatever happened next.

Her eyes narrowed slightly. "Ex-military?"

I paused for a heartbeat before nodding slowly. Okay, so Felix and the rest knew that about me too.

"What branch?" she asked.

"Marines," I answered quickly. Another truth.

She shifted. "Which accounts for the mixture of accents I hear behind that fake Louisiana drawl you've convinced everyone else around here you have. How long?"

I was thankful she didn't dwell on the accent.

"Four years."

"Where, exactly, up north are you from? I'd wager..." She held up a finger when I opened my mouth. Honestly, the lies I'd been telling over the past years rolled off my tongue so easily, I didn't even know what I was going to say. "Chicago," she finished.

My eyebrows jumped just the slightest, giving the answer away.

"Okay, so..." She shifted again, leaning her back against the wall as she ran her eyes over me once more. "What in the hell is a boy from Chicago, turned marine, turned biker slash drug gang, doing in my town trying to convince everyone he's nothing but a good ol' boy?" She smiled slowly. "You thought I was dumb, like the rest of them?" She nudged her chin towards the back door.

I couldn't help it, my appreciation for the woman tripled instantly.

Then she leaned closer to me and whispered, "Like I said, you can't fool me."

I nodded slowly and once again opened my mouth. But before I could say anything, my entire body was yanked out of the booth.

One minute I was sitting there looking into the most beautiful brown eyes I'd ever seen, ready to reveal all my secrets, the next I hit the opposite wall with a thud and saw stars.

Shit.

"Quincy!" I heard Rayne yell through the haze.

Biting the insides of my mouth, I steadied myself and prepared for a fight. Only, the blow didn't come.

Instead, I saw Rayne jump on the back of a man roughly my size and build. His long jet-black hair hung low over his eyes. The man was wearing a leather vest, showcasing far more tattoos than I had.

My hearing had yet to come back so most of what I understood next was from reading lips in the dark, smoky bar. I watched them struggle for a few moments before the man stilled and Rayne pushed her way in front of him.

"Quincy! Leave him alone," Rayne was shouting as she held the man away from me.

"Why in the hell are you hanging around a Reaper?" Quincy asked Rayne, who was now standing nose to nose with the man.

"That's none of your..."—this is when my hearing came back—"damned business," Rayne said as she shoved the man in the chest. The guy didn't even budge.

"He's a Reaper." Quincy pointed at me.

"And you're a cop," Rayne threw back at the man.

Shit. Another cop? Okay, one cop I could explain away with my heightened libido. Two? Nope. No way.

From the way the two were talking to one another, it was obvious they were currently or had recently been an item. Which, I suppose, accounted for the man attacking me from behind. "Starting a bar fight is illegal. I could haul your butt down to the station now..." Rayne was saying.

"Don't bother. We both know it won't do either of us any good." Quincy turned to me. "Go on, get out of here," the man said as if he was shooing away a fly.

I couldn't help it. I arched my eyebrows at the guy.

"Only if the lady wants me to," I replied, knowing full well that whatever happened now, the rest of the Reapers would get wind of what went down. If I didn't stand up now, then I'd look like a wimp. Even if I was standing up to a cop.

Sure, Felix had dragged Declan out of the bar earlier when Rayne had pinned him against the wall. But that was Felix.

I squared my shoulders and waited.

"Quincy, just go." Rayne shoved the man again. I noticed her efforts didn't even make the man budge this second time.

Thankfully, at that moment, Tobias and Aria returned.

Aria instantly got in Quincy's face and started yelling at him while Tobias walked over and helped me.

"Sorry about this," Tobias said quietly.

"Sure." I rolled my shoulders. "Ex?"

Tobias nodded. "She broke things off after she found out he had hooked up with one of the waitresses here."

Stupid, I thought as I watched the two women face off with the other man.

"I'll go," I told Tobias.

"Naw." Tobias took my arm. "That'll just piss her off more. Trust me, you don't want to be on Rayne's bad side," he said with a chuckle.

I nodded since it was something I'd already figured out.

When Rayne and Aria had finally convinced Quincy to leave, the man pushed past me, shoving his shoulder into mine and trying to topple me over. I'd been ready for the move and didn't budge.

"Are you okay?" Rayne asked as Tobias and Aria returned to the booth.

"Yeah, you?" I asked, running my eyes over her once more. Yeah, she would be worth fighting over. Any man who cheated on her deserved what she gave them.

"I'm good." She sighed and glanced around. "Come on, let's get some air." She took my hand and pulled me towards the door.

When we stepped out into the muggy summer night, she stopped. "Which one is yours?" She motioned to the row of bikes still parked at the bar. I noticed all of the bikes owned by the Reapers were missing. Thankfully.

"What makes you think I own a bike?" I asked with a smile. "That could be my car." I pointed to a Mini Cooper and she laughed.

"First off, that's Aria's. She bought it for herself for her twenty-fifth birthday." She nudged my shoulder. "Second off, everyone in town knows one of the requirements to join the Reapers is you have to have a bike. So..." She moved a little closer to me until she was only a breath away. "I'll ask again, which one is yours?"

Damn. Just the sexy scent of her had me pointing to my bike. Yeah, mine. All mine. Even if I didn't have to pretend to be in a drug dealing, backwater gang, I'd ride her.

"Nice," she said, walking over to the bike. Then, to my surprise, she pulled out her phone and snapped a picture of my plates.

"Cop move," I joked and had her smiling. "Gonna run me?"

"You know it." She put her phone back in the pocket of her jacket. "Now, how about a walk?" She motioned and, stupidly, I fell in step beside her. We made our way down the sidewalk to a small parking lot where a green bench sat under a very dim streetlight.

When she sat down, I sat next to her.

"I have a serious addiction," she said softly, causing me to tense for a split second.

"Oh?" I asked, waiting, and counting my heartbeats.

She turned her face towards mine and I instantly got lost in exploring her face with my eyes.

"I tend to fall for guys like you," she finished.

"Which is?" I asked.

She rolled her eyes. "Bad-boy types. Pretty on the outside and jerks on the inside."

"Do you think I'm a jerk?" I asked with a smile.

She chuckled. "I don't know you all that well. But, if you're part of the Reapers, something tells me you don't rescue kittens from trees in your spare time."

"I like kittens," I said, shifting closer to her while my

gaze was locked on her lips. I couldn't stop myself from wondering what she'd taste like. What she'd feel like.

"See, right there." She narrowed her eyes at me. "At first, all men will say or do anything to get what they want."

"And what is that?" I asked, falling for her bait.

"I'd wager the same thing I want at this point. To get into your pants." She smiled.

I leaned in, totally prepared to take her lips but she leaned back and slapped a hand to my chest.

"Nice try, Yank." She sighed and shook her head. "I don't kiss until the plates come back clean."

I chuckled. "They're clean. I'm clean."

"We'll see about that." She cocked her head slightly. "You're not what you want everyone to think." She narrowed her eyes. "You're lying. That's a fact." When I opened my mouth to deny it, she added, "I'll get to the bottom of it. One way or another." She shifted and then stood up suddenly. "I'll see you around town, Jameson Lorenzo." She walked backward towards the bar.

Damn.

Suddenly, I wished it was winter and it was one of those freezing Chicago snow days I'd hated so much growing up. Everything was too hot. My body was on fire and, for the first time in years, I knew there wouldn't be any relief until I had just a sample of Detective Rayne.

I climbed on my hog and rode the few blocks to the apartment I'd been set up in. The massive loft fit the profile I needed along with my needs for the time being. The fact that there was a safe room that held my guns, computers, and a secure phone was a huge bonus.

The massive two thousand square foot, two-bedroom loft was open concept, and my bedroom overlooked the kitchen and living space. I'd turned the second bedroom into a gym to prevent any of the Reapers who just needed a place to crash from doing so.

Most of the furniture in the place was secondhand, but I didn't care. I hardly spent time there except when I needed to reset, eat, or sleep.

The loft sat directly above a café and next to a theater in the old part of town.

Not wasting any time, I let myself into my safe room, which was hidden behind the fireplace in the brick wall that ran on either side of the loft, and sat down at my unregistered computer. Logging into the VPN, I searched for Rayne's information in every database I had access to.

After half an hour, I grew very frustrated at the lack of information. I hadn't even turned up a birth certificate or a social security number. So, I turned to social media sites to see if I could learn details about her personal life.

She had a basic presence there. A photo of her and Aria laughing at what appeared to be a local water hole. The friends sitting on top of a tree branch with a rope swing in hand as if they were ready to jump in. Sure enough, a few photos later, the duo were flying through the air, laughing as they hit the water.

Her profile stated she worked for the local PD. Investigations lieutenant.

Impressive. From what I could tell, she'd held the job for a few years now. Before that, she appeared to be a beat cop in town.

The further back I went on her profiles, the less there was. One thing was obvious, the woman didn't like telling the world every little detail about herself.

But I'd already figured out that she didn't like talking about herself.

Since it had been a few months since I'd checked in, I

pulled out my business phone, turned it on, and called Jasmine.

She answered on the second ring. "Hey. Updates?"

"None so far," I answered, leaning back in the chair.

"Why the call?" she asked.

"I need you to pull some info on someone," I said.

"Shoot," Jasmine said, and I heard her shifting around.

"Rayne." Then I spelled the name out.

"First or last name?" Jasmine asked.

"No last name. Just Rayne. She's the investigations lieutenant for Gemsville," I said as my eyes ran over the attractive picture of her smiling into the camera. This picture was of her and Aria at the local gun range. Aria had a bright pink gun in her hands, while Rayne held a black 35.

"Think she's dirty?" Jasmine asked.

"No, this one's... personal," I added.

"Ohh." Jasmine chuckled. "Damn, Jameson does have a libido."

"Shut up." I groaned. "Just let me know what you can find on her, will you?"

"Sure, just as long as it doesn't interfere with why you're there. I doubt the Reapers will take too kindly to you shaking up with a cop. One they probably know and avoid themselves."

"Yeah, I know," I admitted. "Still, there's something..." I dropped off.

"She got under your skin?" Jasmine said with a sigh. "Jameson, you know the story of how I met my husband Stephen,"

"Yeah," I said quickly, remembering how she'd arrested Stephen for solicitation only to discover he'd been undercover himself to snag her.

"Good, then let that be a warning." She laughed. "Now,

get me real names. Real progress. We aren't paying you to shack up with some lieutenant."

"Right," I said and hung up.

I shut everything down and headed in to take a very cold shower and try to get some sleep.

Chapter Six

*"Rough diamonds may sometimes
be mistaken for worthless pebbles.*
–Sir Thomas Browne

Rayne

The last thing I wanted to do on a windy, rainy Monday morning was stand in front of the City and County Building. There were a dozen or more cameras shoved in my face as I gave an update on the mayor's murder case.

I was upset that I didn't have anything new to tell them from the last time I'd stood there a week ago. What pissed me off was the possibility that whatever I said this time would be taken out of context, like it had the week before.

The photo of me hovering over Sharon Taylor's body had gone viral after the murder, thanks to Sabrina DeRouen.

Okay, so maybe she was a little pissed at me for hauling her butt down to the station and locking her in an interview room for an hour or so until she finally coughed over the camera drive. Hindsight, I should have seized her computer to make sure she hadn't already copied the photo from the drive.

The fact that it had been an entire week since the mayor's death and I was no closer to finding who had stabbed the woman thirty-two times and then tried to skin her face, disturbed me. It wasn't the gruesome details of the crime that kept me up at night, it was the fact that none of the puzzle pieces fit.

Henry Taylor's alibi checked out. The man was at the bar until he climbed the back stairs with Faye to her apartment above the bar, where he stayed until he drove home. Apparently, it wasn't the first time the guy had slept over at the younger bartender's place.

The Taylor twins were both accounted for as well. Just as they'd said, Beau had been in Lafayette for the week for a job and Wyatt had spent the night with Clara Mangrum.

The biggest clues in the case I'd gotten during my interview with Sabrina DeRouen. The woman had been a wealth of information as far as the Taylor family's goings-on.

That fact disturbed me almost as much as meeting Jameson Lorenzo at the BBB.

My mind hadn't been able to relax from the case until after my chat with Aria. She didn't bring her work to the party so I figured I'd better leave mine at the office and enjoy my makeshift birthday party, which had entailed flirting with Jameson.

Yeah, the first thing I did when I got into the station the next morning was to pull up his info. The fact that he was clean only solidified my thoughts about the man.

Every single member of the Reapers had a rap sheet.

Most had several pages full of misdemeanors and time they'd spent behind bars.

Jameson Lorenzo only had two misdemeanors. Speeding tickets.

Which didn't add up. Then I found out he'd been living in my town for a year. A full fucking year!

How in the hell had I missed the man?

Plus, his address was only a few blocks from the station, and he had worked at the Red River Iron Gym for the past eight months.

I wasn't a member of the gym myself but had been there a few times with Aria and Tobias. Not once had I seen Jameson there.

Trust me when I say I would have noticed him. I had a radar when it came to men like him.

Which is how I found Quincy Ingram. The man had transferred to our station a little over two years before from Baton Rouge. We didn't normally get transfers and I'd been upset that we'd hired the position of patrol division captain from outside, but then I'd seen him and, well, you know the rest.

Jesus, why can't I control myself around men like them? I'd learned my lesson with Quincy though. The man was a snake. Still, I was smart enough to know that not all snakes were the same.

I'd gone out on a few dates with a couple of men after that, some of which went against my physical attraction code, and both of those had been even bigger snakes than Quincy.

With Jameson, however, things felt different. There was something that I couldn't quite put my finger on about the man. I hoped to bump into him again, but interviewing everyone attached to the case was keeping me busy.

After running through my pre-planned statement, I was stupid enough to take a few questions. When I spotted Sabrina in the crowd, I purposely avoided her hand and answered a question from a state-run news station.

"Can you confirm whether there are any suspects or persons of interest in custody related to the murder?" the man asked.

"As I mentioned in my statement," I started, trying desperately not to sound annoyed at the question, "at this time we are looking into several different suspects. No one is in custody at this time." I motioned to the next hand raised.

"Can you comment on any potential motives or theories that your team is exploring in connection with the murder?" the woman asked.

"At this time we are exploring several potential motives," I reiterated, sounding one hundred percent annoyed. Didn't they listen to my statement? It was as if the media were nothing more than children.

Finally, Sabrina was the last to have her hand raised, so I called on her.

"Is it true that Mayor Taylor was being investigated by the State Attorney General's Office for public corruption and embezzling?" Sabrina asked with a smirk.

Damn it. How in the hell had she gotten wind of that? I had only just found that out earlier that morning.

"No further questions at this time," I said into the mic. I turned on my heeled boots and started marching through the rain.

"Rayne," Sabrina called after me.

"Go away," I called over my shoulder.

"I can help you," she said, catching up with me.

"Go away," I said after stopping and turning to square up with her.

She narrowed her eyes at me. "I'm sorry about posting the picture," she blurted out. I let my shoulders relax. "You know, you and I used to be friends."

"Used to be."

"Rayne." She reached up and touched my arm. "I heard Edith is doing well through her chemo," she said, a little softer.

I jerked my arm away from hers. "She's a fighter. How did you find out about the attorney general?"

She sighed and then her smile grew. "I have sources."

I raised my eyebrows. "Are you still dating what's his name?"

She shook her head. "Nope, I have a new guy in my life." Her smile doubled. "A little more local."

"Stay clear of me during this, Sabrina," I warned. "Let me do my job."

"Let me do mine," she threw back, lifting her chin.

I closed my eyes. "How about a truce?" I suggested.

"Go on." Sabrina waited.

"If you let me in on any new details you happen to hear before me, I'll call you first when I haul the killer in," I suggested.

Sabrina's left eyebrow arched slightly, then she nodded slowly.

As I turned to go, she held my arm.

"You might want to check into Mr. Taylor's girlfriend," she said. "She has a few other... side hustles."

With this, she dropped her hold on my arm and marched away quickly.

Shit. How in the hell did that woman know what was on my to-do list?

Feeling pissed, I jumped into my patrol car and headed across town. When I pulled into the parking lot of Bayou Brews, I glanced at my watch and winced. They wouldn't be open at nine in the morning.

Shit. Pulling out my phone, I scanned my list of suspects and decided to visit the mayor's office instead. Heading back across town, I somehow ended up passing the Red River Iron Gym.

What the hell? I pulled into the parking lot when I noticed Jameson's hog sitting out front.

Nine in the morning, the gym was pretty empty. It was just past the time for the early morning fanatics that hit the gym before work and too early for the stay-at-home types who were finishing their avocado toast and lattes before hitting their yoga mats.

Seeing Jameson through the wall of glass windows, I narrowed my eyes and watched him talking to a male gym goer.

God, the man looked sexy as hell in a gray T-shirt and black shorts. His hair appeared slightly wet, as if he'd just come inside out of the rain.

Had he just gotten there?

When my phone rang, I answered Randy's call on the second ring.

"Hey," I answered, shifting slightly in my seat.

"Hey, Edith wanted me to see if you'd be up for dinner on Saturday," Randy said.

"Sure," I answered without even thinking. "How was this morning's round?"

Randy grew quiet. "She'd kill me for letting on that she was hurting."

"I know," I said softly. "Even so, you should tell me."

"Right," he agreed. "She says that the chemo is better

than the radiation burns from last time. She's starting to lose her hair."

I closed my eyes to the pain. Edith Cordova had the most beautiful silver-gray curly locks that I'd ever seen. It was one of the first features I could remember seeing in my young childhood. That and her soft brown eyes, which had always been filled with love and kindness, like Randy's were.

"I can take her into Aria and see what she can do?" I suggested.

"She's talking about shaving it all off," Randy said with a sigh.

My chest grew heavy. "I can be there," I said. "Saturday?"

"Saturday," Randy agreed. "See you then."

When I hung up, tears burned my eyes. Until my passenger door flew open and Jameson jumped in the seat beside me.

"You know, if you sit out here much longer, you're going to give the gym a bad rep," he said with a smile.

I moved my hand away from my gun and narrowed my eyes at him. "You know, if you spook a cop like that again, you might just have a few more holes than you'd like."

His smile grew. "Checking up on me?" he asked.

I knew there was no logical reason for me to be sitting outside his work for... shit, had I been on the call for ten minutes? I answered, "It's not a crime."

He chuckled. "You know, my friends and yours don't play too well together. If you want to meet up, we should do so someplace more... private."

I tilted my head. "I haven't made up my mind yet about that," I said honestly. "Why do you only have two misdemeanors?"

He tilted his head to match mine. "Should I have more?"

"It doesn't add up," I pointed out. "You don't add up."

"Not everything in life adds up all the time."

"I don't like puzzles that are missing pieces." My statement had an odd effect on him. He suddenly seemed to be thinking deeply about something.

"Why Rayne?" he asked.

"Why what?"

"Why is your name Rayne and only Rayne?"

I tilted my head. "As I said, I don't know you well enough—"

He held up his hand to stop me. "Okay, how about we agree to an answer for an answer? But..."—he glanced back at the building—"not here."

"Where?" I asked, trying to hide my excitement.

"There's a cabin on Red River Road, on the bend along the river near Barns Street, just outside of town. It's red with a blue door, off by itself," he said.

"I know of it," I said, and his eyebrows rose slowly. "I know my town," I added with a chuckle.

He nodded. "Noon? Don't drive the patrol car."

I didn't know what I had expected, maybe a late-night rendezvous, but the middle of the day worked for me too. I nodded and Jameson climbed out of my car and dashed through the rain back inside.

Glancing at my watch, I groaned. I'd effectively wasted an hour. Deciding to try my luck at Bayou Brews I was happily surprised when I saw a light on inside.

I knocked on the door and waited until Faye Baker opened the door. Seeing me, she quickly glanced up and down the street before pulling me inside.

"What?" she hissed as she shut the door behind me. "I answered all your questions the other day."

"I have a few more," I said, walking into the empty bar. There was only a low light on behind the bar area and by the way Faye was dressed, I'd wager she'd come downstairs for something. She wore hot pink sleeping shorts and a tank top that said "Hot Stuff" on her butt and boobs, and her jet-black hair was at the nape of her neck in one of those messy buns I could never get to look right on me.

"Coffee?" Faye asked, moving behind the bar.

"Sure," I said, pulling down one of the stools and sitting on it.

"Black?" she asked over her shoulder.

"Cream and sugar if you have it," I said.

Faye glanced over her shoulder as her eyes narrowed. "I thought all cops like their coffee black?"

"That's a stereotype," I said with a sigh. "Don't group me in with the rest of the cops in town."

"No," Faye said with a sigh. "I forgot, you're some sort of super-cop."

I rolled my eyes. "Detective."

"Right." She set a mug in front of me and leaned on the counter as she sipped from her mug. Her dark eyes ran over me slowly. "Ask your questions."

"How is it you are lucky enough to live upstairs?" I pointed at my mug before taking a drink. Up until the mayor's death, I hadn't known there was an apartment on the third floor of the building or that Faye was living there.

"I'm friendly with the owner," she said smoothly.

The owner—Jackson Pennington. In my book, Jackson Pennington was a suspected sleazeball in a suit. That didn't mean he had anything to do with my case. He was extremely rich like the Taylors, but that didn't automatically mean that he would stoop to murder. From all the information I had on the man, he was friendly with the Taylors.

Still, I mentally added his name to my interview-again list, just in case.

"Plus, I pay rent and watch out for the building," Faye added. "Next question."

"What do you know about the Taylor's trouble with the State Attorney General's Office looking into them for public corruption and embezzling?"

I watched the sheer shock on Faye's face and knew the answer before she even opened her mouth.

"They're what?" Faye asked, setting down her cup.

I sighed and set my cup down. "Are you friendly with either Beau or Wyatt?"

Faye glanced down at her hands. "Wyatt comes in now and then."

"Who does he hang out with?" I asked.

Her eyes jerked back up to mine. "Who doesn't he hang with? Jocks, bikers, yuppies, ma and pa types." She shrugged. "The man is far more popular than his brother, that's for sure. It's funny," she started, but then she stopped and shook her head.

"Funny?" I prodded.

She rolled her eyes. "It's just... Beau is far better looking than Wyatt." She smiled.

"Does Beau come in often?"

She shrugged. "Sometimes he comes to pick up his father. I've never seen him drink."

"Wyatt's involved with..." I pretended to pull out my notepad to look, but Faye beat me to the name. "Clara Mangrum."

I nodded. Clara Mangrum worked at the station, but I

still didn't know whether in Internal Affairs or records. I was going to make a point to find out.

"They've been going out again for a few months," Faye added. "Before that... we used to be a thing."

"Is that why you started shaking it up with his old man?" I asked, not caring to go light on her at this point. "Couldn't keep the son?"

Her eyes jerked to mine. "Henry takes care of me, unlike Wyatt."

"Financially? Because I can think of a few laws—"

"No, in other ways." She picked up her coffee to sip. "Do you have any other questions? Because I need to head up and shower."

"How often do the Reapers come in here?" I asked instead of asking any other questions about the murder.

Faye looked surprised. "Too often if you ask me." I waited. "At least five times a week. Every day during the winter."

I nodded. "Troublemakers?" I asked, already knowing the answer.

She shrugged. "Sometimes. Only twice we've had to call you guys in to help out. For the most part, I think they know we're the only ones in town that will deal with them, so they play nice."

"Right," I said, knowing that was probably the reason Felix Woolf had pulled Declan O'Malley out of my grip and out of the bar last week. There was no doubt in my mind that Felix and Declan knew who I was. Even though I didn't work the beat, they knew. "What do you know about Jameson Lorenzo?"

Faye's eyebrows arched and she smiled for the first time. "Now that's a man I'd like to sink my teeth into." She purred and when I didn't respond, she continued. "He's quiet. Watchful. Kind. A good tipper. I can tell he doesn't like the shenanigans that a few of the others get into. He seems all business. Like Felix and Ben, though I've seen those two cut loose. I haven't seen Jameson relax so much as a muscle. Oh, he *looks* relaxed, but there's just something..." She dropped off.

"Right," I agreed. There was something unexplainable about the man. The piece of the puzzle I hadn't quite found yet.

I stood up from my stool and downed the rest of the now lukewarm coffee. "Thanks for that." I motioned to the cup. "Let me know if you think of anything else."

"Sure."

"Oh, one more thing." I stopped. "What other tricks do you have going?"

I watched her eyes widen slightly before she lied. "None."

"Make sure it stays that way," I warned and walked out.

I had a couple of hours to kill before I went to meet Jameson. Just enough time to head into the mayor's office and ask the mayor's coworkers the new questions that I had.

Chapter Seven

"To be a diamond, you have to go through a lot of pressure and heat, but in the end, you come out shining.
–Unknown

Jameson

I couldn't believe my luck. Not ten minutes after Rayne's patrol car disappeared from the parking lot of the gym, Ben and Declan showed up. A few minutes later, a few more of the Reapers joined them.

For the next hour, I joked and worked out with the men, trying to act like nothing was wrong. In truth, since the week before, I'd been on edge.

I'd gotten a call from Felix asking me why I hadn't high-tailed it out of the bar when the rest of the gang had. So I told him the truth.

I'd spotted some tail worth following.

When Felix asked for a name, I joked that I hadn't even had time to get one. Thankfully, he'd laughed that off and we'd moved on in the conversation.

Now I was helping five of the other Reapers lift weights

and talking about each of their sex lives while desperately wishing I was anywhere else.

How long had I been dealing with jackasses like these? Years. Never before had I felt so over conversations like this. Not like I currently felt.

When anyone from my real life asked me if I liked my job, my normal answer was that I loved it. Then again, I hadn't been in contact with anyone in the real world much in the last few years.

In truth, the past week was the first time I'd missed having a real personal life. And it was all thanks to Rayne.

The moment the Reapers left the gym, I hit the shower and changed into my street clothes. Thankfully, the rain had let up a little. After pulling on my leather jacket and helmet, I hit the road for the cabin.

Besides my apartment, the cabin was the only other safe space I had in or near town. The DEA had rented the property under a pseudonym a year before my arrival. They'd moved in the basics of furniture and supplied it with everything I'd need during my stay.

Since the road to the cabin was a narrow dirt lane, it wasn't hard to tell if I'd been followed anytime that I drove out there. So far, none of the other Reapers knew or cared where I spent my time outside of the gang activities.

I wasn't surprised to see a white Jeep parked under one of the massive oak trees off to the side. I pulled my bike under the carport, turned it off, and pulled off my helmet.

"So, want to tell me whose place this is?" Rayne asked as she stepped under the carport.

"I would have thought you'd have time to research that before heading over here," I joked.

Watching her eyes narrow, I smiled and waited.

"I did. Who is Caleb Morales?" She crossed her arms over her chest.

I shrugged. "Who is Rayne?" I countered.

She rolled her eyes. "Do you have keys?" She motioned over her shoulder to the cabin. I held up the set and shook them. "I brought lunch," she added and held up a bag from one of the fast-food burger joints in town.

We headed down the pathway, and she stood under the front porch while I unlocked the door. I stood back as she walked in, then stepped inside and flipped on the light switch.

The place was decorated with country-style furniture. In the living room, there was a leather sofa and matching chairs. The dining room had an oak table and chairs, and the bedroom had a king-sized bed, nightstands, and a dresser.

The only thing missing was a television and some other basics. Just the essentials.

I had only been out there twice in the time I'd been in town, both times to meet Jasmine and pass information between us. The place smelled dusty and empty. But the view from the large windows in the back was something I could get used to. The river curved around half of the property and a large grove of oak trees stood beyond the river.

"Okay." Rayne turned on me once we stepped inside. "I'm thinking..." She tilted her head. "Homeland Security?" I arched my eyebrows, then shook my head. She sighed as she set the bag of fast food on the table. "FBI?" I shook my head again. "I'm close, right?"

I shrugged. "Why Rayne?" I asked her.

She sat down and, instead of answering, pulled out a burger and started eating it. "Is there anything to drink in that fridge or is it just for looks?" she asked.

I walked over and pulled out two sodas that I'd stocked in there the last time I'd been here. There could come a time when I'd have to hide out here and I wanted to be prepared. Setting two sodas down on the table, I sat across from her.

"You're undercover." It was a statement, not a question this time. I nodded in agreement and she slapped the table. "I knew it."

"I've been authorized to share my details with any of the local police I deem trustworthy," I added.

A look of surprise crossed her face. "Does this have anything to do with—"

I held up my finger, stopping her. "Why Rayne?"

She sighed and leaned back in her chair. "It was the only word I knew when they found me," she admitted. I frowned and shook my head, not understanding her meaning.

"Whatever agency you're with must not have much access to personal files," she joked as she leaned forward. "I was around five years old when they found me. Not far from here, actually." She glanced towards the windows. "Out there, somewhere." She motioned to the left of the scene, beyond the river.

"Who found you?" I asked.

"What agency?" she countered with a smile. "If you play fair, remember, an answer for an answer." She wiggled her eyebrows at me and I relaxed.

"DEA," I answered.

She laughed, then sobered a little. "Shit, you're serious," she said when I didn't laugh with her.

"Who found you?" I asked again.

"Cops. One of them, Randy Cordova, and his wife,

Edith, took me in when no one stepped forward and claimed me," she answered. "Why is the DEA in my town?"

"Why does the DEA go anywhere?" I countered. She frowned and was quiet for a moment, so I asked, "Why become a detective?"

"I don't want anyone to feel the way I felt. Abandoned. Even after death," she added. "Do you think the Reapers are dealing?"

I shook my head. "There are some answers I'm not authorized to give just yet."

"That's fair." She shifted. "Caleb Morales?"

"Another one of my names. I've gone by Jameson Lorenzo for more than five years," I answered with a shrug.

She tilted her head and smiled. "You look like a Jameson."

I laughed. "It's my middle name."

"Three names to my one," she joked and took another bite of her burger. "Why confide in me?"

My eyes ran over her face. When I watched heat flood into her cheeks, I knew she had the answer.

"Okay, so, we both agree on that point." She took a sip of her drink and leaned back, shoving the finished burger away. I took the last bite of mine and did the same. "How does this work? I'm sure the Reapers won't appreciate you hanging out with a cop."

I nodded. "Yeah. For now, no more impromptu visits to my work. I can explain a few bump-ins but nothing more."

She nodded. "Okay, I get that. I have a few missing puzzle pieces."

I chuckled. "I only seemed to have gotten one from you."

She smiled. "Maybe, when I'm not expected somewhere else, we can do this again. Maybe even a sleepover?" she teased.

Damn. Now that was all I was going to think about. Leaning over, I pulled her chair close to mine and watched her eyes heat.

"This may not work," I told her as she climbed over me, her legs pinning me to the chair as she straddled me.

"It may not," she whispered, her mouth a breath away from mine. "Then again..." She dropped off as I leaned up and took her mouth. Her hands slipped into my hair.

She tasted like heaven. Her lips melted against mine as her body vibrated. My hands glided over her hips, avoiding her holster and weapon. I cupped her butt while she pressed tight against my crotch.

My dick jumped in response to her pressing tight against it while she rolled her tongue around mine and sucked softly on it.

I could have exploded right then and there. Would have if not for her cell phone ringing in the pocket of her jacket.

"Shit." She leaned her forehead against mine. "Don't speak," she warned as she pulled the phone out and answered the call.

"Yeah?" she practically barked into the phone. "When?" She waited. "Shit. Okay, yeah, I'll be there in ten." She hung up. "This has been fun," she said, running her eyes over my face. "How do I reach you?"

I smiled and took her phone from her and entered my private cell number. "Leave a message. I'll get it." I handed her the phone back.

She took it and then leaned in and rubbed her lips across mine. I cupped her butt one last time and then watched as she climbed out of my lap, grabbed her jacket, and left without another word.

Shit. I leaned back in the chair and had to take a full five minutes to calm the fuck down after the napalm she'd just set off in my system.

Since I was there, I unlocked the hidden safe in the floorboard, pulled out the duplicate phone, and called Jasmine.

"Updates?" Jasmine answered on the first ring.

"I let a local badge in on the operation," I said.

Jasmine was quiet for a moment. "Your cop?"

"Rayne," I answered.

"She's the one you had me look into. The daughter of the COP," Jasmine said. She was quiet for a moment, no doubt re-reading every detail of Rayne's life, much like I had done several times since meeting her. "Okay, what did you tell her?"

"Nothing about why I'm here. Just that I'm DEA."

Jasmine was quiet. "Fine. I can set up a meet and drop?"

"No need. I'll fill her in, if and when it becomes necessary."

Jasmine was quiet. "Is this going to be a problem?"

"Nope," I said quickly.

"Jameson, I know you've been under a long while. If you need time..."

"I'm good," I said, growing a little agitated. "Really," I added a little softer. "We agree that whatever this is, it can't get in the way of why I'm here."

I heard Jasmine sigh. "Okay, keep me updated. Is there any other reason you're calling me?"

"There's a shipment coming into town later this week. I don't know the details yet, but something big is happening." I looked out the windows as the rain started falling harder. "When I know more, I'll send it to you."

"Good. Jameson?"

"Yeah?"

"Be careful." She hung up.

"Yeah," I said, shutting off the phone and putting it back in the safe.

I sat in the chair, watching the rain until it let up some, and then headed back into town.

Since I was off work for the rest of the day, I drove to the bar where I knew some of the Reapers would be. Sure enough, everyone was there except Ben and Declan.

I tried to nurse a beer for the next few hours but was thankful for the burger when Ben finally showed up and bought a couple of rounds for the entire crew.

Everyone seemed to be in a good mood, which made me very cautious for the rest of the night. Then Declan showed up with Evelyn in tow, and the cheerful attitude changed.

The guy was already drunk, and from the bruises covering Evelyn's face and arms, it appeared that he'd started on her before they'd arrived.

I didn't see the two Taylor brothers arrive, and when the fight started, I initially stood back and watched all their jock friends mesh with a few of the Reapers. Then I took a fist to my left ear and out of the corner of my eye caught Ben watching for my reaction.

Shit. I guess I'm all in at this point. Jumping into the fray, I took down the brother who had punched me.

When the cops showed up, I figured I'd earned Ben's appreciation as I and six of the other Reapers were cuffed and shuffled into a paddy wagon. I smiled knowing the two brothers and a few of their friends were being hauled into a second paddy wagon.

"That was fun," I said and spat some blood onto the van's floor.

"Don't worry, Felix will get us out." Declan laughed.

"What a rush. Those pussies deserved a beatdown. They've been sticking their noses around town, asking about us."

For the rest of the ride to the jail, I leaned my head back and pretended not to listen to Declan's rant about the Taylor twins.

Two and a half hours later, I sat in the cell with my mates and waited while we were all processed and released. Ben was first, followed by Declan.

"See you at the swamp this weekend," Declan called out as he half-danced out of the jail, turned, and double-flipped me off as he laughed. "Later."

"Yeah." I laughed back at him. I knew that there'd be an even bigger party at Felix's place this weekend. Everyone was gossiping about some big news Felix wanted to share with everyone.

Being arrested was to the Reapers like a badge of honor. One I'd just earned.

After almost an hour of waiting for Felix to post my bail, I realized the second part of today's stupid game. The get-yourself-out-of-jail badge. No doubt, they expected me to earn that badge today too.

I lay back and decided to get a little shut-eye before finishing the game. I was dog-tired. The fight hadn't been a rough one, not compared to some of the brawls I'd been in. But I was working on four beers—no scratch that, five and two shots—and the burger and fries I'd shared with Rayne earlier.

"This is fun." I woke to Rayne smiling down at me.

"Hi." I smiled.

"Are you drunk?" she asked, her eyes narrowing.

"Coming down from it," I admitted. "Which is why I was sleeping it off before I post bail."

She tilted her head slightly. "Your friends just left you in here?"

"I think it's another initiation." I sat up and ran my hands over my face and then through my hair. "What time is it?"

Rayne glanced down at her watch. "A quarter past seven."

"In the morning?" She nodded and I groaned. "I guess I missed work."

"Guess so," she said, watching me.

"I heard you and the gang had a little fun with the Taylor brothers and their friends last night."

"Yeah," I said, glancing around the room. "Later," I whispered when I saw the dark-haired cop sitting at a desk across the room watching us.

Rayne nodded. "I think he's sobered up," she called out to the other cop. "Come on," she said to me and helped me stand. "You're free to go."

"I am?" I asked softly.

"The brothers decided not to press charges. So you're free to go." She walked with me out of the cell.

"Great." I followed her through the building and realized I couldn't remember much of the previous night. "I guess I did drink a little too much," I admitted under my breath.

"I take it that doesn't happen often?" she asked as they made their way down the hallway.

"Never," I admitted. "You?"

"Only on my fake birthday," she answered as we stepped into a large, empty waiting room. "Need a ride back to the bar?"

I glanced out the window and groaned at the heavy rain falling outside.

"How about to my place? I can walk over and get my bike after this rain stops," I suggested.

She nodded and motioned for me to follow her. We walked back down a different hallway and out a back door.

I was surprised that she led me to her Jeep instead of a patrol unit.

I sat in the passenger seat as she drove me through town. When we pulled into the drive-through at a coffee shop, I was grateful.

After ordering a large coffee and two breakfast sandwiches, we sat in the rain and enjoyed the food and drinks in silence.

"How many of those initiations have they put you through?" she asked.

"Too many," I admitted. "I had to catch three alligators. Three." I groaned. "We grilled them up. I'd never even seen a gator before they tossed me in a swamp with bait and told me not to come back until I had three of them in the boat with me."

"I bet that was scary," Rayne said with a smile.

I shrugged. "I've had worse," I admitted with a chuckle.

"It's interesting. What we do for our jobs." She rested her head back. "Who we have to talk to, be friendly with, when all you want to do is punch them in the face and haul their butts down and lock them up."

"Who's on your shit list?" I asked, curious.

She glanced sideways at me. "Most of the Reapers, for starters."

I nodded. "Agreed."

"Second, I'd like to lock up the mayor's husband and sons." She frowned. "But I can't quite pin her murder on any of them. I'm pretty sure they had something to do with her death. The husband is just..." She visibly shivered.

"Sleazy. The boys..." She rolled her eyes and took another sip of her coffee. "They've been bugging me since grade school."

"Then I'm glad to report I kicked one of their asses last night," I said between bites.

"Which one?" Rayne asked.

I shrugged. "I can't tell them apart."

She laughed. "Everyone can tell them apart. They're not identical. Wyatt is shorter and a little bit stockier and Beau is usually described as the better-looking one."

I thought about it. " I guess it was the husky one."

"Good." She smiled. "He's a bigger ass."

I chuckled. "I had thought that the guy was friendly with Felix at one point."

Rayne was quiet for a moment. "You'd tell me if you thought the Reapers had anything to do with the mayor's death?"

I glanced at her, looked into her eyes, and promised. "If I thought there might be a connection, I wouldn't hesitate to tell you."

"Good," she said, finishing her sandwich and starting the Jeep again. "I'll take you home."

When she pulled up to my building, I couldn't help but glance around the empty back lot. The café guests usually parked out front on the main street and the employees used the side parking area.

"Thanks for the lift," I said, starting to get out. Then I said, "Screw it," and took Rayne's face in my hands and kissed her until I felt steadier. When I felt her body vibrating again, I released her and dashed through the rain to the stairs that led up to my place.

I was damned to hell, I thought as I stood under the cold

shower, trying to clear my mind and body from the woman. This was hell. For the first time in years, I couldn't have what I wanted more than anything else in life.

Chapter Eight

"The divine is in us,
in our own intrinsic humanity,
like a diamond in a mine."
–Juan Ramon Jimenez

Rayne

The moment I stepped foot into the house I'd grown up in, I knew there was trouble. Normally, there would be warm smells of food or baked goods to greet me at the door.

The Cordova home sat on five acres of grassland surrounded by large oak and pecan trees, many of which I'd spent my youth trying to climb. Even though the place was smaller than the other homes on the street, with three bedrooms, two baths, and an office off the back porch area, it still felt huge to me.

"Mom?" I called out.

"Back here," Edith Cordova answered from the back of the home.

Shortly after I'd moved out, Randy had turned the covered porch into a sunroom of sorts by closing in the three walls. Now, Edith spent most of her days enjoying the sunny views of their backyard.

The Cordovas were the only parents I could remember having. They were my folks, yet for some reason, I had a difficult time calling them or thinking about them by anything but their names. It was as if my brain was broken. The pair of them had been so patient with me when I was growing up and called them by their first names instead of Mom and Dad. Most of the time it didn't bother them. At least they didn't show it.

As an adult, I noticed that when I did force the words, it made them so much happier. So I tried my hardest to show my appreciation in that small way.

I walked through the formal living area and down the long hall that passed the kitchen and dining room, and then stepped out onto what used to be our back porch. Now, the room was so much cozier. Oak French doors opened into the space. The entire back wall was floor-to-ceiling windows that Edith currently had propped open, letting in the warm breeze.

There was an old, oversized sofa, a small television set, a bookcase that was overflowing, and Randy's old plaid chair in the space.

When I saw Edith, I had to hold in a gasp.

"Is it that bad?" Edith said with a sigh as she sat up. She'd been lounging on the sofa and, from the looks of it, I'd woken her.

"I didn't mean to wake you," I said, ignoring her question.

She ran her hands over her once thick and shiny hair.

Now, massive patches were missing and the silver-gray had turned to a dirty gray color.

"You didn't," she answered. "I had hoped to make you some cookies or some of my crumb cake you like so much. But I suppose I lost track of time."

"It's okay." I sat next to her and pulled her into my arms. When had she gotten so fragile? Breast cancer was stealing the only woman I loved right in front of my eyes.

"We can head into town?" I suggested suddenly. "Grab a coffee and treat at Creole's?" I added.

Creole Coffee Company was one of Edith's favorite places to go.

"I don't know," she answered with a sigh. "I just don't feel like being seen right now."

I reached up and touched her face, noting that it was puffy and slightly odd-colored. The chemo was doing a trick on her. Still, she was here. She was still fighting.

"Mom," I sighed. "Let me take you to Aria." Edith closed her eyes as a tear slipped down her cheek. "She has these wigs..." I started.

Edith's eyes flew open. "I don't want to wear a goddamned wig." Then she sighed. "Sorry, sweetie. It's just..."

"I know. You don't have to apologize to me." I hugged her again.

"No, I suppose I don't."

I felt like the world was ending as I held her and she cried for a few moments.

"Okay, fuck it." She leaned back. "I'm so over feeling sorry for myself." She straightened her shoulders. "Enough tears." She nodded once as she wiped her face. "It's past time I did this." She reached up and I watched her eyes turn sad as she touched her hair. "Call Aria. See if she can fit me in. She glanced down at the gray sweats she was wearing. "I'll go put on something more appropriate."

I smiled and nodded and pulled out my phone as she walked out of the room.

"Hey." Aria answered on the third ring.

"Hey, tell me you have a slot empty in half an hour," I asked.

Aria was quiet. "Your mom?"

"Yeah," I answered.

"I'll make the time. Come on down," Aria said and hung up.

Leaning back, I closed my eyes and thought of all the good times I'd had thanks to Edith.

Just before Randy and James Lee, an officer who had died of heart failure five years ago, found me, the couple had just lost their only son, Randy Jr., to SIDS. It had been a miracle that they'd gotten pregnant with Randy Jr. The chances of it happening again were practically zero.

Then I'd come into their lives. If not for them, who knows where I would have ended up? Since becoming a cop, I'd seen many kids enter the system. Our county had implemented a new registry a few years back, thanks to Randy and Edith.

Our state had one of the highest numbers of children under the age of eleven in the foster care system. The last time I checked, there were over four thousand kids in the system, and only a quarter of that was for registered families.

I'd thought about adding my name to that list, but my job and my current life could not handle such an endeavor. At least not at the moment.

"Are you sure about this?" I asked Edith as I drove us

into town. "I don't want you to feel like I strongarmed you into this."

She chuckled. "Sweetie, I was never the one who fell for your big puppy dog eyes. It was your father who always caved to your demands."

I chuckled. It was true. Edith had always been the stronger parent while Randy, well, he was slush when it came to me. The man had always given me everything I'd ever asked for. If I wanted two helpings of dessert, he'd give it to me. Whenever I got in trouble or received a bad grade, I'd tell Randy first. The punishment was always lighter than what I received when Edith found out first.

Still, in the past few years, we'd grown closer than we had when I'd lived under her roof. I never doubted her love for me. Not once.

When we'd found out the first time about her cancer diagnosis, it had hit all of us hard. That first surgery, the double mastectomy, I'd taken off work to be by her side. I'd been the one to watch over her, empty her drains, and give her a sponge bath. I'd stuck by her side for weeks until she'd fully recovered.

The next two surgeries, the removal of lymph nodes and her thyroid, I'd been there as well. Maybe seeing her in such a vulnerable state when she'd always been the strong one changed the way I saw her.

My personality and hers were so much alike that often, when I spoke out, I'd hear her voice in my head saying the same words.

I parked in front of Jazzed Up Hair Salon.

Aria waved at us through the large windows.

"Ready?" I asked Edith.

"As ready as I'll ever be."

For the next hour, the salon was filled with tears and

laughter. This wasn't the first time that Aria had to shave a woman's head or fit her with a wig. It was, however, the first time I'd witnessed it.

To my surprise, halfway through the process, Charlotte walked in carrying pink roses and balloons along with cupcakes for everyone in the room.

Somehow, they'd managed to turn it into a celebration instead of the death of what some considered to be a woman's most important beauty feature.

I had to admit, the wig looked so much better than the patches of scraggly hair she had earlier.

"I feel like a new woman," Edith said, reaching out and taking my hand and squeezing it softly. "Thank you." She took Aria's hand too. "Both of you. All of you." She laughed as she looked over at Charlotte.

"You look amazing." Charlotte smiled.

The silver wig matched Edith's old hair almost perfectly. Aria had purchased it with her in mind when we'd found out she had to go through chemo this time.

Honestly, I couldn't have found a better friend to watch out for the woman who had watched out for me.

"Thank you," I said, hugging Aria.

When we drove back to the house, Randy's eyes teared up when he saw Edith. The hug that followed warmed my heart. In thirty years of marriage they'd been through the hell of losing a child, fighting cancer twice, and raising me. Yet they were still so strongly in love.

No wonder I struggled with relationships. Nothing I'd found so far had sticking power like what I'd grown up with.

"I feel good enough to make us dinner," Edith said as we walked inside.

"Nope, not tonight. I've got some steaks on the grill.

Tonight, I'm cooking." Randy took my hand in his and mouthed, "Thank you."

Having dinner with my parents was always a joy. I tended to leave more relaxed than when I'd arrived. One of the rules that Edith had was no shop talk at the dinner table.

I knew Randy itched to ask me how the case was going, and I wanted to ask him his opinions on a few things. But we stuck to lighthearted topics instead and talked about the county fall fair coming to town in a few months. We replayed some fun gossip going around town and talked about world events and news.

As Randy walked me out to my Jeep, only then did we touch on work.

I filled him in on a few key details, and he helped shed some light on what path to take next.

I turned to leave but stopped when something dawned on me.

"You'd have to be notified if any undercover agents were working on cases in your town, right?" I asked.

Randy's expression didn't change. "What do you mean?"

"Like, say, if a DEA agent was in town." I watched his expression change ever so slightly. "You knew?" I asked.

"Knew what?" He shook his head.

"Jameson Lorenzo." I crossed my arms over my chest.

"How'd you find out?" Randy asked.

I smiled. "I'm thinking of dating him. Only..." I frowned. "It's not such a great time for that."

He nodded slowly. "I'd agree. The man has an impressive background. One that has to be kept between us, for now."

"Why?" I narrowed my eyes slightly. "What is it you're not telling me?"

He shrugged. "Let him do his job. You do yours." He turned and started walking inside. "Night. See you at work tomorrow."

"Night," I called out.

Driving through town on a Saturday night, I knew all the hot spots that would be active. Mainly, around the bar areas.

There was a long row of bikes outside of Bayou Brews, and I almost drove past but slowed when I spotted both Jameson's bike and Aria's Mini.

Pulling into a parking spot, I debated going in for a full five minutes. I pulled out my phone and shot a text to Aria.

"What are you doing at the BBB?"

I didn't have to wait long for an answer.

"Tobias and I are having a drink. Come on in and join us. Since it's obvious you're outside."

What the hell? I thought as I climbed out of my Jeep.

Bayou Brews and Blues was a three-story classic brick building in the heart of the oldest part of town. Sometime when I was in high school, a couple purchased the building and refurbished it. After their hard work, they'd sold it to the current owner, Jackson Pennington, who had opened the blues-style bar. In all honesty, it was one of the nicest bars in town.

The fact that it was the place the Reapers hung out didn't normally deter other guests. Every Friday and Saturday, the place hosted live jazz and blues music. They served basic bar foods upstairs in a small dining area. There were three pool tables, dart boards, and four large-screen televisions behind the bar that always played whatever sports games were currently on.

The moment I walked into the crowded bar I instantly wished I'd gone straight home. Normally, you would never find me in such a crowded place. It wasn't that I hated people. Well, okay, I hated most people and tolerated some.

"Rayne," a few people I'd known since school called out to me as I passed them by. Smiling, I yelled over the loud saxophone music if they had seen Aria.

One of them pointed upstairs, so I made my way to the bar and ordered a beer before heading up. A few Reaper members were sitting at the bar talking, none of them Jameson. I spotted a few more near the pool tables along with a few of the women that always hung around them.

Isabella Sinclair had been a few grades lower than me. She'd been a troubled girl as far back as I could remember. My theory was that she'd come from an abusive home and had practically raised herself. She was an attention hog. In classes, she'd learned early that any attention was good attention. Often, she'd start fights or bully the weaker girls. She laughed when she made any of her victims cry, almost as if she got off on tears.

Isabella, or Izzy as everyone called her, could have easily been the all-American, small-town princess, if not for the rotten core inside. As with the rest of the Reapers, she was covered almost head to toe in tattoos, except for that face of hers, which could have easily been on any magazine cover. She'd dyed the ends of her long blonde hair with bright pink, purple, and, this week's color, blue.

Then there was Nadia Monroe. The woman was a gym rat who could probably outlift most men in the Reapers. But since she had ovaries, she was kept from achieving full member status.

Nadia's parents had moved out of town shortly after her graduation, around the same time she'd joined the Reapers. She was shorter than I was and had long jet-black hair with bleached tips. Her toned and tanned body had even more muscles than tattoos, which covered almost every inch of her arms, shoulders, and legs.

Out of the two of them, Nadia Monroe was the one I would pick to watch closely. The woman never showed emotions. Her intelligence was, according to her records, off the charts.

Someone that smart didn't stick around the gang for scraps. She was after something.

Not spotting Jameson in the mix, I took my beer and headed upstairs.

Aria and Tobias sat in a low circular booth area with a round coffee table. Seeing the handful of empty beers and shot glasses on the table, I sat next to Aria.

"Hey, kids," I said, leaning back. "What are we celebrating tonight?"

"Nothing." Aria leaned over and hugged me. "Everything."

"We finally picked a date," Tobias said with a smile.

"Finally?" I laughed. "You mean, out of the half dozen dates you finally picked one of them?"

They both looked at one another. "We've decided on a new date," Aria said cheerfully.

"Okay, shoot. What's the date?" I asked.

"October tenth." Tobias smiled. "It's easy to remember. Ten, ten."

"Plus, it's on a Saturday this year and I called the hall and they're open so we booked it." Aria squealed and hugged Tobias. "We're getting married."

I laughed and picked up my beer. "And to think, it only took three years."

"Three years, six months, thirteen days, and"—Tobias glanced at his watch and narrowed his eyes—"twenty-two hours."

I'd been there less than half an hour before finally spotting Jameson downstairs playing pool.

I didn't know if he'd spotted me yet so I watched him as I leaned on the railing overhead.

Izzy was trying her best to get the man to notice her. Her black leather corset top had her solid Ds hiked up to her chin, and half of her butt cheeks hung out under the matching leather skirt she wore with it. The thigh-high boots completed the woman's outfit, which made me instantly wonder how anyone could be comfortable in an outfit like that.

I glanced down at the black jeans, blue button-up shirt, and heeled boots I'd dressed up in for dinner at my folks' place. This was my standard attire.

Except for the handful of sundresses I owned for occasions such as attending church with the Cordovas or special party events, this was as dressy as I got.

I glanced up just in time to see Izzy press her chest against Jameson's side and whisper something that had him laughing.

There wasn't an ounce of jealousy in my bones. Not normally. But at that moment, I wanted to kick in the other woman's teeth.

Turning away, I leaned on the half wall and watched Aria and Tobias together. What did it take to have something like they did?

The pair had pretty much fallen for one another at first sight. Tobias was a good man. One who had helped raise his younger sister after his father had been shot and killed in a drive-by shooting when he'd been thirteen. Randy had been the cop to put the two twenty-year-old shooters behind bars. Shortly after that, Randy took the chief of police gig.

Aria's story wasn't as sad as Tobias's. Aria came from a

middle-class family. They lived in a nice house just outside of town. Had good-paying jobs. Went to church every Sunday. Her mother volunteered at the school and the nursing home, while her father donated his time as a volunteer firefighter.

They were the stereotypical small-town family. With one exception. Aria was adopted. Both of her parents were black and had chosen to adopt Aria, a very pale white girl with flyaway blonde hair, at the tender age of six.

I think it was this fact that made us so close. The fact that neither of us knew our real roots was one of the first reasons we'd become friends. After that, well, we just sort of melted together as best friends.

"Taking in the view?"

I glanced over to see Jameson leaning against the wall next to me. How had he gotten there without me noticing?

"Sure." I took a sip of my second beer as Jameson glanced over to watch Aria and Tobias for a second. "It appears as if you were enjoying the game downstairs," I said, turning around to look over the crowd below.

"Pool isn't my sport," he replied, leaning next to me.

"Oh?" I asked, bumping his shoulder with mine. "What is your sport?"

Instead of answering, he smiled quickly and my knees wobbled. If I hadn't been leaning on the wall, I wondered if I would have fallen.

"Looks like Izzy is signed up to play on your team." I motioned with my head to where the woman had been below.

He leaned closer to me and lowered his voice.

"I've already picked my team," he whispered. "We need to talk." He ran his hand down my arm and squeezed my hand, placing a piece of paper in it before turning and walking away.

I waited until I was locked in a bathroom stall before reading his message.

"They found out about us. Meet me at the cabin at one."

Totally sober now, I closed my eyes and took a few deep breaths.

Shit. Just how big of trouble was he in thanks to me?

Chapter Nine

"There are three things extremely hard: steel, a diamond, and to know oneself."
—Benjamin Franklin

Jameson

In all my years on the job, I had never been put in a tight spot like I was in now. Waiting for Rayne to show up, I paced the cabin and tried to think of my next move.

Of course, I had to warn her of Felix's plans.

When he and Ben confronted me about seeing us last week, I'd easily blown them off with the whole "I was trying to get laid and didn't know she was a cop" bit.

Then, they'd somehow heard that Rayne had walked me out of the cell and driven me home. That news had seemed to force Felix and Ben into plotting.

During the weekend party at his house the night before, he'd pulled me aside.

"You see, Jameson, we need someone to keep us posted on a few things. You could use this flirtatious relationship you have with the pretty detective"—Felix wiggled his eyebrows at me at that point and slapped my shoulder a little too hard—"to our benefit."

"Like I said, I didn't even get to first base," I had countered, hoping the matter would be dropped. I did not want to bring Rayne into the spotlight of the Reapers.

"Yeah, yet." Felix laughed. "What if you could get the pretty detective to trust you?"

"Meaning?" I asked.

"You see, there's a... gray spot we need to shed some light on in this town," Felix added.

"A gray spot?" I had asked, instantly wondering what he meant, but then he sprung his and Ben's plans to have me use Rayne to get information about the mayor's murder. Why in the hell were they concerned about that?

"We need a few details, you know, to make sure she's not poking her nose where it doesn't belong," he'd said. "I'll get you more details soon."

From what I could tell, none of the Reapers had so much as looked in the mayor's direction before. Sure, a bunch of them took issue with the mayor's twin sons. The brawl that week hadn't been the first between the groups. Nor, I'd wager, would it be the last, since the Reapers were already plotting their revenge.

Hearing a car drive up, I glanced out to see Rayne park her Jeep and shut it off. I watched the road to make sure she hadn't been followed, then opened the door for her.

"How big of trouble are you in?" she asked, stepping inside.

"First things first," I said, pulling her into my arms and covering her mouth with mine.

I'd missed the taste and feel of her next to me. I'd

dreamed of nothing else but her since the moment I'd seen her across the bar.

"Now I feel steadier," I said, pulling back a little.

"You do?" She chuckled. "I think my entire body is vibrating." She smiled up at me.

I took her hand and led her into the living room.

"How bad is it?" she asked after we sat down.

"They want me to use you for information," I blurted out, causing her to laugh. Then she sobered.

"Information on what?" she asked.

I tilted my head slightly.

"Oh shit." She stood up and walked to the dark windows as she wrapped her arms around herself. "I had pretty much ruled out anyone in the Reapers for Sharon's murder." She turned back to me. "Now..." She shook her head.

"Yeah." I nodded. "So what's your game plan?"

"Mine?" She balked. "Shit." She closed her eyes. "Shit," she said again. She sat next to me again. "Who asked you to use me?"

"Felix."

Her eyes narrowed.

"George Felix Woolf, age thirty-two. Six foot two, two hundred and fifteen pounds. Six convictions and four years behind bars. He was last released about two years ago," she rattled off.

"Do you have a computer in that head of yours?" I asked, amazed at her recount of details.

She chuckled. "Eidetic memory." She tapped her head. "It's a curse in my personal life but a benefit to the job."

I nodded. "Something tells me Ben was in on the request too. Felix doesn't make a move without consulting him first."

"Ben Blackwood. Do you know I once went out on a date with him in junior high?" She shook her head. "Dodged that bullet. He beat up his high school girlfriend on the night of prom when she glanced at another boy. That was the first time he spent time in jail. He has six more convictions and did time with Felix for a year or two."

I nodded. I knew all there was about each member of the Reapers. Far more than any police report could tell anyone.

"In school, he used to brag about some of the crap he did. I've wanted to lock him up for years." She leaned back. "If you're here, DEA, that means drugs. Are we talking more than the shit that flows through every small town?" she asked, and I nodded. "Okay." She took a deep breath. "Do you know anything about the attorney general's investigation into Sharon Taylor?"

I guess my surprised look answered the question.

"For?" I asked.

Rayne shifted slightly.

The moment her leg brushed against mine, I wished we were there for anything other than work.

"Apparently, corruption and embezzling," she answered.

"Apparently?" I asked. She shrugged.

"I've got a request in for more details and to be added to the loop, but since Sharon's death, I doubt they'll give me much. It seems like their case hit a dead end." She rolled her head towards me. "No pun intended. I have known Sharon Taylor my entire life. Even though I never had a personal friendship with her, she was there when I received my badge. What happens now? What do Felix and Ben have in store for you?"

"I'm to use you," I answered and saw a twitch in her

lips. "Yeah, Felix is expecting all the juicy details of our sex-capades."

She chuckled. "Well, we'd better make sure our stories match then." She shifted and moved over me. Her legs straddled my hips.

"Oh?" I smiled and gripped her hips with my hands, digging my fingertips into her softness. I'd dreamed of this. Of this very moment. The feel of her, the soft subtle scent of leather and flowers that she carried on her. "And how do you propose we do that?" I asked, trying to keep my heart from exploding in my chest.

Instead of answering, she brushed her lips across mine softly. The featherlight touch was almost my undoing.

How long had I gone without the feel of a soft woman next to me? Too damned long, that was for sure.

While she ran her mouth over mine, tangling our tongues in tantalizing play, I moved my hands all over her body. Even though she was probably the tallest woman I'd been attracted to, she was still so much smaller than I was. Her body fit tight up against mine and when she started moving her hips, I about lost it.

I was holding back years of pent-up desire, so I lifted Rayne in my arms and carried her the few dozen steps or so into the bedroom.

Her body slid down mine, and we both took a moment to remove our weapons—my Glock, which I slid into the finger-coded safe on the nightstand, and her Beretta.

"Nice piece," I said as she sat it and her holster down on the same nightstand.

"It's my personal piece." She smiled. "I have a few different ones. We can compare and appreciate each other's weapons later." She laughed as she unbuttoned her blouse.

My mouth watered when she exposed a simple skin-colored bra underneath. She was lean, toned, and had tan lines that crossed over her perfect skin, indicating she'd spent some time outside recently.

She tossed the shirt onto the chair next to the bed and reached to start pulling my shirt over my head.

"God," she purred as she ran her hands over my chest. Then she traced one of my tattoos with her fingertip. "I'm a sucker for these. I have a few myself." She smiled up at me.

I nodded and started tracing the small, curved flowers on her shoulder.

Pulling her closer, I kissed her until we both felt unsteady as we frantically peeled off layer after layer of clothing.

When we finally fell onto the bed, every bit of clothing was gone. The feeling of her skin against mine sent shock waves through every fiber of my being.

This was new, I kept telling myself. This mattered.

How long had I managed to avoid letting down my guard while on the job? Not caving to any of the pleasures dangled in front of my face for years. And trust me, there was plenty of pretty fruit willingly offered.

None of them had mattered. Not one was worth taking that step. This step. The one I so desperately wanted with Rayne.

I'd asked myself why. Why her?

Then I'd think back to the handful of conversations we'd had. How the time I'd spent with her had mattered more to me than any I'd had over the years.

Besides my boss, Rayne was the only person who knew me.

Now, I was lucky enough to be able to spend these moments with her and vowed to stretch the time out for as long as I could. I was going to explore every inch of her soft sexy body so that I could memorize every curve. I knew there might come a time when things changed. In my line of work, things could grow dark very fast. I might not always get to be here with her in the future.

I ran my mouth down her neck and lapped at each breast while her fingers dug into my hair, holding me, pushing me where she wanted.

I followed all of her demands until I settled between her thighs, which wrapped around my shoulders.

When I tasted her for the first time, I knew there was no way in hell I would stop at having her taste on my tongue just once.

I dipped one of my fingers inside her as I continued to suck at her skin. She arched. Bucked. Moaned.

Every movement and every sound that she made affected my body, and I knew I was running out of time.

I pulled on one of the rubbers I'd purchased the previous week for just such an occasion and slid up her body. I covered her while she tangled her legs around mine.

"Before," she said, holding still, "one last question." I smiled and nodded. "What's your real name?"

I hovered over her, looking deep into her dark eyes. Her hair was fanned out on the pillow in long straight lines. Her lips were plump and pink from our kisses. She looked like a woman who was already sated, yet the vibration coming from her body told me that she was still in need. "The truth is, I can't even remember," I said as I slid into her.

"Jameson," she whispered as I started to move.

Yes, that felt right. The man I had once been, long ago, was nowhere to be found.

Even now, being here with her like this, I was reborn. Remade.

What I was feeling now, I'd never felt before. I was sure of it.

Her tightness wrapped around me. The taste of her on my lips. The feeling of her heated skin next to mine. Every new feeling and thought I had was like exploring the world for the first time.

We moved together, seeming to know what the other needed, wanted.

Our fingers tangled over her head as I pumped long slow strides deep inside her. When the speed quickened, our eyes locked for a moment.

There, deep inside her soft brown eyes, I could see the same things I was feeling. The same wants.

She shouted my name as I felt her convulse under me seconds before my release, one that rocked my core and shattered every hope of getting out of the small town unscathed.

I was lost. There would be no coming back from this.

I collapsed next to her, pulling her heated body up tight against my side.

We lay in the quiet, listening to the cicadas and crickets outside the cabin.

"I can't stay," she said after our bodies had cooled.

"Yeah," I agreed. "I can't either."

"Where do we go from here?" she asked, rolling over to hover over me as she rested on her elbow. Her eyes scanned my face, my chest.

"I suppose we need to make some sort of public appearance for the cause," I suggested.

"Bayou Brews?"

I shrugged. "I work tomorrow from eight to three."

She smiled. "I could hit the gym during my lunch break. I'll make sure to wear something... just for you."

I instantly thought of seeing her in one of the skimpy gym outfits most of the women wore when they worked out and felt myself grow hard again.

In one quick move, I spun us around, pinning her under me, and had her laughing.

This time, when we came together, there was no speed. Instead, laughter filled the room as we tested each other's limits.

Her nails scraped my sides and back, no doubt leaving slight marks there. Still, when she flipped me over, I willingly went and watched in amazement and wonder as she climbed on top of me and took what she wanted from me.

This time, we jumped over the edge together. The moment our bodies cooled, we retreated to the shower, gathered our things, and dressed.

"It's morning." Rayne groaned softly. "I'm going to kill you if you make me do burpees," she warned as they walked out into the early morning air. The sun was just starting to cast shadows through the thick trees.

Before she could climb into her Jeep, I pulled her back into my arms, needing to feel her once more against me. This time, when I kissed her, I allowed everything I was feeling to pour from me.

"Wow," she said, resting her forehead against my chest.

I closed my eyes and nodded. "Yeah, wow."

Riding back to the apartment, I parked and figured I'd stop in the café downstairs for a cup of coffee and something sugary to help me get through the rest of the morning.

By the time I gathered my gym bag, I was almost refreshed.

When I stepped out onto the balcony at the top of my stairs to head back down to the bike, I spotted two of the

Reapers sitting in an old truck across the street, watching me.

Shit. Had they been there when I'd arrived? I'd been too tired to notice. Did it matter? Double shit.

Acting like I hadn't seen them, I climbed on my bike and went to work.

In the safety of the locker room, I pulled out my phone and sent Rayne a coded text.

"Thanks for last night. I enjoyed watching the movie *The Surveillance* with you."

I hoped she'd get the clue and waited, watching my phone screen for her reply.

"It was a great movie. Next time, you can pick, I trust you can find something that will entertain us. I'll see you at lunch."

I smiled. Yeah. Okay, so I was falling fast for her. Her brains and wit far outshined anyone I'd met before. Plus, she was sexy as hell.

I didn't know how I was going to get through the hours until I saw her again.

Chapter Ten

"Diamonds are to be found only in the darkness of the earth, and truth in the darkness of the mind."
—Victor Hugo

Rayne

Even after two cups of coffee with three times the sugar I usually put in, my mind was still a little foggy. I doubted it was from the lack of sleep but more due to the fact that I'd had mind-melting, body-slamming, ultimate sexcapades last night.

How in the hell did one man know just what my body needed? It was like he was a freaking mind reader, a magician when it came to manifesting my deepest, darkest desires.

My body was still vibrating when I stepped into my office. Before my computer could even boot up, Sherry was there, leaning on my doorjamb.

"What?" I asked with a groan, causing her to smile.

Today's outfit was a dark blue jumper that somehow

made her look slim and fit. I knew that if I ever wore something like that, I'd probably look like an Oompa Loompa.

"I finally tracked down the two Bobbys," she said slowly.

"Okay." I leaned back in my chair. "Where are they?"

I had yet to talk to the two men who had made that initial call on the day of Sharon Taylor's murder. The duo often went MIA for weeks and months in the swamp lands to hunt or fish. So it wasn't a big concern of mine in the case. Still, it was on my list to talk to them when they did return.

I needed to know exactly what they'd heard and why in fuck they'd called it in when everyone in town knew they hated the cops. Almost as much as they hated the IRS and the Feds.

"They're back home," Sherry answered, her eyes narrowing as she scanned my face. "You're glowing."

"I'm..." I shook my head, not understanding.

Sherry smiled. "Aria told me you were flirting with someone. I couldn't get a name out of her and something tells me I won't get one out of you either." She crossed her arms over her chest. "If I ever found a man that made me glow," she nodded with her head as she sighed heavily, "I'd know he was the one."

Wiping my hands over my face I silently agreed. "I'll head out to see the Bobbys." I started to get up but stopped when my computer was finally done booting up and signaled I had an email.

"Take your time. I told them you'd swing by today. They're busy cutting up their catches," Sherry added over her shoulder as she walked away.

Before I had a chance to open my email, Quincy poked his head in my door.

"Good, you're here," he said, stepping in and shutting my door behind him.

"Not for long," I said, opening the few emails I had. One was from Randy with Edith's updated chemo schedule.

"We need to talk," Quincy said, sitting down and leaning forward.

"About?" I asked as I opened the second email. I froze in place when the fuzzy image of Jameson and me filled the screen. The image of us embracing while standing on the porch of the cabin that morning had my heart pounding so loudly that I couldn't hear or focus on what Quincy was saying.

I shut down my system by quickly hitting the button on the tower. "I... need to head out."

"We haven't talked..." Quincy called after me as I rushed from the room.

"Later. After lunch," I called back. I'm pretty sure I bumped into a few people as I retreated out of the building.

Before I could climb into the patrol car, I got a text message from Jameson.

"Thanks for last night. I enjoyed watching the movie *The Surveillance* with you."

Shit. Yeah. We had been watched. That message was loud and clear now. Obviously, the cabin was no longer a safe place. Why? Why were they watching us? Who were they watching? Him or me?

I typed back. "It was a great movie. Next time, you can pick. I trust you can find something that will entertain us. I'll see you at lunch." I hit send.

I got into the patrol car, slid on my sunglasses, and, as I backed out, I glanced around.

As I took off down the street, I rolled my eyes at the

obvious sedan occupied by two Reapers parked across the street from the precinct.

I must have been tired or stupid not to spot them following me earlier. Now, however, as they tailed three cars behind me, I wondered why. I wanted to pull over and confront them, but instead I headed out to the Bobbys' place. The second I turned into the driveway, the sedan disappeared.

Lost interest or knew where I was going?

I parked behind a massive black truck and climbed out of the car just as Bobby Sr. walked out onto his porch.

"Morning, Bobby," I said, stepping onto the porch.

"Rayne." He nodded. "Coffee?" he asked, holding up the mug he had.

"No, I got my own, thanks." I sat on the chair he motioned for me to take, and he sat across from me.

From there, I could see the side of the Taylor's massive house, which sat less than two hundred yards away.

"We didn't like Sharon much. She always complained about us not having our property clean and tidy, but she didn't deserve what was done to her," Bobby said, leaning back in his chair.

For a man in his sixties, Bobby Elwood Sr. was in great shape. There were only a dozen or so lines that crossed the man's face. He was in good enough shape that he could probably outrun a boar.

The Bobbys were known for causing trouble in town but their home life was quiet. They'd never had a call out to their property for fights or complaints. Bar fights were their usual thing and normally involved a Reaper or two. Hell, most good people in town mixed with a Reaper on a regular basis.

"Want to tell me what you heard that caused you to call us?" I asked.

"Not me, my boy," Bobby said. "Junior," he called through the screen door. "Rayne's here to talk."

Bobby Jr. was the spitting image of his dad. Same build, same shaggy mud-colored hair and eyes. Junior had been a few years before me in school. I'd heard he'd been the star of the football and basketball teams in high school. He was good-looking enough that everyone wondered why he was still single.

"Hey, Rayne." Bobby sat across from me while he sipped his mug. "Coffee?"

"No, thanks," I answered. "What did you hear?" I asked.

Bobby sighed. "Screaming. Like a banshee in the middle of the night. I'd stepped out to take a smoke. Paw doesn't like me to in the house. My maw never allowed it when she was alive." Jr. smiled. "I thought of heading over to the big house myself, you know, to check and see if all was all right, but then it stopped." He shrugged. "Figured it was a bobcat, you know. They scream just as loud when they've been cornered by a bear or boar."

"Right," I agreed. "Time?"

"Oh, about oneish." He shrugged. "Maybe closer to one-thirty."

"What made you call this one in?" I asked.

Junior shrugged. "Just a feeling. Right here." He tapped his gut. "We were heading out for our hunt, packing up first thing that morning." He frowned into his mug. "The screams kept playing in my head. Something just wasn't right. So I called. Figured it wouldn't do no harm."

"You were right to call," I told him. "You didn't by chance see a car in the drive?"

Junior shook his head. "No car. Heard what sounded like a bike sometime in the night before though."

"A... motorcycle?" I asked, jotting down the note. "What time?"

Both men looked at one another and shrugged.

"Before the screams?" I asked.

Junior nodded. "I guess about an hour before."

I made a note. "And after the screams?"

"After that, it was quiet till we left. I guess right before you arrived and found..." He dropped off.

I nodded. "Anything else you can remember about that night or morning?" I asked. Both men shook their heads. "Happen to know when Mr. Taylor left?"

"Sure, early evening. Watched that stupid-looking pink car pull out around six." Sr. chuckled. "No man should be caught driving a pink car."

Both men laughed then sobered as they glanced over to the pink car still in the driveway.

"We know how hard it is, losing someone," Senior said with a sigh. "Speaking of which, how's your ma doing? Chemo can be really tough. My Louisa, she was a fighter." He shook his head.

"She's... holding up," I offered, remembering only then that breast cancer had been the cause of his wife's death.

My gut twisted and my heart did a little jump that felt like I'd need paddles to get it started beating normally again.

"Next time you see her, give her our best," Senior added.

"Thank you," I said, standing up, unable to bear any more talk about Edith's journey. "If you think of anything else, let me know."

"Will do," they both said at once.

As I drove back to town, I watched my rearview mirror

for the sedan. It surprised me that they had lost interest in following me at first, but then I realized they probably knew exactly where I had been heading. There wasn't much out on the county road that led to the Bobbys' place and the Taylor's plantation.

Since it was on my list and I still had a few hours before lunch, I dropped by the city building, hoping to get a meeting with Jackson Pennington. The man had been busy the few times I'd tried to get an interview with him. Maybe today he'd have time?

When I stepped into the man's office, which sat across the hallway from the mayor's now empty office, the differences were immediately obvious.

The mayor's office was filled with pinks, lace doilies, and what some would consider cheap and tacky items. Jackson Pennington obviously liked the finer things in life.

Rich warm hues mixed with dark woods. Expensive-looking furniture, rugs, and artwork filled the massive space. No doubt everything inside belonged to Pennington himself. Gemsville didn't have the kind of money to purchase so much as the rug she was currently standing on.

It was interesting that the man's office was at least twice the size of the mayor's. He must have removed a few walls to extend the space to the size it was. How had this been allowed? Why?

Emma Boudreaux sat at the front desk, watching me walk in behind the heavy glass doors.

"He's in a meeting," Emma said before I had even made it halfway across the large circular rug.

"Good, then you'll have time to answer a few of my questions until he's free," I said with a smile.

It was clear that Jackson had asked Emma to play

blocker, and I couldn't fault the woman for simply doing her job.

"I'm not..." Emma started, but when she noticed me raising my eyebrows, she sighed. "What questions?"

"Schedule questions," I said, pulling out my notepad. For the next few moments, I asked Emma every question I thought she could answer. Most of them were about Pennington's whereabouts before, during, and in the days after Sharon's murder.

Emma rattled off the man's schedule and, after I requested a copy, she shot me an email. I noticed that none of the information provided was after business hours with the exception of one evening dinner with a client in a town almost an hour away.

I was just about to ask another question when the dark wood double doors opened and Pennington stepped out with a dark-skinned woman with jet-black hair who looked to be in her mid-thirties. I had never seen the woman in town before. Her business attire spoke of money, yet her neon purple lips and the matching purple tips of her hair spoke of something else.

The woman was quite stunning and spoke in a deep voice laced with Southern charm. I pegged it for a Georgia accent, not Louisiana.

"Thank you, Mrs. Caldwell." Jackson's smile slipped slightly when he noticed me leaning against the secretary's desk.

I smiled at him and waited, watching the interaction.

"I'll get those numbers to you later this week," Mrs. Caldwell said easily as she shook Pennington's hand. "I look forward to doing business with you."

Pennington nodded and stood just inside his doors until Mrs. Caldwell passed me.

The woman's eyes narrowed slightly as she assessed me, then she nodded at me before leaving.

"Rayne, please come in." Jackson motioned as he stood back, allowing me to pass through the doors. "Emma, hold all my calls," he said before shutting the door behind us. "What can I do for you today, Rayne?"

I moved into the massive office and sat down in one of the high-back red leather chairs.

The chairs sat almost half a foot shorter than his chair, so he towered over anyone who sat down across from him, which told me exactly what kind of man he was. He wanted control, and power over anyone he met with.

Still, I knew how to deal with power-hungry men and straightened my back just enough that we sat almost eye to eye.

"Emma was kind enough to fill me in on your schedule during the last few weeks," I informed him as he settled into his chair.

"By you still being here, I'm assuming you have more questions?" he asked.

I smiled slightly, not letting my irritation with his tone show.

"Your assistant can only confirm your whereabouts during business hours. I require some after-hours information." I pulled out my notepad.

"Such as?" he asked, his tone laced with annoyance.

I rattled off the dates and times and then jotted down his responses. Most of his time was spent traveling between Gemsville and Lafayette, where he claimed he had several business meetings with investors.

"You missed one," I pointed out. "The night of Sharon's murder." I waited.

He tilted his head and glanced at his phone before answering.

"If I didn't mention it, I was at home. Alone," he said dryly.

I nodded several times as I thought. "No missus at home?" I said as I tucked my notepad into my pocket.

"No." The man's left eyebrow arched up.

"No prospects in that area?" I asked.

"Rayne, is this a futile attempt to ask me out?" he said with a sneer.

I put on my fuck-you smile and remained quiet for a moment. Long enough that he started to squirm for a split second.

The man was tall, skinny, too refined for my taste and probably didn't have a tattoo on his body. He wore suits like they were his comfort clothes and, to be honest, there was nothing less appealing than the way he spoke to women as if they were his slaves only here to do his bidding.

"Is there anyone who can corroborate you being home? Alone?" I asked dryly.

"No, detective. No missus. No prospects. I'm married to my work," he said with a slight sigh. "Now, if you don't mind..." He started to get up.

"Did you know that Sharon Taylor was being investigated by the state attorney's office for corruption and embezzling?" I threw at him and watched anger and fake surprise cross his eyes.

"No," he said slowly as he sat back down. "Is it true?"

Instead of answering, I added, "Did you know that Sharon was having multiple affairs?"

This time the surprised look was so obviously fake I almost laughed. "I suppose that makes sense. Rumors are that Henry has a few... friends on the side."

I nodded and watched the man closely while I asked my next question. "You own both the Red River Iron Gym and the Bayou Brews and Blues."

Again, the irritation was in his demeanor and tone. "I own a lot of buildings, a lot of businesses in this town."

"And you're about the only business owner who single-handedly employs more than a dozen members of the Swamp Reapers Motorcycle Club." I smiled when his eyes narrowed at me.

"I personally am not involved with the running of any of my buildings or businesses. I keep at arm's length from all of them. It's better this way. In other words, I am not responsible for hiring any employees other than Emma, out front." His smile was strained.

I shifted forward, laying my elbows on my knees. "Let's make this official, shall we?"

"Sure." He threw up his hands in frustration.

"Mr. Jackson Pennington, do you possess any information pertinent to the investigation into the homicide of Mayor Sharon Taylor, or are you refraining from disclosing any relevant details that could aid in the apprehension of any individuals implicated in Mayor Sharon Taylor's murder?"

By the time I was done speaking, Jackson was standing up.

"No, now please leave my office." He motioned towards the doors.

"Thank you for your cooperation," I said as I slowly stood up to leave. But then I spotted a small silver picture frame sitting on a side table that held a coffee pot, a plant, and a printer.

I walked over to it and smiled down at a picture of Jackson Pennington, Faye Baker, and Kenya Jackson on a boat somewhere. The trio looked very comfortable together, with Jackson in the middle of the group. The two ladies were wearing very skimpy bikinis, and Jackson's chest was bare.

There was another picture of Jackson and Quincy Ingram on the same boat. Obviously, the men were on a fishing trip.

There were other pictures in similar frames—some of a large boat on the river, others of him, and a few of him with some of the other townspeople, including one of him and the mayor at the opening of one of his businesses—but this one for some reason stood out to me.

"Nice picture," I said, tapping the frame before walking out of the office.

Chapter Eleven

Jameson

Trying to keep my mind busy until Rayne showed up wasn't hard. Everything I did was scrutinized by one or two members of the gang. It was as if they were blatantly watching over me.

"What's up?" I asked Felix. He had joined me at the gym almost an hour before Rayne was scheduled to be here.

"Just watching out for our investment." Felix had slapped me on the back.

"Investment?" I chuckled. "Dude, I'm getting laid." I wiggled my eyebrows.

"Yeah." Felix laughed, then lowered his voice. "She's currently visiting the city building. We need to know why."

"I'm sure she's..." I was going to say, working the case, but was afraid it would sound too cop-like. "She's doing her job," I finished with a shrug. "Don't the police work at the city building sometimes? You know, to go to hearings and shit?"

Felix laughed slightly. "Find out why." He slapped me on the shoulder and then, instead of working out, waved his hand, and the two Reapers that were currently in the building followed him outside.

It was almost as if they knew Rayne was about to make an appearance. If Felix had given him free rein to do what he wanted with her, why in the fuck were they watching them?

Shit. That meant no matter what, he still hadn't earned their trust.

After they left, I tried to go about my business, looking out the windows, eager for Rayne to get there.

When she finally did show up, I felt both relieved and anxious. Were they still watching us?

Since they knew that we'd spent the night together in the cabin, I pulled her into my arms and kissed her.

"For show?" she asked against my ear.

"Both for that and to settle my nerves. I'm pretty sure they know about last night," I said as I pretended to hug her.

"Oh, they do. I received a lovely photo of us on the porch of the cabin from this morning in my email."

"Shit." I pulled back, my entire body tense.

"Who do they think owns the cabin?" she asked.

"I told them it was a friend. Someone who owed me a favor."

"Now," she said in a normal voice, "how about you show me what equipment your gym has that can help work out the kinks."

"Sure," I agreed and took her hand to lead her back to the locker rooms where she could change into the workout clothes that she most likely had in the gym bag on her shoulder.

After she disappeared into the women's locker room, I signed her in at the register computer as my guest and then waited. I tried not to glance out the windows too much but from what I could tell, it appeared the Reapers had left us alone. It appeared that way, but I still felt like someone was watching.

When she came out, my heart pretty much stopped when I ran my eyes over the skin-tight dark gray yoga outfit she had on.

"Okay," I said, then had to clear my throat when my voice cracked. Rayne instantly smiled. "Let's start with a warmup," I said, taking her hand and walking to the mats.

I was under no assumption that Rayne didn't know how to work out. I'd run my hands all over that body and knew full well that she was toned everywhere.

Once we started lifting weights, she matched me stride for stride. Even though I had more weight, her form was perfect, assuring me she knew what she was doing.

"Think it's safe for us to talk here?" she asked.

I shrugged. "Probably not. But if we keep our voices low, we'll be okay."

"Have you figured out what they want from me yet?" she asked softly, between reps.

"They want to know what you were doing at the city building this morning," I answered as I glanced up towards the windows.

She was quiet for a moment. "They followed me out to the Bobbys' place, and I spotted them after I left the city office."

I nodded. "I'm almost one hundred percent sure that they're out there right now, watching."

"Oh, I know it. They're really bad at tailing." She chuckled and then sat up straight. "If you want to tell them, I was interviewing Jackson Pennington."

I frowned. "The investor and owner of this place?"

She nodded. "He owns most buildings in town. But the important part is that his office is directly across from the mayor's." She stood up as I moved over to add more weights to the bar. "And since Sharon's death, he's filled in as mayor."

"Dotting all the I's?" I asked.

"Twice." She rolled her shoulders. "Is that all they want?" she asked with her back to the windows.

"For now," I admitted and moved to sit on the bench.

"Just how far are they wanting to take this?" she whispered.

Instead of answering, I pulled her close and wrapped my arms around her hips, letting her settle between my thighs. When I pressed my face into her chest and her hands moved up into my hair, I answered.

"They expect me to fully use you."

She sighed. "Then I suppose you'll just have to let me come over tonight."

I chuckled. "I suppose. You know where I live. Stop by anytime."

"I'll bring dinner." She glanced at her watch. "I'd better go, I've got a meeting in half an hour." She turned and glanced towards the windows, then added a little louder, "With the mayor's husband."

I held back a smile and nodded. "I'm glad I could make you sweat. I look forward to doing it again tonight."

The edges of her lips curved slightly before she turned and walked towards the locker rooms.

When she came out again, she was back in her standard

detective uniform of dark pants and button-up shirt. She had a worried look on her face, but when I stepped up to her, it disappeared.

"Problems?" I asked softly.

She shook her head. "See you tonight." She reached up on her toes and brushed her lips across mine.

Less than half an hour after she'd left, Ben strolled through the doors.

"Got a minute?" he asked me.

I glanced at my watch and nodded. "I get off in ten."

He nodded. "Meet you outside." He turned and walked out.

Whatever it was, I could tell that it was serious. After showering and clocking out, I stepped out front.

"Declan's been arrested," he said as I stuffed my gym bag into my saddlebags.

"For?" I asked.

"Evelyn's in the hospital," Ben said with a frown.

"Shit," I said, wanting to ask if the woman was okay. Only, I knew Ben wasn't upset that the woman was hurt.

"I need you to come with me tonight on a run," he said quickly. "Declan was supposed to, but now I guess you're going to have to fill in for him since your woman's the one who put him behind bars."

"My..." I had to glance down to hide the smile. "Right," I said, controlling my voice. "When and where do you need me?"

"I'll swing by your place around eight," Ben said. "Be ready."

"Sure thing," I said and then watched Ben drive off on his newer Harley.

Shit, I'd been working on this gig for this long and all it

took me to be added into the middle circle was for Rayne to arrest Declan?

I wanted to call or text her. Instead, I drove slowly through town, past the bar, where there were still two cop cars and four uniformed officers standing out front.

When I reached my apartment, I locked myself in my room and updated Jasmine about the plan for that night and tried to find out how Evelyn was doing.

Using my private phone, I shot a text message to Rayne.

"Heard you had a productive afternoon. I've got to call tonight off since I have work now that Declan's busy. Rain check for tomorrow?"

I waited for her response and almost fell asleep in the chair.

"Sounds good. See you then. Sorry I didn't tell you. I've been kinda busy."

"Understood. Night."

After shutting everything down, I set an alarm and crawled into bed for a few hours before Ben would arrive.

When the man finally knocked on my door, I'd dressed in black jeans, a shirt, and my leather jacket. I had both my guns on me—one in the holster where Ben and everyone else knew I wore it every day and the other one tucked in my motorcycle boot. I also had the knife I always kept in my other boot.

"Ready?" Ben asked after running his eyes over me quickly and approving of my attire.

"Yeah," I said, following him down the stairs.

"We're leaving the bikes tonight," he said as he walked towards his truck. I climbed in the passenger seat and sat back as we drove out of town.

I didn't know what I had expected, but almost an hour

later, he pulled off the county road and onto a dirt lane choked with overgrowth.

"We walk from here," he said as he climbed out and pulled an empty bag out of the bed. There were a few bags and boxes in the back of his truck that I hadn't noticed before.

"Who?" I asked. Ben just chuckled.

"You'll see." He started walking.

What in the hell had I gotten myself into?

We walked for almost twenty minutes. The pathway got a hell of a lot narrower. I was thankful Ben had brought a high-powered Mag flashlight that lit up the way.

When we made it to a clearing, he shut off the light and we stood there like idiots in the middle of swamp land for almost ten minutes. I wanted to ask questions but felt like Ben would have just told me to shut up.

I vaguely worried about gators. Did they attack at night? Shit. After that thought, every sound I heard caused me to tense.

When my eyes finally adjusted to the dark, I realized just how many stars there were overhead. The trees blocked out a lot of them and the moon was nothing more than a sliver in the night sky.

I'd never really been one to enjoy hiking or camping. But even with the mosquitoes buzzing around me, no doubt sucking my blood wherever my skin was exposed, I thought it was a beautiful night.

Then I heard a noise.

"Who dat?" someone called out in a thick Cajun accent.

"His name is Jameson," Ben answered.

"Where da oder man?" the voice asked.

"Jail. You get me and Jameson tonight," Ben said firmly.

The quiet stretched on. "Follow me," the voice said, and

Ben started moving without turning on the light. I followed him, the both of us tripping occasionally on vines or roots.

When I spotted a light coming from a hut, I realized Ben had been following a boy. The kid was no taller than my hips. Skinny too. I'd wager no older than six or so. He wore baggy clothes that had many holes in them and didn't have any shoes on.

"Who dat?" a deeper voice asked, almost causing me to jump.

"Jameson. Declan couldn't make it," Ben said, sounding slightly annoyed. "Are we good?"

The quiet stretched out for almost two full minutes, during which time I was barely breathing. I had no idea if they had weapons on me, how many there were, or even how in the hell to get out of the place.

Then I heard something land by Ben's feet. He bent over and picked it up, turning it over in his hand a few times. "Where's the rest?" Ben asked.

"Da boy will show you where da rest at," the man said, his Cajun accent so strong that he was hard to understand. "Where is our stuff at?"

Ben pulled out a small bag from his jacket pocket and tossed it to the shadow standing a few feet away.

Seconds later, a lighter flickered, and I held my breath. I'd never seen anyone as skinny as the old man standing before us. You could practically see every bone in his body. He was wearing a pair of old jeans and nothing else. His gray hair reached down to the waist of the jeans, and his eyes... there was something about those eyes. Like a wild animal that had seen one too many days in a cage.

How many times had I seen that look before on the men and women I'd locked up? Too many.

This man would, undoubtedly, kill.

The amount of drugs Ben had given the man wouldn't last someone this deep in addiction long. I guessed the Reapers had regular meetups. The only question was, what was the man giving them in return?

By the size and shape of the package he'd thrown to Ben, I doubted that it was drugs.

"Show dem, boy," the man said, waving his hand as he turned to go back into the dark hut.

"Follow me," the boy said, and we turned to walk through the darkness again. "Right dar," the boy said when we stopped by a small boat floating in the dark bayou waters.

"Thanks," Ben said and tossed a small package to the boy.

"Drugs?" I asked with a frown as the boy turned and disappeared back towards the hut.

Ben laughed. "Sugar. Candy. He likes hard candy. Chocolate melts and his pa finds it and whoops him. Hard candy he can hide." Ben shrugged. "I'm not a monster. The kid is only eight."

"Right," I said.

"Help me with these." Ben motioned to the similarly shaped packages that practically filled the small boat.

The first time I held one bundle, I knew exactly what was inside. Cash. Judging by how many bundles, I'd wager almost a hundred thousand dollars' worth.

The old man was a mule and a user. Bad combo for the kid.

"Now what?" I asked Ben when we were heading back to the truck.

"On to the next stop," Ben said with a sigh. He tossed the bags of money under his seat as I climbed in.

We drove back towards Gemsville, taking the main

route this time. I realized we'd only been about half an hour away from town using the main road. Why had Ben taken the back road to get there?

My only guess was that he could explain away the money, but if he'd been caught with the drugs...

When he pulled into a long drive and turned off the truck, this time I knew exactly who he was meeting.

"You can stay in the truck for this one," Ben said, getting out and shutting the door behind him.

Shit, I thought. What in the hell was Ben doing meeting with Henry Taylor?

Chapter Twelve

"The family is like a diamond, with a rock solidity and divine splendor, held by love."
–Skender Nitaj

Rayne

The day had had the potential to be the best day of my life, but then I'd seen that email when I'd gone into my office in the morning. My workout with Jameson had settled me some at lunch, but then I'd gotten the call about the disturbance at the bar.

What had Declan been doing at the bar that early anyway? The place was scheduled to be open in about an hour, but Evelyn and Declan had been the only ones there. Why?

When I arrived, Owen and Abe, another beat officer, were trying to get into the building.

"We had complaints of a loud argument inside, followed by screams," Owen said.

"They don't open for another hour," I said. "What's the issue?"

Both men nodded to the building. I heard it then. Something inside broke followed by a shout and then another scream.

Pulling out my service weapon, I banged on the door. "Police. Open up," I shouted.

"We tried that," Owen said. "We were just about to go in."

Without hesitating, I broke the glass with the butt of my gun and pushed through the door.

Declan O'Malley was kneeling over the unconscious body of Evelyn Hart. I shouted for him to get his hands up as the other two officers held weapons on the man.

Then I watched Declan's arm jerk back as if he prepared to hit Evelyn and something deep inside me snapped. I flew across the room and jumped on the man, taking him with me to the ground.

We scuffled for a few seconds, during which time I made sure my elbow connected to his gut and groin before rolling him over and slapping my cuffs on him.

I prayed that the man would continue to fight me. Thankfully, he did. Two quick moves and he was pinned like a pig under my knees.

"Call an ambulance," I said when Evelyn coughed up blood.

"I didn't do nothing," Declan screamed. "It's not me. I didn't do nothing," he said again. "Someone else did that to her."

"Well now," I said leaning right next to his ear, "this time she doesn't have to file charges since you just had three officers witness the whole thing."

Declan bucked, trying to get free from my hold. I shoved my knee deeper into his back and heard him grunt.

"I'm playing nice," I warned him. "You know the drill. This time, you're not getting off so easily."

Then Declan started screaming. "You'll pay, bitch."

Seeing the man hauled away and locked in the back of a patrol car had to be the highlight of my afternoon.

Seeing Evelyn being taken away in the back of an ambulance dulled that moment of justice for me.

"We can handle this from now," Abe said to me.

"This is mine," I told him, meaning it. I wanted to see this one through. It mattered to me. Evelyn mattered.

I'd spoken to the woman a handful of times in the past week. Warned her about Declan. Talked to her about her six-year-old son, Tristan.

From the amount of blood coating the floor and her clothes, she'd be lucky to survive the night. Her head and face were so swollen that the only way I knew it was her was by the color of her hair and the clothes that she was wearing.

Jesus, this job sometimes made me think.

After talking to witnesses, and making sure the crime scene photographers took enough photos of the mess, I headed back to my office to work on the paperwork to keep Declan locked behind bars.

When I finally saw the text from Jameson, I had just sent my report over to my captain.

"Heard you had a productive afternoon. I've got to call tonight off since I have work now that Declan's busy. Rain check for tomorrow?"

Well, shit. There went my evening. I had been looking forward to a repeat of the night before. Still, I knew I'd probably be better off catching up on my sleep.

"Sounds good. See you then. Sorry I didn't tell you. I've been kinda busy," I responded.

"Understood. Night," he texted back almost immediately.

Glancing at my watch, I sighed and rolled my shoulders as I leaned back in my chair.

I watched Quincy walk into the bullpen. He eyed me and made a beeline towards me. Shit.

I should have faked being busy. Instead, I waited until he walked in and shut the door.

"Rayne," he said, sitting down across from me.

"Quincy." I mimicked his tone.

At one point, I had fallen for the man's charms. We hadn't gone out for a long, two short months. The sex had been good, not as knock-your-socks-off good as it was with Jameson. Still. I respected the man. What I didn't respect was him hiding things from me. Not little things either. Days would go by and he'd lie to me about being somewhere when I knew for damned sure he wasn't.

The stupidest being on the planet was someone who lied to a damned good detective and thought they'd get away with it. When I found out he'd been spotted at the bar with another girl's tongue down his throat, well, I simply don't tolerate having a relationship with a cheater.

He leaned forward, his eyes running over my face. "I think we need to talk."

"About?" I asked, arching my brows.

He cleared his throat and shifted as if he was uncomfortable.

"You aren't pregnant, are you?" I tried to joke.

Instead of laughing, he sighed and ran his hands through his hair.

"There are things, people, you should be careful about associating with," he said slowly.

My temper grew. "Such as?" I asked just as slowly.

"You don't like games, so I'll just say it. There's a rumor going around town that you and Jameson Lorenzo are... tangled."

I chuckled. "Since when do you care about rumors?" I asked dryly.

Quincy's eyes narrowed. "The Reapers are no joke."

"I'm not laughing." I waited, wondering just what his game was. Was he concerned for my well-being or was he just trying to win me back? He'd tried for the first few weeks after I'd broken things off with him. Tried and failed miserably.

"There are holes too deep even for you to crawl out of," Quincy said as he stood up and walked out of my office.

Shit. Now I was in a piss-poor mood. I pulled out my phone and sent a text to Aria. "What are you doing tonight?"

Her response was almost immediate.

"Whatever you want. You can come in for a trim and girl time? My last appointment leaves in about half an hour."

"Perfect," I added.

"I'll have the wine ready," she sent back to me.

"See if Charlotte can hang and make it margaritas. I need some hard liquor."

"Woohoo! Fun times. I'll have her run next door and get what we need. See you when you get here."

I smiled as I tucked my phone away.

I was very lucky to have friends who were available when I needed them. Friends that I would drop everything for in return.

Since I had time, I opened the email I'd quickly closed earlier that morning and tried to figure out who had sent it.

The email address was a long line of numbers and, after a quick search, I found out that the account was closed.

I scanned the attached image and tried to mentally figure out where the photographer would have been to get the shot. My answer was somewhere in the woods that surrounded the cabin. Which meant they could have been there, watching us, all night.

Thankfully, the bedroom windows had thick curtains covering them.

There was no text with the image. No threatening words. The image was meant to do that job. That morning, I had been pissed off, not scared. Now, however, I started wondering if it was one of the Reapers or someone else. After all, they weren't hiding the fact that they were watching me.

I chuckled as I shut my computer down. Then again, maybe they thought they were doing a great job of being inconspicuous.

Stepping out of my office, I passed by Owen, who was on the phone.

"Have a good night," I said to a few people.

"You off tomorrow?" Abe asked as I passed his desk.

"For the next two days," I added with a nod. "Night."

The man turned back to his computer.

Quincy stood at the break area watching me as I knocked on Randy's door.

"Yeah," he called out and I opened the door. "Hey, sweetie." He stood up and stretched. "Heading out?"

I nodded. "I'm heading over to hang at Arias for a while."

His smile was quick. "Girls' night?"

I nodded. "How's Mom doing?"

His smile grew bigger. "She loves the new do." I

watched his eyes and saw them turn slightly sad. "It's given her a second wind. She'll need it for this next round."

"That starts in a week?" I asked, trying to remember the schedule he'd sent me earlier.

"Yeah. Her friend Carolyn is going to be with her for the first bit. She's flying in from Florida." He smiled. "I know you're working the big one, so we called in a favor."

"I could have..." I started, but Randy held up his hand.

"Do your job. We'll take good care of her until you solve this one. Speaking of which?" He motioned for me to shut the door. I did and leaned against it. "Updates?" he asked.

"I'm working a couple of leads." I moved closer and lowered my voice. "Something stinks about the whole corruption and embezzling angle."

"I talked to the state attorney's office. They're going to shoot you what information they can. But obviously, the case is dead as far as prosecuting Sharon Taylor."

"Did they mention anyone else on their radar?" I asked.

Randy shook his head. "They wouldn't say. I was lucky to get what information I did. It seems their case is pretty hush-hush at this point."

"Right," I nodded, understanding that when you're working a case this big, you held your cards tight to your chest.

"What about Jameson? How's that going?" he asked.

"The Reapers are doing a shit job of tagging us. Jameson says they want him to use me to see how I'm dancing around the Taylor murder."

Randy frowned. "Why do the Reapers give a shit?"

"That's a very good question," I added with a smile as I glanced down at my watch. "But look, I'm officially off duty."

He chuckled. "Have fun tonight." He sat back down in his chair.

"Aren't you heading out?" I asked.

He shook his head. "I've got a new report from my lead detective in my inbox I have to look over."

I laughed. "Lance auto-sent that to you?"

"You know it." He laughed.

"Why did you make him captain?" I asked.

Randy rolled his eyes. "Because you wouldn't take the job."

I laughed and walked out of his office.

I was in a better mood as I headed towards Jazzed Up. The moment I stepped inside, Charlotte handed me a drink, and I laughed.

"Bad day?" she and Aria asked at the same time.

"No, not really," I said after taking a sip of the salty delight. "I got to kick Declan's ass."

"We heard," Charlotte said as I moved over to sit in Aria's chair.

I sank into the plush salon chair, reveling in the smell of chemicals and lotions, and listening to the soothing jazz music that filled the room. Jazzed Up always felt like a sanctuary, especially when accompanied by my two favorite troublemakers.

Aria today had hot green highlights amongst her platinum blonde locks. She flashed me a mischievous grin as she mixed up whatever gunk she was going to put in my hair.

"So, are you ready for your next transformation?" she joked. "Ready for something wild? How about bright red?"

I rolled my eyes playfully. "Yeah, right. Just don't make me look like a walking highlighter pen like you."

Aria laughed. "Your standard caramel color is already mixed." She showed me.

Charlotte, the queen of sass, chimed in from her chair as she sipped her drink. "Hey, if anyone can pull off red highlights, it's you, Rayne. Someday you'll let your wild side shine through."

I mock-glared at her, taking a sip of the margarita that Aria had given me. "Thanks, but for now, I'll keep my wild side saved up for kicking assholes' butts."

While my friend got to work adding my standard caramel highlights to my hair, I told my two friends everything that had happened to me since that morning.

"How is Evelyn doing?" Charlotte asked.

"Stable. She's not awake yet. I called the hospital before I came over here. A broken arm and two loose teeth."

"Tell me you busted his balls?" Charlotte said.

I laughed. "Twice. His voice was so high-pitched when they loaded him into the back of the patrol car, I doubt it'll drop for weeks."

Aria laughed as she worked her magic by expertly applying the foils with precision.

Over an hour later, my head looked like a huge aluminum antenna as I sat under the heater.

"All right, while we wait for this to set, how about a little pampering? Charlotte, why don't you do Rayne's nails and then a facial when she's done under the heater?" Aria said as she disappeared into the back to clean her equipment.

Charlotte smirked, wiggling her eyebrows suggestively. "Oh, this is going to be fun. Get ready to glow, Rayne."

I settled back in my chair, letting the stress of the week melt away as Charlotte worked her magic with my fingernails. She applied a soft pink color and even did the same on my toes.

When I was done under the heater and Aria had

washed my hair and applied some other gunk that had to sit on it for a while, Charlotte started my facial.

"Ah, this is the life. Who needs therapy when you have margaritas and facials with your best friends?" I said as I closed my eyes and Charlotte yanked the wax strip off my eyebrows.

Once my face felt so clean it almost burned, Aria finished rinsing my hair out. We moved back over to her chair and she got to work trimming all those split ends I had before blow-drying and styling my hair in ways I could never mimic.

I admired the new highlights in the mirror, feeling like a brand-new woman.

"You've outdone yourself. I feel like a million bucks," I told them as I swung my chair and held the mirror.

I felt good. My skin felt like it glowed thanks to the facial Charlotte had given me. I loved the soft pink on my nails. It wasn't too bright or flashy.

It was strange to look at my reflection and see the changes they had made to me in such a short time. I looked... like a woman. Felt like one too. Not that I didn't normally, but now I felt girlie.

"I love my job. Now, who's ready for another round of margaritas?" Aria laughed.

Almost two hours later, the three of us stumbled to Tobias' truck and climbed in.

"Thanks for the lift," Aria said as she leaned over and planted a long heated kiss on his lips.

"It looks like you ladies had a blast. I like the new highlights," he said, glancing back at me.

"Thanks!" I pretty much shouted my response, then fell into a fit of laughter against Charlotte.

Tobias dropped his sister off first since her apartment

was only a few blocks from the salon. I was next. My home was in the opposite direction as Aria and Tobias's place and, after Charlotte was gone, the drive seemed to drag on.

When the car finally came to a stop, I jerked awake.

"Want me to walk you in?" Tobias asked.

"No, I got it. Thanks." I started to get out and then realized that I'd left my purse in the seat and had to reach across the seat for it. "Night. Thanks for the new me," I told Aria, who smiled and waved funny at me.

Tobias kept the truck lights on my front door area as I unlocked it and stumbled inside. I waved to the bright lights and shut the door as I heard him drive off.

Leaning against the door, I sighed and thought about falling into my bed as I was. Instead, I felt my body sliding down the door, and I laughed when my butt hit the ground.

How long had it been since I'd allowed myself to let go? A year? Two?

I never drank this much. Sure, I'd have a few beers on the occasional girl's night or my fake birthday, but nothing like tonight.

I suppose I felt there was a reason to celebrate. I'd not only locked up one of the worst scumballs in town, but I'd had great sex the night before.

Since the world was spinning, I started crawling across the thick rug runner that I'd purchased a few months ago.

In the past three years, I'd transformed the little wooden home with its wraparound porch. It was just the right size for my needs with two bedrooms, two baths, and the smaller front office. I glanced over at my desk and smiled as I crawled past it.

The kitchen was the only thing that I had spent real money on. When I'd moved in, it had been seriously outdated. Now, I had all new appliances, cabinets, and countertops.

Off the back of the house, where my bedroom sat, I had a massive deck that overlooked a small pond area. Since the property had come with five acres, I was secluded enough that I didn't have to deal with any neighbors.

Not that I didn't like people. I just didn't want to wave at them over a fence or hear them arguing next door. Smell their cookouts. Hear their dogs barking. Those types of things.

I liked being alone. Well, at least I had.

My mind turned towards Jameson. God, I had been looking forward to spending the night with him. Feeling his hard, toned body against mine. Just the way he moved had my mind going to mush. How had the man done that to me so quickly?

It wasn't just his body that I craved.

I daydreamed about spending time with him. Laughing and joking with him.

I had made it halfway across the living room rug when my front window shattered along with a glass vase that had been full of wildflowers that Randy and Edith had given me for my birthday. It exploded, sending glass and water spraying all over me.

Even in my inebriated state, I knew a gunshot when I heard it. I spread my body out flat on the rug as a barrage of bullets flew through my shattered front window, hitting my sofa and chair and embedding in the wall separating the living space from my kitchen.

I had my gun in my hand and my cell in the other. As I dialed 911 and rattled off my address, I kept my eyes and weapon trained on the window and my front door.

Seconds ticked off as the spray continued. Pain filled my mind for a split second then dulled.

When the spray of bullets finally died down, I counted my breaths and cursed the alcohol in my veins causing my eyes to blur. Blinking the water from the flowers out of my eyes, I wondered why it was red.

When I finally saw the flashing lights from a patrol car out my window, I relaxed as someone called my name. Was that Randy?

I blinked and then he was there, standing over me.

"Shit," he said, kneeling next to me. A look of sheer terror filled his eyes. "Shit," he said again, just as everything went blank.

Chapter Thirteen

"Many individuals have, like uncut diamonds, shining qualities beneath a rough exterior."
–Decimus Junius Juvenalis

Jameson

By the next morning, news of what had happened to Rayne was everywhere in town. Since I had to be at work at the gym at six, I'd heard it shortly after I arrived and unlocked the doors.

My first inclination was to turn everyone out, lock up, and head to the hospital to see how she was doing.

Then Felix showed up. Felix hardly ever came to the gym. Since he wasn't carrying a gym bag, I knew he wasn't there to lift weights.

"What's up?" I asked when we stepped into the empty waiting area.

"Heard your side piece got in some trouble last night." Felix chuckled as he ran his eyes over my face. Was he wanting to gauge my reaction?

"Yeah, I heard," I said, trying to sound unfazed. The

truth was, I could think of little else. I desperately wished I could text Rayne even if I couldn't go see her.

"Ben tells me last night went smooth," he added.

I shrugged. "I just took a ride," I said, acting bored.

"Yeah, well, we appreciate you stepping in. It won't happen again now that Declan is out. He promised me that he is going to fall in line."

I frowned slightly. "Okay."

Felix narrowed his eyes. "Until things cool off, I think we gained everything we can from your lady friend. I hope you got your fill of her."

My eyebrows shot up. "Not really," I said slowly. "I was hoping for last night."

Felix laughed and slapped me on my back. "Do what you want. From here on out, the cop is yours to toy with."

Before I could ask him what that meant, he turned and walked out.

Shit. Declan was out of jail already. Was he the one who shot up Rayne's house? If the timing matched up then there was no doubt in my mind Declan was the shooter. Which just pissed me off.

Deciding I was in the right place to get rid of that anger, I lifted weights until I couldn't feel my body.

Once I clocked out for the day, I headed straight home to shoot Rayne a text from my private phone.

"Are you okay?"

When no response came, I tossed the phone back on the desk and paced the small safe room. Shit. Shit.

After an hour, I decided to head to the hospital, not caring if anyone saw me.

After all, I'd just admitted to Felix I wasn't done with Rayne. Maybe they'd see it as a sign that I just wanted to keep that relationship going.

When I stepped outside my place, a silver-haired man walked up to me. I instantly recognized Randy Cordova, the chief of police.

"We need to talk," he told me. "Not here." He motioned towards the coffee shop. "Don't worry, I made sure no one was around." He started walking.

I fell in step with him and asked, "Is she okay?"

He nodded. "Tell me that you had nothing to do with last night."

I almost winced. "No, I was somewhere else," I said quickly.

The man nodded as we stepped inside.

"How bad is it?" I asked. "I was just heading over..."

"Don't. She's home with us now. Resting," Randy said as we took a seat at a table in the back.

I frequented the place since I lived upstairs, and so did Randy. The waitress walked over and poured us each a cup of coffee.

"Anything else for either of you?" she asked.

"No, thanks, Katie," Randy said and then waited until we were alone again. "Declan was released half an hour before."

"Shit." I ran my hand through my hair. "I knew it. That son of a..." I started to get up, only to stop when Randy laid a hand on my arm.

"Don't. I've known who you were and what you were doing from the moment you stepped foot in my town. Now, I've let you be. Done what I had to clear my town of... well, people like Declan. I hadn't expected you to take so damned long nor did I for one minute believe you'd drag my daughter into the mess."

I nodded slowly, understanding.

"Do what you have to. Shut them down. Then, get the

hell out of Gemsville, and by god, don't look back," he warned. "I'll be damned if I let anything happen to Rayne. I hated the day she decided to become a cop like me. Hated the day I pinned the badge on her. Proud as hell but hated it. Knowing what could happen to us always getting in the line of fire. But let's face facts—as bad as we have it, you have it a hundred times worse. Your entire life becomes a lie. The things you have to do..." He shook his head. "You're made of stronger stuff than most. So I'll say this once. If you have any feelings for my daughter, you'll step away now before something goes down. Before you break something in her by leaving. We both know that Felix and his gang aren't the brains, they're the brawn, and they'll gladly burn the whole damn town down before they give up who it is they work for."

I nodded again. "If it was Declan, then last night had nothing to do with me," I pointed out.

"Don't give me that crap," Randy said, almost spilling his coffee. "If you'd done your damn job faster, Declan wouldn't be a problem." He stood up. "Do your goddamned job. Before someone gets hurt."

"Sir," I stopped him from leaving. "Tell Rayne I'm sorry."

He nodded and then walked out, leaving me to brood in my lukewarm coffee. After feeling sorry for myself for a few more minutes, I headed back upstairs and did what Randy suggested. I got to work.

Felix was hosting another one of his big parties that following weekend, which meant everyone would be in attendance. Including Declan.

One thing Felix never discouraged was fighting at one of his parties. If any of the members had a problem with the other, the party was a safe place to air your grievances.

Until then, I had a few people I needed to look into. First and foremost was Henry Taylor.

The deceased mayor's husband was getting a middle-of-the-night visit from the Reapers for a reason. All the money we'd moved had disappeared into the Taylor's massive mansion.

Since I was revved up, I geared up and snuck out of my place shortly after dark. I made my way in the shadows as I headed down the street to where I had a car stashed in a garage. Then I drove the side streets out of town and headed to the Taylor's massive place. I needed a look around.

I'd scoped out a place to park the car in the brush and hiked almost two miles to the old plantation. I was surprised at the lack of security.

Lying in the tall grass a few yards from the home, I scanned every inch of the place through my night vision scope.

I didn't spot any cameras anywhere on the home or surrounding trees, not even a doorbell with a camera on it.

There were also no guard dogs. Which meant I could get as close as I wanted to the place without being recorded or seen.

There were no cars out front and, as I'd driven out of town, I'd spotted Henry Taylor's pink Cadillac parked behind the BBB. So I knew the man was... occupied.

I let myself in the back door, and it took me less than ten minutes to find the hidden safe in the main bedroom's closet. There were two other safes in the house. None of them held the money, which meant either he hid it somewhere else or the money had been handed off.

I was betting on the first option since it was obvious the man had enough money now that his wife was out of the picture. I'd done a few hours of research on the Taylor family.

Sharon Taylor had married Henry Taylor when she'd become pregnant with their twin boys. The marriage appeared to be happy for the first decade or so. After that, there were profiles on online dating apps for the pair of them.

The house was filled with stuffy items, furniture from past centuries mixed with newer items. There was no real style to anything, and it had an almost chaotic atmosphere.

After letting myself out, I hiked back to my car. Since it was on the way, I drove by the Cordova's place, which sat not too far off the road. All the lights were off, so I kept going back into town.

I returned the car to its garage and changed into my normal street clothes. Then I made my way towards the bar, knowing the gang would be there.

When I walked in, to my shock, Evelyn was sitting on Declan's lap, laughing, her casted arm held tight up against her body. There were bruises all over her face and legs.

I wanted to ask what in the hell was going on, but instead, I acted like I was brooding and went to sit down in my usual spot. Izzy was there and within minutes she was all over me.

"I heard you've been slumming it with Rayne." She chuckled. "That bitch has always gone after men out of her league."

"I'll take that as a compliment," I tried to joke. What I wanted to do was walk away, but Randy was right. I was here to do a job. I should have used Izzy to get as much information as possible long ago.

Wrapping my hand around her waist, I pulled her

closer. "How's that going?" I asked, motioning towards Declan and Evelyn.

She sighed and leaned against me, and I could tell and smell that she was seriously wasted.

"I think they've both learned their lesson." She sighed as she brushed her fingers through my hair. "Have you?"

I tilted my head slightly. "Me?" I asked.

She smiled. "Reapers don't fuck cops."

Everything in my body tensed as a light bulb went off over my foggy head.

Shit. How fucking far off had I been?

Yeah, of course, it had been Izzy who had shot up Rayne's place.

She would have been jealous the second she'd found out I was with Rayne.

"Yeah," I said, trying very hard not to clench my back teeth. "That was you?

She laughed and shook her head. "I don't know what you're talking about." I could see the truth in her eyes.

She straddled my leg and started grinding it slowly. "How about we head to my place? I know just how to scratch that itch you have."

Thankfully, just then, Ben walked over and grabbed Izzy's arm.

"Give us a minute," he told her and yanked her off my leg.

Izzy frowned at Ben, then pouted as she walked back towards Nadia and a few other Reapers playing pool.

"What's up?" I asked.

"I might need you for another job tomorrow night," Ben said, sitting down beside me. "Felix wants Declan to tag along but I still think he has to cool off. He almost blew the last run I took him on."

"Sure," I said, trying hard not to sound excited. "Same time tomorrow?" I asked.

Ben shrugged. "What time do you get off work?"

I thought about it for a second. "I have the day off."

Ben nodded. "Then we'll leave around eight tomorrow night."

I nodded. "Gear?" I asked.

Ben ran his eyes over me. "What you're wearing is fine. We'll take the bikes for part of the journey." I nodded and he stood up. "Can you swim?"

I laughed and then nodded. "Sure." I pretended to doggy paddle, causing Ben to chuckle and slap my shoulder hard.

Since I'd accomplished more than I'd imagined, I decided not to take my chances with Izzy again. I downed my beer in one gulp and headed towards the back door.

Unfortunately, Izzy beat me to it.

"Ready?" she asked, taking my hand in hers.

"I'm heading home. Alone," I added. "I'm not in the mood tonight." I pulled my hand free.

She pushed her hand against my chest until I backed up against the door.

"We're having serious thoughts about your loyalty," she hissed.

"We?" I chuckled.

Her eyes narrowed. "I am," she corrected. "I'm through playing games with you."

"I don't play games," I warned and removed her hand from my chest. "Nor do I fuck someone I don't want to."

I turned to walk out and then was blindsided when a half-full beer bottle crashed into the side of my head. I was stunned for a moment before I recovered to duck the next one as blood oozed from my head just above my left ear.

"Crazy bitch," Ben hissed as he yanked Izzy back a few feet and wrapped his arms around her to stop her from throwing anything more. "Go on, get out of here. I've got her," Ben told me.

Seeing the blood on my hand, I straightened and nodded.

Shit, I thought as I headed towards my place, thankful that it was only a couple blocks away.

By the time I climbed my stairs, everything was blurry.

"What in the hell happened to you?" Rayne asked from my doorway. It was dark enough that I couldn't see her face. Hell, if I hadn't climbed my stairs, I wouldn't have known she was there.

Without answering, I quickly unlocked my door and pulled her inside. Making sure to keep my lights off, I held onto her for a full minute before talking.

"Why are you here?" I asked. I tried to remember why she shouldn't be there, but my head hurt too much.

She reached up and touched my head. "You're bleeding."

"Yeah." I took her hand and cupped it. "I'm okay."

"No, you're not." She glanced around. When she reached for the light switch, I stopped her.

"Wait," I said, taking her hand and pulling her into my bathroom. Then I switched on the light and we both gasped when we finally got a look at one another.

There was a large bandage over her forehead and smaller cuts and bruises over her face and hands.

Cupping her face in my blood-soaked hands, I leaned in and kissed her gently. "It was Izzy," I said and felt her tense. "She pretty much bragged about it to me just now. Right before she threw two beer bottles at my head for turning her down tonight."

When I moved my hand, I realized I'd smeared her face with blood. Taking a towel, I started to wipe it clean, but she took the towel from me and held it to my head. I winced with pain.

"I think there's still some glass in here. Sit down." She motioned to the side of my tub. I sat. Well, more like fell.

"Do you have a first aid kit?" she asked, walking over to the sink.

"Under," I said, holding the towel to my head. "What are you doing here?" I asked as she bent to get the kit.

"I came to talk to you." She set the kit on the counter and then dug through it. "Randy said he had a chat with you earlier."

"Yeah," I sighed, remembering suddenly that I was supposed to steer clear of Rayne. She turned towards me and we locked eyes. "I can't do it." I shook my head.

"What?" she asked, moving closer to me.

"Stay away from you," I said, running my eyes over her. How could I stay away? Why would I?

"Then don't," she said as a slow smile spread on those luscious lips of hers. God, I wanted to kiss her. Needed to.

In a daze, I pulled her lips to mine, tasting her, feeling her, and then I poured everything I felt into that one kiss. My hopes and dreams for us, for my future, for our future. What I had come to feel for her in the short time I'd known her. What I wanted from her was so obvious it was a wonder it didn't burst from me. Could this work? Could we get through this unscathed?

Whatever happened, I was going to make damned sure we did.

Chapter Fourteen

"There comes a moment when the silence between two people can have the purity of a diamond."
–Philippe Djian, *Betty Blue*

Rayne

I had taken a chance to sneak out of my old home shortly after Randy and Edith had gone to bed. It wasn't the first time I'd tip-toed out the back door, but it was strange doing so as an adult.

I couldn't blame them for wanting me close. Not after what had happened today.

Knowing it was important for me to stay hidden, I'd driven my mother's minivan. Because of all her medication, she hadn't driven it in months anyway. I left a note for my folks so they wouldn't worry, something I'd never thought of doing as a teen when I'd snuck out to hang with Aria.

My plan, however, was to be back in their guest room, my old bedroom, before sunup.

When I arrived at Jameson's place and realized that he wasn't there, I figured he was still working. After waiting almost fifteen minutes, I had just talked myself into leaving. Then I spotted him walking down the street and immediately knew something was wrong.

The way he was holding himself, I could tell he was in pain or in trouble. I glanced around for someone shadowing him and knew that we were alone.

The fact that it had been Izzy who had unloaded more than two dozen rounds into my home made sense. Seeing the damage she'd done to Jameson's head somehow pissed me off more than all the destruction that she'd done to my place.

Windows and furniture could be replaced. The jagged scar that Jameson would have just above his left ear was forever.

"Here," I said, pulling back from his kiss, "let me fix you up."

"I'm okay." He groaned and tried to pull me back between his legs. God, it felt so good there, caged in his body.

"You're bleeding all over the place," I said, holding out my blood-soaked hand.

He frowned down at my fingers and then nodded. "Okay, but after..." His hand moved up to cover my butt and I held in a moan.

"Why do you think I'm here?" I joked.

Okay, I was there for a lot of other reasons. First, I'd wanted to make sure whatever he did last night hadn't involved a drive-by of my place.

I knew what agents had to do undercover. The fact was that they couldn't sweat the small stuff. In his time undercover, he'd probably had to witness or be part of countless illegal activities, all with the singular goal of catching that one really big fish. The one pulling the strings. There was no doubt in my mind that he'd do what it took to get his job done. I just needed to make sure I wasn't collateral damage along the way.

However, the kiss we'd just shared assured me of several things. First and foremost were his feelings for me. And that meant he would have done anything to ensure that I didn't get hurt.

After cleaning up the cut and removing a few pieces of glass from his scalp, I used butterfly bandages to seal up his skin nicely.

The bleeding would continue for a while, so I tapped a thick piece of gauze over the spot, using more tape than was probably necessary.

"I should shave your head here so these will stick," I mumbled.

"So do it. Clippers are under the sink," he said, keeping his eyes closed.

"No, I like your hair." I frowned at him.

"It grows back." He opened his eyes and looked at me.

Without answering, I grabbed a washcloth and got it wet. Then I took my time cleaning the blood from his hair and skin.

When I was done, I used a few more strips of tape to hold the bandages more tightly over the spot.

"It's as best as I can get," I admitted. Then I leaned down and brushed my lips over his.

He chuckled, then lifted his hands and gently ran them over some of my cuts. "Are you okay?"

I nodded. "Cuts. Bruises." I smiled. "My front window is being replaced tomorrow. I'll need a new sofa and lamp."

He cupped my face. "I wanted to strangle the crazy bitch."

I nodded. "I'll pay her back."

He shook his head. "You can't. She only mentioned it to me. She'll know—"

"I assume she told you at the bar?" I broke in. He nodded slowly as I smiled. "Everyone in town probably knows by now. I'll wait until the rumor hits me, then seek my revenge." I rubbed my hands together and laughed, causing him to smile. "Besides, I owe her for this." I touched the bandage on his head. "Tell me we don't have to stay in this bathroom all night."

He stood up, then surprised me by lifting me into his arms and carrying me through the dark rooms. He nudged open a door and walked through it.

When he flipped on a low light and set me down on a small bed, I realized this was a safe room. There were no windows, only a computer on a small table, a lamp, and a twin-sized bed.

"We're good in here." He smiled as he removed his coat before reaching for my sneakers.

I toed my shoes off before he could help and then whipped my shirt over my head.

He hissed and moved to sit next to me, his eyes running over the cuts and bruises that covered my arms and chest. He cursed under his breath.

"I'm good," I assured him. "Believe it or not, I used to get worse playing softball."

"Yeah." Jameson smiled. "I'm a huge baseball nut. I pitched my school team all the way to state champs."

"We'll have to start a team." I laughed before pulling him towards me for another kiss.

I matched his speed and desire as our needs pushed us

forward. Clothes hit the floor as our hands ran over one another.

I felt as if I couldn't get enough of him. Felt as if I could take forever exploring, enjoying, wanting.

I felt so much when he laid me down on the bed. My heart surged as I wrapped my legs around his hips.

The way he moved his mouth over me sent shivers to my very core. His fingers slipped deep inside me while his tongue circled my nipples, making me ache deep down.

This time, when he slid inside me, I felt something I'd never felt before. Something primitive, something that transcended all time and space.

Had I ever felt like this before? My mind burst along with my body when I felt our release together. I'd never felt so in sync with anyone before.

"Rayne," he murmured, his voice soft in the quiet of the night. "We need to talk about us. I don't know what this is," he said into my hair as his breathing slowed, "but I'll be damned if anyone, including your father, is going to stop us from exploring it further."

I smiled as my hands slowly ran over his shoulders. "Agreed." I turned to face him, my heart quickening at the seriousness in his tone. "It's not going to be easy, but we can't keep pretending that this isn't real."

While the darkness of the room enveloped us, a shroud of secrecy seemed fitting for our clandestine conversation. Jameson's presence beside me was both comforting and electrifying, his warmth seeping into my skin as we lay tangled in the sheets.

He reached out, his hand finding mine in the darkness, our fingers intertwining as if seeking reassurance. "I want to be with you. More than anything. But you know the risks. My job, the danger... we can't let anyone know about us."

I nodded, understanding the weight of his words. "I know. And I want to be with you too. But it's not just about hiding our relationship. It's about what could happen if you're discovered. The Reapers, to my knowledge, don't dally in murder. That doesn't mean they won't if you're exposed because of me."

"Felix has pretty much told me to end this. Now that there is a lot of attention on you after today, I think he's scared you'll come after them harder," he said with a slight sigh.

I nodded, understanding, as tears stung my heart. He was right. I wanted to set my sights on the Reapers and take them down. Even before I'd known it was Lizzy who was behind all the destruction.

He sighed, a heavy exhale that seemed to carry the weight of the world.

"But suddenly I can't imagine my life without you. I'm willing to take that risk if it means being with you."

"I feel the same way. But we have to be careful." Tears rolled out of the corners of my eyes, a mix of longing and apprehension swirling within me.

"I promise. I'll do whatever it takes to protect us, to protect you." He squeezed my hand, his touch a silent vow in the darkness.

As we lay together in the darkness of his safe room, after whispering promises of devotion, we both knew that this would always be our greatest secret.

"Do you have to get back?" he asked after a moment.

I nodded and closed my eyes, silently wishing my life was different, normal.

"How did you get here?" he asked, leaning up on his elbows to look down at me.

"My mother's car."

He nodded slowly as he ran his eyes over my face. "I wanted to strangle Izzy for this." He brushed a finger gently over my cheek.

"I will for this." I smiled up at him as I gently touched his head.

"Declan is out of jail," he said, and I nodded.

"Yeah, he only spent a few hours behind bars. Long enough for Evelyn to wake up and clear him of charges. She claims someone else broke into the bar while she was opening up and hurt her. She claimed that Declan was trying to perform medical help when we arrived."

"She was with him tonight at the bar, laughing and joking while she sat on his lap. With a broken arm. They acted as if nothing had happened." He shook his head. "She looked twice as bad as we do right now."

I nodded. "It's not the first time he's done this to her. I was hoping it was the last. She was unconscious forever. I can't believe she didn't stay in the hospital longer," I said. "What makes a person go back to the one that has done something like that to them?"

He shook his head. "Not knowing there is more out there? Fear?" He shrugged. "This." He motioned between us. "I meant what I said. I don't want anything getting in the way. As long as you're willing, I'd like to ride it out. See where it goes."

I smiled. "I'd like that."

He frowned a little more. "Even if that means putting things on hold until I have everything wrapped up."

"Your job is important. What you do, what I do, it matters. This can wait," I assured him.

He sighed and rested his forehead against mine. "I wish it didn't have to. I wish we could spend the night wrapped in each other's arms."

"Same," I agreed.

He kissed me and my heart ached. It caused me more pain than all of the cuts had.

"I wish I had the energy to go another round,"

I shook my head. "I'm too tired. If we did, I wouldn't be able to make it back."

He nodded and then his weight and warmth were gone as he sat up.

We dressed in silence, but he stopped me from leaving the room once I was fully dressed. Then he pulled me back into his arms and kissed me.

"Can you tell me where you were last night?" I asked, my voice laced with a hint of concern as he pulled away.

He shrugged a casual gesture that belied the gravity of our conversation. "Another run," he replied, his eyes flickering with something unreadable. "There might be something..." He paused, his gaze drifting to the distance. "I'll let you know if it goes anywhere. For now, I think it would be best to follow this new lead on my own. However, I will tell you that we dropped a ton of money off at the Taylor's place."

"How much money?" I asked, my mind reeling at the implications.

He shrugged once more, the nonchalance of his demeanor unsettling. "I didn't count it, but my guess was about a hundred grand or so."

"Shit." My thoughts raced. "The Reapers dropped off a hundred thousand dollars to Henry Taylor?"

He nodded solemnly. "Yeah, at least I think it was to Henry Taylor. I mean, I didn't see the man since I stayed out in the car."

"Where did that money come from?" I asked, my voice tinged with urgency.

"That's the lead I want to follow up on," he said cryptically, his expression inscrutable. "For now, at least I've confirmed that the money is no longer at the Taylor's place."

"You've..." I narrowed my eyes, a mixture of curiosity and frustration coursing through me. "How?"

He smiled enigmatically. "I have my ways."

I groaned. "Do not tell me you broke into the house."

"Okay." He flashed a mischievous grin. "I won't tell you."

I threw up my hands in exasperation. "I know you have to do what you have to for the job, but from here on out, keep me in the dark about any illegal activities."

"Will do." He chuckled.

"Why would the Reapers be giving Henry Taylor money?" I asked.

"That's what I'm hoping to find out. From what I know about the man, he's not the type I'm looking for. Running an undercover drug ring that stretches over more than a dozen states just isn't his cup of tea. Besides, I don't think he has what it takes up here"—he tapped the undamaged side of his head—"to be an evil mastermind."

As I ran through my mental dossier on the man, the intricate tapestry of the Taylor family's history unfurled before me like a dark, tangled web. They had always been shrouded in controversy, their legacy tainted by the shadow of their past deeds.

First, as one of the largest slave owners in the area, they had wielded their wealth and influence to maintain their stranglehold over both land and people, clinging desperately to their way of life even as the Civil War loomed on the horizon. Theirs was a legacy built on the backs of others, steeped in the blood and sweat of generations enslaved.

But even after the abolition of slavery, the Taylors had

found new ways to exert their dominance, using the laws and the weight of their money to crush any competition that dared to challenge their supremacy. Gemsville, once a small town beholden to their every whim, had grown beyond their control, but the Taylors had adapted, their grip on power only tightening with the passing years.

Henry Taylor, the scion of this dynasty, had inherited his family's legacy of entitlement and privilege. His upbringing had been steeped in the trappings of wealth and power, his path in life paved with golden promises and silver spoons. But where his forebears had thrived, Henry had faltered, his reputation tarnished by whispers of incompetence and indolence.

Rumors had long swirled around him, painting him as a ne'er-do-well, a mere shadow of his illustrious lineage. He had coasted through school only due to his family's influence, his diploma a hollow testament to his lack of ambition. Afterward, he had taken a position in his father's company, a cushy job that demanded little and offered even less.

His forced marriage due to Sharon's pregnancy was surrounded by whispers of scandal back in the day. The untimely death of Henry's parents and his subsequent ascension in the family threw more fuel to the rumor mills.

The pair stayed under the radar for years until Sharon ascended to the mayor's office. Then Henry's ambitions had suddenly ignited, fueled, no doubt, by a burning desire to prove his worth. No longer content to be a mere footnote in his family's storied history, he had seized every opportunity to assert his authority, his hunger for power driving him to grasp control wherever he could.

It was as if he were trying to outrun the shadows of his past, to carve out a place for himself in a world that had long overlooked him. And now, as I contemplated his meteoric rise to prominence, I couldn't shake the feeling that there was more to Henry Taylor than met the eye. Beneath the facade of respectability lurked a man driven by ambition and haunted by the ghosts of his family's legacy.

I felt an urge to move him up on the list of suspects in his wife's murder. Had I fallen prey to his ploys like everyone else in town?

"Text my private number and let me know when you get back to your parents' place safely," Jameson broke into my thoughts. I nodded as he shut off the lights in the hidden room and slid open the doorway. "I'll walk you as far as I can," he added.

We stepped out of the secret room, and I realized that an entire brick wall had slid silently open to allow access to the space.

From what I could tell, his loft apartment was huge. The light from the massive windows that overlooked the street lit the space well enough that I could see he kept things tidy. He helped me through the dark living room, past the kitchen, and to the front door.

"Later, I hope I can visit your place in the daytime. I'd like to see what kind of house you keep," I joked.

He chuckled. "I'm a clean freak. I suppose it comes from having to keep my shit hidden. My real shit at any rate."

He opened his door and stepped out, looking around. I waited until he came back.

"It's clear, from what I can tell. Still, stick to the shadows. I've turned off the porch light. There are twenty-two stairs to the pathway."

"Thanks." I leaned up and kissed him again. "Night."

After descending the twenty-two stairs, I turned right and followed the dark alleyway, pausing at the entrance to scan the area. It was a quarter past three in the morning. The bars had closed at one, which meant the town was dead quiet. If I was being watched, whoever it was was damned good at keeping hidden.

The darkness of the night seemed to swallow me whole as I made my way down the dimly lit alley, every step a silent prayer that no one was following.

The streets were deserted, the only sounds the distant hum of a passing car on the highway almost half a mile away and the buzzing of the summer night bugs. I hugged the shadows, my senses on high alert as I navigated the empty sidewalks, acutely aware of the need to remain unseen.

A sudden rustle in the bushes ahead sent a jolt of fear coursing through me, my pulse quickening as I froze in place. Was someone watching? Was I being followed?

With bated breath, I strained my ears for any sign of movement, my heart pounding in my chest. I pressed myself against a brick wall and stood there for a full two minutes, but all I heard was the whisper of the wind through the trees, the night silent once more.

Relief flooded through me as I cautiously resumed my journey, my footsteps barely an echo in the stillness. Sweat rolled down my back as the summer heat soaked my clothes. Every shadow seemed to hold a threat, every corner a potential danger, but I pressed on, determined to reach the van quickly.

Finally, I stepped into the alley where my mother's van was parked. I could see it at the other end of the street, a beacon of safety in the darkness. I quickened my pace, my heart racing as I fumbled for the keys in my pocket, desperate to escape the suffocating grip of the night.

I had only parked three blocks away from Jameson's place, yet the journey had seemed to take forever.

I'd been so focused on reaching the van and concerned that someone was following me that I wasn't paying attention to where I was walking. When I tripped and landed on my hands and knees, I cursed under my breath.

I'd fallen into something sticky and immediately cringed. Then I turned and looked at what I'd tripped over and gasped.

Evelyn Hart lay in the center of the alleyway, her body twisted at odd angles as her eyes staring blankly up into the night sky.

"Well, shit," I groaned.

Chapter Fifteen

"Invest in the human soul. Who knows,
it might be a diamond in the rough."
–Daniel Defoe

Jameson

Since I had the day off, I didn't catch wind of Evelyn's death until I swung by the sandwich shop around noon. My first gut reaction was a mix of relief and hope that maybe now Declan would get what was coming to him.

Then I heard the buzz about Rayne stumbling upon the body during her late-night drive, and it sent a chill down my spine. There was no doubt in my mind that she'd found Evelyn on her way back to her car.

I'd been so exhausted after she'd sent me a text that she was safe, that I'd fallen asleep immediately. Why had she sent that message if she'd found Evelyn? Why not tell me?

Deep down I knew why. I would have hauled my butt down the street to be with her. No matter who saw it. Then it would have been obvious where she had been.

I needed more information, but I didn't want to fuck up the run I was supposed to go on that night with Ben, so I couldn't head down to the station.

The best place in town to hear gossip was the bar, especially since Evelyn worked there.

After finishing my lunch, I strolled down the sidewalk and headed towards BBB.

When I saw the patrol cars and the police tape blocking off the alley a few blocks away, I changed course and headed over there. There were almost two dozen other bystanders huddled around, so I figured I'd blend in.

Two officers stood around as a woman in a black coat took photos of the street.

"What's up?" I asked the blond man.

The dark-haired cop answered instead. "Hit-and-run last night." The man looked me over. "You're Jameson, right?"

I nodded and wondered how this cop knew my name. I'd seen him once, somewhere. Maybe when I'd been booked?

"She okay?" I asked.

The man's eyes narrowed, but then he shook his head slowly.

"DOA," he answered.

"Bummer," I said, trying to act casual. Since the guy was now staring me down, I shoved my hands in my pocket and turned to head back to the bar.

I was half a block away when I realized my mistake. I'd asked if she was okay. The cop had just told me it was a hit-and-run. Not that a woman had been hit. No wonder he looked at me funny.

Shit.

Okay, I was losing it. Get yourself together, I told myself as I stepped through the back door to the bar.

Seeing Felix sitting at the bar alone, I moved to sit next to him.

"Hey," I said casually.

Felix glanced over at me. "Your day off?" he asked.

I nodded. "Heard there was a hit-and-run," I said, keeping the details to a minimum.

"Evelyn Hart," Felix said and then downed the shot sitting in front of him.

"What?" I acted shocked, then I glanced around. "Does Declan know?"

"We're taking care of him," Felix said. "How's the head?" He motioned to the small bandages I'd put on the spot after my shower that morning.

"I'm okay." I ran my hand gently through my hair, as if I wasn't emotionally affected by Evelyn's death. In truth, I was. I was pissed that a kind young woman had her life snuffed out because she'd fallen for the wrong kind of man.

Faye, one of the other bartenders, moved over to take my order. Her eyes were puffy and red, and I could tell that she was upset about her coworker's death.

"Beer," I said, and then motioned to the empty shot glass. "And two more of those." Faye moved to fill my order. "What now?" I asked.

Felix shifted towards me. "For now, you and Ben have a meeting tonight. After, you'll fill in for Declan for a while longer. Until he's... back in the game."

I nodded, taking in this information. "Sure," I said as the drinks were set in front of me.

"To the family," Felix said and tapped my shot glass against his.

"Family," I agreed and downed the drink.

We sat at the bar for a few hours while I nursed a single beer. When Ben and a few of the other guys finally strolled in after work hours, we all grabbed burgers and sat in a booth.

Shortly before dark, Ben slapped me on the shoulder and nodded and we took off. I'd walked over, so he met me at my place and waited while I grabbed my jacket and changed into my bike boots. I also slipped my other gun and my knife under my boot.

I followed Ben as we weaved our way down county roads. Honestly, if I hadn't studied the entire surrounding area on a map, I would have been lost.

When we finally stopped along a branch of the Red River almost thirty miles outside of town, I mentally made a note of the exact spot.

"What now? Another hike?" I asked, shutting off my bike.

"For a while. There is too much sand on the pathway for the bikes. After that, we take a boat." Ben started walking down a dirt path. We walked for about ten minutes before coming to the edge of the river, where a small jet boat was tied to a dock.

Ben got behind the wheel, and we headed downriver. Several times we had to duck to get under the overgrowth. We made our way more than ten miles down the widest part of the river. Ben pushed the boat at top speeds while I held on and tried to pretend that I was enjoying myself. When he finally cut the engine, I wondered just how in the hell he knew where we were going in the pitch dark.

Then I saw the green light he was aiming at. It flashed a few times, and Ben cut the engine as we coasted towards the shore.

I was surprised to see Declan standing on the dock.

"Hey," Declan said, grabbing the rope to the boat and tying it off.

"Hey," I said back.

Once the boat was secure, I followed Ben and Declan up the dock to a massive cement structure with a tall iron fence surrounding it. It was a fortress in the middle of nowhere.

"What is this place?" I asked, stepping inside the gates.

"Welcome to the Nest." Declan laughed. "It's totally off-grid. Runs on diesel generators and has no roads in or out."

The building itself was bigger than the Taylor plantation, although far less fancy with its simple cement floors and walls.

It reminded me of the bunkers I'd read the mob used to have, only on a much larger scale.

The moment we stepped inside, I saw why it was hidden. It was set up like a normal house inside with a living room and entertainment area. There was a leather sofa and a large-screen television that was currently paused on a shooter game that Declan must have been playing.

There was even a makeshift kitchen area with a fridge, microwave, and cabinets. I assumed there were a few bedrooms and bathrooms down the hallway.

Weapons of all types hung on the walls or sat lying around. Ready for anything, I thought.

I turned and saw a massive table in the middle of the space covered with large stacks of cash. Hundreds of thousands of bills sat right next to more drugs than I'd seen in my entire lifetime. I saw everything from marijuana to coke to pills of all shapes, colors, and potencies.

This right here would easily be the largest bust ever

recorded. But I knew Declan and Ben weren't worth the trouble. Whoever was behind this could have ten other places just like this one hidden somewhere.

"Want anything?" Declan waved towards the table.

"No, thanks," I answered. Felix and Ben both knew I had made a stand about not sampling the drugs. I didn't mind selling them, or making money from them, but never touched them myself. I gave them some sob story about a friend who had OD'd in school. Thankfully, they never required me to mess with the stuff to work for them.

I was under the assumption that it was one of the reasons I'd moved up so quickly in the gang. There were a few Reapers that did dally in drugs and often messed up to the point that Felix stopped using them for big runs.

"Make yourself at home. We've got a while before we need to head out again." Ben walked over to the fridge and pulled out a soda. "Want?" he asked me. When I nodded, he tossed one over. I caught it, tapped the top, and opened it, drinking half the can in one gulp.

"Hot as balls out there," Declan said as he sat back down and picked up his game. "Thank god there's AC in this place."

I leaned against the edge of the wall to watch him play the game.

"Hey, heard about Evelyn," I said, trying to keep it casual.

If I kept quiet, he might think I was onto him. Still, if I said the wrong thing, he might think the same.

Declan shrugged and kept his eyes on the game. "I told the cops I didn't touch her," he said. "When I showed up the other day, she was all beat up. I'm just glad she was okay. Sucks about her broken arm, but she'll heal."

I frowned. "I meant the other—" I started, but Ben poked me in the ribs and shook his head.

Shit. Seriously? From the looks of it, Declan didn't know that Evelyn was dead. Which meant he had nothing to do with her murder.

Just then Ben's phone chimed and he turned to me. "Ready?"

"Sure." I set the empty soda can down as Declan paused his game and followed us back into the main room.

"I've got you all loaded," Declan said, motioning to three large black duffle bags. "Everything's in there." He walked over and took an AR-15 and an AK-47 off the wall and handed one to each of us. "You were ex-military, you should know how to use these." I nodded. "See you in about an hour." He winked at me and then turned back to his game.

I strapped the weapon over my shoulder and took one of the bags Ben offered me. As we made our way back outside and down the narrow pathway toward the boat, I instantly knew that the bag wasn't loaded with money. It weighed too much.

If I could, while Ben was driving the boat, I'd sneak a glance at what was inside just to confirm.

"It's guns," Ben said as he tossed the two bags inside. "Tonight, we're running guns." He took the bag from my hands and tossed it down. "We got a shipment of bangers and are trading for cash. It's a simple drop-and-grab." He motioned towards the boat.

"Why the heavy artillery?" I asked, sitting back down on the boat.

"Let's just say, the last time we made a trade with this group, things didn't go so well," Ben answered as he unhooked the boat, jumped in, and turned the engine back on.

"Should I be worried?" I asked as he slowly maneuvered the boat away from the dock.

"Naw, Felix and I taught them a lesson." Ben smiled. "These are just for show."

I nodded but still felt uneasy as we traveled further down the river.

I could see dim lights from a large town ahead of us along the river but before we hit the brighter lights, Ben cut the engine and aimed the boat towards a small beach area.

Before the boat hit the soft sand, two men just as armed as we were appeared.

"Ronny's expecting you," they said at the same time.

Ben chuckled. "Jameson, meet the twins." He handed me one of the bags.

Now that I could see both men in the dim light, I could tell they were identical twins.

We followed them up a sandy pathway to an old cabin. Ben knocked on the door and waited.

Someone shouted, "Come in," and we stepped inside.

An old black man sat in a rocking chair, smoking a joint as he watched us. I noticed he was missing half of his left leg and a few fingers.

Instantly, I wondered if that was what Ben had meant about teaching them a lesson.

"Bout time," he said to Ben. "New guy?" he asked, motioning towards me.

"Jameson," Ben said, setting the two bags at the man's feet. "This is Ronny." I walked over and set my bag with Ben's, then stood back.

The man ran his eyes over me. "Looks like the rest of ya." The man chuckled. I kept my mouth shut as the man bent over and looked in each bag. Sure enough, there were dozens of handguns in each bag. "Go on. The twins will get you what you need." He waved his hand and took another hit.

When we were safely back on our boat with two bags full of cash, I asked Ben, "Declan really doesn't know about Evelyn?"

"No." Ben glanced at me. "And Felix wants to keep it that way until..." He dropped off. "For a while."

"Sure." I nodded.

"Felix convinced Declan to switch spots with..." He sighed. "Shit." He stopped the boat and turned to me. "Until further notice, you're my right-hand man. Got that?" I nodded. "There are still things I can't tell you. You'll know a lot more than before, but some things are just... a need-to-know basis. Got it?" I nodded again.

Ben nodded and started up the boat again.

"Who do you think killed Evelyn then?" I asked.

Ben sighed and ran his hands through his hair. "Hell if I know. I liked the girl. Unlike Izzy, she wasn't trouble."

"Right," I agreed.

"You're smart to avoid that one. Izzy is... fucked up. You're just lucky she was aiming at your head. This time," Ben joked.

For show, I grabbed my balls and winced, causing Ben to laugh.

After dropping the bags of cash back with Declan almost an hour later, we headed back to our bikes.

When we strolled back into the bar, it was a quarter past midnight and almost the entire gang was still there.

Including Izzy. Upon seeing me, she wobbled over and started hanging on me like she hadn't tried to take my head off the night before.

I hadn't noticed at first, but half an hour later, I happened to glance towards the bar area and spotted Rayne sitting alone, watching all of us.

I had yet to unwrap Izzy from around myself and had pretty much given up trying. When my eyes locked with Rayne's, I could tell she was sympathetic to my plight. I wanted to smile at her but knew there were too many eyes on us.

No doubt, she was staking out the bar, waiting for Declan to reappear.

Just as I was about to turn around and give my attention to keeping Izzy off me, Nadia shoved past Rayne, knocking her drink over. I stilled and watched Rayne face off with the woman.

Rayne's jaw was set, and her eyes flashed with a mixture of anger and defiance. Nadia's expression was cold and calculating, her lips curled into a sneer.

As the tension crackled between them, I hesitated, unsure whether to intervene or let them handle it themselves. But before I could make a move, Rayne spoke, her voice low and controlled, despite the rage simmering beneath the surface.

"Watch where you're going," she said, her words sharp and pointed.

Nadia's laugh was mocking. "Or what, Rayne? You'll arrest me?"

Rayne's fists clenched at her sides, but she held her ground, refusing to be intimidated. "If you give me a reason to, you'll spend the rest of the night as uncomfortable as I can manage," she replied, her tone icy.

Nadia's eyes narrowed slightly, then she shoved Rayne with her shoulder and walked away with a smile. Rayne stood there, her shoulders tense with unresolved tension.

"She's such a bitch," Nadia hissed as she passed me. She gave me a disdainful glance, her lips twisted into a scornful smirk as she noticed Izzy clinging to me. "As for you," she scoffed, her voice dripping with contempt, "why not stop messing with the uptight cop bitch and put Izzy out of her misery." With that parting shot, she sauntered off.

"Yeah." Izzy started laughing. "Let's go somewhere and fuck." She jumped up and down several times and then took my hand and started pulling me away from Rayne.

Thankfully, as we passed by the pool table, someone asked me to play and I had yet another excuse not to disappear with Izzy.

By the time the bar closed, Rayne had left and, thankfully, so had Izzy. I'd seen her hanging on the arm of one of the other Reapers, one that she often left with, and was relieved.

I let myself into my apartment and had my weapon out of my holster seconds after spotting a dark shadow.

"Easy, cowboy," Jasmine said smoothly.

"Shit," I said, putting my gun away and waiting for my heart to return to its normal pace.

"Sorry," she said smoothly. "You were, occupied."

"Right," I said, moving over in the dark and opening the hidden room.

Jasmine followed and when we were safely inside, I flipped on the light.

"What's up, boss?" I asked as she moved over and sat down behind the computer.

"You were busy tonight." She glanced at me.

"Yup, I was just about to write my report." I motioned to the computer as I sat on the edge of the bed.

"Don't bother." She smiled over at me. "I watched the whole deal."

"How?" I frowned.

She laughed. "Ronny's place is bugged."

I laughed. "Okay." I thought about it. "So, you know about the Nest?"

I watched her eyebrows rise slowly. "Why don't you tell me what I missed."

Chapter Sixteen

"Perhaps time's definition of coal
is the diamond."
–Khalil Gibran

Rayne

There was little that I liked to do less on my day off than babysit a bunch of criminals. I had started staking out every place I knew Declan could be shortly after they'd driven Evelyn's body away.

A knock on the man's trailer door had turned into me obtaining an early morning warrant. I did a quick search of the small and extremely dirty place and found a handful of party drugs, a lot of alcohol, and a few firearms with their serial numbers filed off.

The man's car had been in the barn and we had towed it in. But after a glance, I could tell it wasn't the vehicle that had plowed into Evelyn in the alleyway. It didn't even have an engine in it and wasn't running.

Since the only other vehicle registered to the man was a motorcycle, which I assumed he was currently riding around somewhere just out of reach.

One thing was sure—it wasn't a damned hog that had done that to the woman. More like a large truck or something bigger.

I hadn't been the one to knock on Mrs. Hart's door and tell her that her daughter was dead. I hadn't been there to see the woman's son, Tristan, cry when he was told his mother would never return. That wasn't my job.

My job was to find the SOB that killed her.

Hit-and-runs happened all the time but this one felt personal. If Declan hadn't been released, I was positive Evelyn would still be alive.

After I found the man and hauled him down to jail again, my next step would be to find out exactly why he had been released.

I watched the man's home and workplace all day. I knew the rest of the Reapers were at the bar, so I sat waiting. When Declan didn't show, I followed Ben. Everyone in town knew Declan followed the man around like a shadow.

Watching Jameson and Ben disappear on their bikes together shortly after sundown, I knew that whatever was happening, I'd get an update from Jameson when possible. So I held back and returned to my place to eat dinner, shower, and change before heading back out to sit at a smoky bar for the rest of the night, waiting for Declan to show.

Randy had hired a company to come in and replace my front window and remove everything that had been damaged. Gone was my comfortable sofa, replaced with an old one that had sat in my parents' den for years. The lamp and end tables would have to be replaced when I had time.

At least for now things were as normal as they could be. While I downed a cold turkey sandwich, chips, and sweet tea, I watched the local news.

The report on Evelyn was brief and to the point. They'd left out a few major details at my request.

When my doorbell rang, I glanced at my security system and groaned. I debated whether to open the door to Sabrina. When she started hitting the button repeatedly, I sighed and walked over and yanked the door open.

"It's not a slot machine," I said as she smiled at me.

"Have a moment?" she asked with a bright smile.

"No," I said, starting to shut the door in her face. I should have seen the old stick-a-foot-in-the-door routine and planned accordingly. But I had yet to sleep and was extremely tired. "Go away," I groaned.

Sabrina easily pushed open my door and stepped inside.

"Hey sister, that's called breaking and—" I started, but she held her hand up for me to stop.

"I have something you will want to hear," she said firmly.

I took a few deep breaths and then motioned to my new sofa. "Five minutes," I warned.

She nodded and moved over to sit down. "Can I have some of that?" she asked, motioning towards my tea.

"This isn't a diner," I warned, but when she tilted her head and just looked at me, I rolled my eyes and poured her a glass. Since I didn't have a coffee table any longer, I handed her the glass. "Talk."

"I have information that Declan O'Malley is not in Gemsville," she said after taking a sip.

"Where is he?" I asked as I sat across from her.

She shrugged. "Felix disappeared with him shortly after you found Evelyn."

My eyes narrowed. "Felix himself?" She nodded. I had seen Felix at the bar before following Jameson and Ben out of town. If he was back in town without Declan, then he was the man I had to talk to.

She pulled a picture out of her purse and held it out for me. "I also have information that this guy is not who he says he is."

I reached for the photo and my hand paused halfway through the air when I heard this. Frowning, I took the image of Jameson from her fingers. "Oh?" I asked, trying to sound bored.

Sabrina chuckled and held out another photo. "And I think you know something about it."

I took this photo and frowned at an image of Jameson and me at the bar that first night.

"Who do you think he is?" I asked, holding onto the images. There was no way I was going to give them back to her.

She shrugged. "I'm on the fence there. Whoever he works for has connections." She leaned back on the sofa. "FBI, DEA." She chuckled. "IRS. Does it matter? There is no way that man is who he says he is."

I leaned my elbows on my knees. "What do you know?" I asked.

She mimicked my moves. "Nothing."

I narrowed my eyes. "Sabrina," I warned.

She smiled and suddenly leaned back again. "I know you." She pointed at me. "I know there is no way in hell you'd be caught dead with a Reaper" She pulled out another photo, this one of me sneaking up Jameson's stairs the night before. "Which means you know exactly who he is. And since I know you like men who are bad boys on the outside but you wouldn't be caught dead messing around with someone who was bad on the inside, that makes Mr. tall, dark, and"—she made a hissing sound with her teeth—"sexy as hell an honest-to-god good guy on the inside." She tucked the last photo back into her bag.

"You're treading on thin ice," I warned. Sabrina smiled back at me, waiting. "Your five minutes is up," I said, standing up.

"Tell me, off the record," she said. "Rayne." Her voice changed as she motioned around. "I'm worried about you. We used to be friends."

"Used to be," I added, motioning towards the door.

"There is no way I'd run with the story," she said, and I walked over and yanked her arm until she stood up. "Like I'd want his or your death on my hands." She scoffed. "Seriously, I'm smarter than that."

"What's your angle?" I asked when she wouldn't budge.

"My angle..." She turned suddenly and looked at me. "Seriously?" She motioned towards my house again. "Someone shot at you." She frowned at the sofa. "Wasn't that in your parents' den?"

I rolled my eyes and took several deep breaths. "Sabrina."

"Rayne," she retorted. "Just... assure me he's a good guy and I'll drop it. But when the story does break, I get the scoop."

I stared into her eyes for a moment. I'd known her my entire life. At one point, we had been a trio—me, Aria, and Sabrina. I had trusted her with my early teenage secrets and she'd trusted me with hers.

But this wasn't some teenage crush I had on Jameson. If I spilled his secrets and she dropped her guard to the wrong person, it was the life of the man that I was growing to love on the line.

"I can't." I shook my head. "If you trust me, then that should be enough."

Sabrina reached up, took my shoulders, and surprised me by pulling me into a hug. "That's enough for me," she said easily. "Be safe. Please."

I stood there in total shock as she let herself out of my house.

When that wore off, I headed down to the BBB and watched Felix as I waited for Jameson and Ben to return.

When Nadia purposely bumped into me, I was ready for a fight. I wanted nothing more than to knock the woman's teeth in. It was obvious the entire Reaper gang was out in full force that night except Declan. Which meant they were all hiding a murder.

Did Evelyn mean so little to them? She'd been part of their gang. Part of their family.

Did Izzy and the other women realize how little their lives mattered to them?

After that run-in with Nadia, all of my energy seemed to drain. Besides, watching Izzy paw the man I wanted to be with more than anything sucked the life right out of me.

After heading home and clocking out for a handful of hours, I headed into the office first thing after sunup. I was eager to find out all I could about Evelyn's death.

"Isn't it your day off?" Sam Davis, a younger cop, asked. Sam was one of the men in town who was a constant flirt. He used his charms on both women and men and usually walked away with whatever he wanted. I liked the guy but knew better than to work side by side with him, lest I fall prey to those charms.

Instead of answering, I glared at him.

"Okay." He held up his hands as if he were surrendering. "Maybe it will cheer you up to know there are donuts in the break room." He quickly turned away.

I smiled as I took a large chocolate-covered, cream-filled donut. I usually never got anything more than a stupid glazed one when someone brought them in.

I poured myself a mug of fresh coffee, balanced my donut on top of my mug, and headed back to my office.

The scent of freshly brewed coffee and the sugary aroma of a giant donut instantly lifted my spirits. It was going to be one of those days fueled by caffeine and carbs, and I was ready to dive headfirst into the case that had kept me tossing and turning last night.

With a satisfied sigh, I settled into my chair and waited for my computer to boot up. The stack of files on my desk beckoned, each one representing a piece of the puzzle in the mysterious death of Sharon Taylor.

I was no further on that case than I had been the day I'd discovered her, which just really pissed me off. For now, I needed to set that aside.

First things first. I needed to dig into the autopsy reports for Evelyn. I pulled up the documents on my computer screen, my fingers flying over the keyboard as I scanned the details. It didn't take long for the pieces to start falling into place. Based on the severity of her injuries, Evelyn had been struck by a large vehicle. Time of death was just before three in the morning, which meant she'd lain there for less than half an hour before I'd discovered her.

Just as I was about to delve deeper into the evidence, a knock on my office door interrupted my concentration. I looked up to see Quincy standing in the doorway with a curious expression.

"Hey." His voice was casual but with an underlying tension that set my senses on edge. "Got a minute?"

"Sure thing," I replied, gesturing for him to come in as I tapped my keyboard and set my computer to sleep. "What's on your mind?" I leaned back and took a sip of my now lukewarm coffee.

Quincy stepped into my office, his eyes darting around the room before returning to me. "I was just wondering if you'd made any progress on the mayor's murder case," he said, his tone carefully neutral.

I felt a prickle of suspicion at his question, but I brushed it aside, chalking it up to the usual curiosity among colleagues. "I'm following a few leads," I said, deciding to keep my response vague.

Quincy nodded, but there was something in his gaze that made me uneasy. Was it just my imagination or was there a hint of fear behind his eyes?

We'd only officially been an item for a few weeks, maybe a month, but I liked to think I knew the man. This behavior was different than I'd seen from him before. He looked on edge for some reason.

"Didn't you have today off?" he asked, suddenly.

"Evelyn is mine," I told him firmly. He slowly nodded.

"What's the word on that?" he asked.

"I just started."

This wasn't the first time he'd poked his head in my door. Actually, I think it was one of the reasons we'd gotten together in the first place. That and he was my type.

But since I didn't do cheaters, he was now off that list forever.

"Anything else?" I asked.

He took one more glance around and shook his head. "Just, uh..." He glanced around and then stepped inside my office and shut my door. "There's a new rumor going around about you and that Reaper. I thought we talked about this." There, there was the old Quincy. The man who thought he could tell me what to do because we'd spent a few heated nights together.

I rolled my eyes and tried to blow him off. "Since when are you into gossip?"

"So it's not true?" he asked, crossing his arms over his chest.

"Quincy," I warned, "you gave away all your rights to know what is and isn't going on in my sex life when you cheated."

He sighed and then nodded. "Fine, but at least let me warn you."

I held up my hand. "Step down," I warned him.

He threw his hands up. "As a friend," he started again, but stopped when I cocked my head.

"I hear you're seeing Clara," I countered. From the look on his face, I could tell that I'd hit a nerve. No one in the office, and I do mean no one, knew that I'd seen Clara and Quincy heading into the file room together. "I thought she was with Wyatt Taylor?" I countered.

Thankfully, Quincy turned and stormed out of my office without another word. There, I'd put him in his place at last.

I returned to my task and scanned over every inch of the report from the coroner. He had taken into account her broken arm, cuts, and bruises from the previous attack and determined that Evelyn had been killed by a simple hit-and-run.

For the next few hours, I ran through every vehicle registered to any past or present Reaper member, including those associated with the gang, such as the countless women that hung around the male members.

By lunchtime, I was so frustrated I needed a walk to clear my head.

The police station sat next to a very nice large park. When I'd been in grade school, we'd had many class trips to explore the flora and fauna in the area.

I'd been more interested in pretending to find clues and trying to match the footprints of the school kids than paying attention to the names of the plants. Picking a park bench, I sat down for a while and replayed Evelyn's last day in my head.

She'd been released from the hospital a few hours after she'd woken up and had some scans that cleared her. Her medical report showed that she'd had a blow to the back of the head along with the broken arm, which had been put in a bright blue cast. She also had some cuts and bruises which had been treated.

From what they could tell, she hadn't been hit in the face, just the back of the head.

I replayed the scene of Declan hovering over Evelyn. He'd pulled back his arm as if preparing to hit her. Hadn't he? Maybe I was biased? Maybe I'd seen what I had wanted to see?

In Declan's interview, he'd stated over and over that he'd found her that way. When he'd shown up to hang out with her while she opened up the bar and she hadn't opened the back door for him, he'd busted through it. Which could have accounted for the banging I'd heard. The back door had been broken off its hinges. If Declan had shouted after finding Evelyn unconscious, that would also match the timeline.

But then, who had Evelyn argued with? The officers had initially been called out to the scene because of shouting and screaming. Maybe she'd been arguing with the real perp? The one who, possibly, ran her down.

Could Declan be innocent?

Did Evelyn's death have anything to do with the mayor's murder?

The lines just weren't crossing. I couldn't see any connection. Still, when Jameson had told me about the Reapers dropping money off at the Taylor residence in the middle of the night, something had felt off.

I had to try and connect the two deaths and the place to start was by looking fully into Henry Taylor.

But first, I needed food. Real food. I locked up my office and headed down the street to the sandwich shop. I downed an entire Italian sub along with their largest chocolate chip cookie

When I stepped back into my office, I could tell someone had been through my things. This time, I was sure of who it was.

When I stormed into Randy's office, he was on the phone and the stack of files, my files, sat in front of him.

"What in the hell?" I said, not caring who he was talking to.

"I'll call you back," Randy said and hung up the phone. "Problem?"

"Those are mine." I pointed to the files.

"You are supposed to have the day off," Randy returned.

"Well, I'm here." I crossed my arms over my chest. "Can I have my files back?"

He nodded but then put his hand over them. "If you agree that you'll take tomorrow off."

I narrowed my eyes at him.

"You need time to rest. I can tell when you're burning the candle at both ends. Go spend time with your mother or, better yet, hang out with Aria and Charlotte. Go out for a movie, to a bar. Do something to relax."

I deflated and sat across from him. "This is relaxing to me."

He smiled. "I never imagined when I found you all those years ago just how determined you'd become. I should have known. I mean, no kid survives what you did without being stubborn." He chuckled. "Take your files. Just promise me that you'll get some rest tonight."

I nodded and smiled, then picked up the stack of files and returned to my office. I was riding on the high of the win as I sat back down and dove into exploring the new angle.

Every day that week, I stayed late, hoping to find something, any clue connecting the two cases.

They had buried Evelyn days after her death. It was sad to see how few people showed up for her funeral. Besides her family, members of her mother's church were the only guests. Not a single member of the Reapers had been in attendance.

I'd seen Jameson a handful of times. Every time, he'd been surrounded by Reaper members or Izzy. From what I could tell, he was still successful at keeping the woman at arm's length and was growing extremely frustrated at the woman's advances.

I desperately wanted some alone time with him. Even though we'd texted one another on his private number a few times, I wanted face to face time soon.

Having spent so much time in my office looking at computer screens and the small print in the files, I was exhausted and just wanted to go home. I grabbed my keys from the desk and stepped out of my office.

"I'll see you in the morning," I told Sherry as I passed her desk. She glanced up from the phone and waved at me.

Even though it was just past noon, it was the dead middle of summer, and I was drenched in sweat just a few seconds after stepping outside. This time of year, people shuffled from the air-conditioned indoors to their cool cars quickly and only enjoyed spending time outside in the early mornings or long after dark.

I wasn't surprised to see Jameson's Harley in front of the bar along with a row of other bikes next to it. When I walked into the place, I ran my eyes over the normal after-lunch crowd. Most of the Reapers who had the day off or didn't work sat in the back at a booth. It looked like the smaller group was holding a meeting.

None of the groupies were in attendance, which I found odd.

Deciding not to play it cool just this once, I walked straight over to the table and sat down next to Felix.

"Hey, gang." I smiled at each member. "What's shaking?"

I watched Jameson's eyes narrow slightly at me.

"Detective," Felix said slowly.

"Is this a bonified card-holding, members-only event or can anyone have a beer?" I waved at Faye and shouted, "A round for the table on me."

Faye stopped in her tracks, blinked a few times, and then hurried away.

I turned back to the eight men, all of whose files I had just spent days extensively studying, except for Jameson.

"Plotting your next bake sale?" I leaned on the table. When no one answered, I turned to Felix. "I noticed not a single member or groupie of your little group attended Evelyn's funeral. I thought Reapers took care of their own?"

"You're overstepping," Felix said in a low tone. Then he turned to Jameson and growled, "Rein your bitch in."

"Oh no." I laughed, getting everyone's attention again. "He's *your* bitch. So is each man at this table." I leaned closer to him. "So why didn't you give a fuck about Evelyn?" I stared Felix directly in the eyes. "Only boys are family members?"

The man was easily twice my size. He stood at six-two and his dark blond hair was shaved on the sides of his head, leaving the top flopping over his eyes. A makeshift mohawk of sorts. My guess was that he styled it that way to showcase the tattoos above each ear. His full beard was slightly red, and he'd even added a few braids to his beard at one point.

The man, as with most of the Reapers, was packed with muscles and always seemed to be wearing black or leather.

"You're pushing your luck, detective." Felix leaned closer to me.

All I could see in his cold blue eyes was power. The power he either believed he held or the power he used to control his emotions.

"Do yourself and Evelyn's son, Tristan, a favor. I don't give a damned where you get it, but her mother is struggling to pay the bills now that her daughter isn't working here to support them." I motioned around the bar. "If you, any of you"—I glanced around the table slowly—"ever gave a damn about her, you'd anonymously donate to the boy's fund." I stood up suddenly as Faye delivered a tray of beers. "I don't give a fuck if the money is dirty in any way. Not when I've seen firsthand just how that kid felt after losing his mother." Setting a couple of twenties on Faye's tray, I added, "Otherwise, everyone in town will know you're all pieces of shit. Enjoy the beer." I decided I'd had enough fun for one day, so I stormed out of the building and drove home.

Chapter Seventeen

Jameson

Whatever I had felt for Rayne before easily doubled after she stormed out of the bar.

"It's possible that woman has actual balls," Felix joked, causing everyone at the table to chuckle.

I had been asked to take the day off for this meeting and another run into the bayou. I had yet to determine where the funds or the drugs were coming from.

"She's not wrong," someone said. I turned and looked at Remy. He was probably the oldest member of the gang. Usually he just hung out with his old lady, Candy.

"No, she's not." Felix nodded. "I'll see to it." He sipped the beer that Rayne had purchased for the table.

"What about her?" Remy asked, motioning to where Rayne had just disappeared. "Now that Jameson isn't keeping an eye on her, how do we know she's not poking those pretty little tits where they don't belong?"

"She's not. She's way off course." Felix smiled. "I have someone watching her. If she gets close, I'll know about it."

I instantly wanted more information, but then Felix started talking about another party at his place. This party, according to Felix, was going to be the big one.

Most people involved in illegal activities liked to show off their wealth with the scum that worked for them. Felix was no exception.

The elaborate parties he hosted were filled with booze, drugs, guns, money, and, one time, a fight-club event.

"Jameson," Felix said, gaining my attention. "Tonight I need you to pick up the party favors for tomorrow night's festivities. I have a little surprise in store for this party. Something different."

I nodded quickly as Felix turned to the next member and rattled off more requests.

It wasn't the first time I'd picked up drugs for Felix. Most of the time it was small stuff. I figured this would be no different.

I knew the drill. I'd get a text message minutes before with the location and time for the pickup. It still made me wonder why he didn't use any of the drugs at the Nest. Since Evelyn's death, Declan had remained hidden. I didn't even know if the man knew of her death yet.

Felix and Ben weren't talking about it and something told me not to ask. I was on their good side and needed to stay that way. One positive thing about Declan being away, besides not having to deal with him, was that I was now Ben's number-one guy. Which made me number three in the entire operation.

When a few more members walked into the bar and

Felix had finished delegating for the party, everyone scattered.

I headed over to play a round of pool and desperately tried to avoid Izzy. At least for a little while.

It was funny that Bayou Brews and Blues was where the Reapers chose to hang. The dimly lit bar was a place where they felt they could let loose. They acted as if they were home.

Tonight, the air was thick with the scent of beer and whiskey and the sound of laughter, music, and the cheers of the patrons glued to whatever ball game was playing on the television sets behind the bar.

Felix was in top form that night. He walked around and gave each member his attention, his presence commanding respect from everyone. It was as if Rayne's earlier challenge had stoked his need to feel important.

As I nursed my drink at the far end of the bar, I saw Henry Taylor stumble into the place. I could tell that he was very inebriated. After glancing around, he pushed his way over to Felix, who was sitting a few barstools from me, talking with Nadia.

Henry jerked Felix around and exchanged hushed words with him. I couldn't hear what they were saying, but Henry's face was twisted with rage and when he started to raise his voice, Felix yanked the man into the hallway right behind me.

"I trusted you!" Henry's words echoed in the dimly lit hallway, making it so I could hear them perfectly. "And you repaid me with murder!"

My heart skipped a beat. Was Henry accusing Felix of being involved in the murder of his wife, Sharon?

I strained to catch more of their conversation, but the

noise of the bar swallowed their words, leaving me with more questions than answers.

As the tension continued between Felix and Henry, Izzy practically fell in my lap. She flashed me a dazzling smile, her eyes sparkling with mischief.

"Oops," she giggled as her breasts pressed against my arm. "Hey there, stranger," she purred, leaning in close enough that I could smell the scent of her perfume mixed with the unmistakable odor of alcohol on her breath.

I offered her a polite smile, trying to keep my distance. "Hey, Izzy," I replied, my voice carefully neutral.

But Izzy wasn't one to take a hint. With a careless laugh, she gestured wildly, sending her beer sloshing over the rim of her glass and onto my shirt. "Oops," she giggled, her fingers trailing dangerously close to the buttons of my shirt as she attempted to wipe away the spill.

I jumped up from the barstool and stepped back instinctively. "Izzy, don't you think you've had enough?" My voice was firm but gentle as I gently pushed her hands away.

But Izzy wasn't about to give up so easily. With a petulant pout, she glared up at me, her eyes flashing with anger. "You're such a buzzkill, Jameson," she spat, her voice rising above the sound of the bar as she stumbled away, leaving me with a sinking feeling in the pit of my stomach.

As I watched her disappear into the crowd, I wondered what other trouble she would get into before the night was over. For now, I had more pressing matters to attend to—like figuring out what the hell was going on between Felix and Henry.

I'd missed a lot of the conversation and now, as Felix and Henry parted ways, I debated following Henry and trying to get more out of him.

Then my phone chimed with the pickup time and

place, and I had to leave to fulfill my role. When I left, both Felix and Nadia were gone.

There were some rumors that the two were involved. It was strange how little Felix acted like he cared for women, yet Nadia still stuck close to the gang. She didn't strike me as a woman who would allow herself to be pushed into the background.

Hell, she probably could out-bench me. She often came into the gym with Felix, but it was very apparent she had her own set up somewhere else. You didn't get arms like hers without lifting daily.

Jumping on my bike, I headed to the pickup spot, a cheap motel on the other side of town.

I staked the place out first, watching who came and went for almost half an hour before it was time for me to head over to room two-twelve.

I knocked on the door and was completely shocked when someone familiar opened the door. Ryan West, six foot two, one-ninety pounds, and all muscle. His jet-black hair was longer than I remembered and was pulled back into a ponytail at the base of his neck. He still wore stupid gamer shirts and jeans with holes in them along with his cowboy boots and hat, which was sitting on the bed next to a backpack that I assumed was full of the drugs I'd come there to purchase.

The guy looked like your all-American country kid just making a buck on the side.

"Shit," I said under my breath and quickly glanced around.

Ryan smiled brightly at me and, much like I had done, glanced around outside.

"We're clean," Ryan said under his breath.

"Ditto," I told him. "I'm solo."

He jerked his head, motioning for me to come into the cheap motel room, which stank of cigarettes, booze, and sex.

When I stepped inside, he shut the door and then held out his hand and shook my outstretched one.

"Fancy meeting you here." Ryan laughed.

"What in the hell." I shook my head. "How long has it been?" I asked, sitting down when Ryan motioned to the chairs.

He narrowed his eyes. "LA?" He shrugged. "I heard you did good work in Vegas."

I nodded and glanced around. "Heard you were in Houston. I expect this is the same setup as LA?"

Ryan nodded. "The guys are in the next room," he said. "Stand down, he's DEA," Ryan said firmly. "After this gig, I'll head back to Houston. I'm just standing in on this one."

"This is just a simple pick up for me." I sighed. "If it goes south, it will ruin what I've got going. I'm hoping to tag much bigger fish on this one."

I'd worked with Ryan on a couple of small-time busts. He'd been the rookie back then, and while I had gone on to larger stings, apparently he still worked the small hotel gigs.

"I'll have my guys check with..." He waited.

"Jasmine Thompson, Supervisory Special Agent, DEA," I supplied and knew that the agents next door would call Jasmine to confirm my gig. No doubt, I'd walk away with whatever drugs had been arranged for the pickup.

"Lucky, I guess, that you got the gig to pick up." Ryan sat down and got comfortable. "If anyone else had shown, we'd have hauled them away."

"Yeah," I said with a frown.

"Think it was on purpose?" Ryan asked.

"Do I think they knew this was a bust?" I asked.

Ryan nodded.

I thought about it quickly. If Felix knew this pickup was a sting and had sent me along for the sole purpose of figuring out if I was a narc, then if I brought the drugs back, he'd have his confirmation. Then again, if he knew Ryan was a sting and I got busted, Felix would trust my loyalties.

But in truth, I'd made a dozen or so pickups since Declan had gone into hiding. Each one had been from different people and places. Any of those could have been stings. If he was questioning my loyalty, why now?

I quickly played through the last week or so and knew deep down that I hadn't done anything to raise his suspicions.

"No," I said, shaking my head. "Not unless you were obvious. Knowing you, you weren't," I added.

Ryan nodded. "So, what's new?"

I shrugged. "I'm thinking of taking a break after this gig."

Ryan's eyebrows rose. "Washing out so soon?"

I laughed. "I found someone worth the break. I'd like to explore what's there. This"—I motioned around me—"is hindering it."

Ryan's smile grew. "Yeah? Does she know what you do?"

I nodded. "She's local PD. A detective." I thought about Rayne. Of how ballsy she'd been facing off with Felix earlier. "What about you?" I asked.

Ryan laughed but his eyebrows were furrowed. "You don't find too many women willing to put up with what we do. Besides, I'm still young." He laughed. "And I'm currently married to my job."

"Ever get back to Texas?" I asked, remembering he'd left his family, a twin brother, just before I'd met him.

He shook his head and I saw sadness flash behind his

green eyes. "Not yet. Next gig has me heading back to Houston." He shrugged, then he paused, his eyebrows shooting up. He smiled. "Looks like you get to take the prize home tonight." He motioned to the bag of drugs on the bed.

I nodded and stood up, holding out my hand again to him. "After this, we should meet up for a beer and swap stories."

"I'd like to hear all about Vegas. I heard you had to ride a horse?" Ryan asked as he shook my hand. "It's been years since I got on the back of one. Sure do miss it."

I laughed. "It was a camel."

Ryan laughed as he shook his head. "Damn, I bet that was crazy. Good luck out there."

"Thanks." I took out the envelope of cash Felix had given me. "Gotta cover our tracks." I handed him the cash. "I'm sure Jasmine has told your SSA to clear out of these parts," I added. "I guess I'll be seeing you sometime." I shook his hand again. "Stay safe."

Ryan nodded and tossed the envelope of cash on the bed as I took the bag of drugs and threw it over my shoulder.

"Later," I said and walked out. The ride back to the bar was pleasant until the rain started. By the time I parked next to Felix's truck and tossed the bag in the back, I could barely see a foot in front of me. There was no way I wanted to ride the bike the few blocks in this mess to my place, nor did I want to head inside soaking wet.

Most of the bikes were gone, which signaled that everyone who had ridden there had left before the rain started. I was pulling my bike under the stairs that led up to the apartment above the bar and was just about to step out of the shadows when Henry Taylor stumbled out the back door with Faye.

"I told you," Henry said as Faye opened an umbrella

and held it over them. "All my money is tied up in this deal."

"But rent is due," Faye whined.

"Once things settle, you can move in with me," Henry promised as they started up the stairs.

"Promise?" Faye asked.

"This is the big one. The last time. After what happened to Sharon, I'm through being indebted to anyone," Henry said. "Once I pay him back, no one can touch me or anyone I care about ever again," Henry added as they disappeared into Faye's apartment above my head.

Henry Taylor owed someone. Someone powerful enough that he believed they killed his wife and were now threatening his livelihood.

Once the couple had disappeared up the stairs and into the apartment above, I glanced around and figured the rain wasn't that bad. There was no way in hell anyone knew I was here. I rolled my bike two blocks and parked it in the garage next to my car. Then I pulled the car out and headed towards Rayne's place as the rain continued to flood the streets.

I made sure to check the mirrors several times to make sure I wasn't being followed. I pulled up into the dirt lane a few yards from her place and slid my car into the bushes. Then I hiked through the rain once more. When I stepped onto her front porch, soaking wet, I wasn't surprised that she jerked open the front door, a gun pointed at my chest.

"Jesus!" she gasped. "What in the hell?"

I smiled at her. "Hi."

She frowned and glanced around, then gripped my jacket and shirt and yanked me into the house.

When I stepped inside, I almost slipped on the tile floor as she turned off the lights in the hallway.

"What in the hell are you doing here?" she hissed. But before I could answer, she pressed her body and mouth to mine. "Don't answer that." She sighed after she pulled away. "Wait, do." She shook her head. "I don't have a safe room."

"You won't need one," I said, my hands running over her hips. "Everyone's occupied tonight running errands for Felix's party this weekend."

"Okay," she said slowly.

The news I had come here to give her could wait. What I wanted—no, what I needed—far outweighed the update on her case.

"You're soaking wet," she said with a chuckle. "And now, so am I."

"Then let's put our clothes in the dryer and shower. I need to warm up." I started to tug her shirt over her head.

I hadn't realized it before, but she was dressed in cotton pajamas with little hearts on them.

Hell, I didn't even know what time it was or how she'd known I was on her porch. Later. I'd ask her later.

Once her shirt hit the floor, I leaned down and sucked her nipple into my mouth as my hand explored the rest of her. The amount of desire I felt for her was overpowering. We fell towards the wall and I used it to hold us up while I took what I needed from her, using her as much as she used me.

When her fingers wrapped around my cock, I jerked in response and then had to concentrate really hard on not just exploding in her hand.

I became an animal in those few moments. My body and desires completely took over from my mind. It wasn't until after I'd slipped inside her and we started moving together that my needs settled some.

Her legs wrapped around my hips as I pushed deeper into her, wedging her between me and the wall. I felt her convulse around me as she cried out my name and followed her. The burst came in waves as I held onto her, wanting to never let go.

"We should get some sort of award," Rayne sighed against my shoulder.

I chuckled. "I honestly didn't come here for this," I said into her hair. "It's a nice bonus though."

I felt her nod. "Why don't you let go of me and we can dress before you tell me exactly why you are here?"

"Part of me doesn't want to let you go," I said honestly as I looked at her. She smiled and brushed her lips across mine.

Then I remembered everything I'd learned earlier and eased away from her.

We dressed quickly in the dark. Since my clothes were soaking wet, I slipped on a pair of sweatpants she swore were her father's. After stuffing my clothes in her dryer and turning it on, she took my hand and led me to her bedroom. She shut the window blinds before she turned on the light.

Her bedroom matched who I imagined she was perfectly—no-fuss furniture and a minimalistic esthetic. I expected the rest of her house to be the same.

She sat on the edge of the bed and motioned for me to sit next to her. I did and quickly filled her in on everything I'd overheard that evening.

"Who is the 'he' in the conversation?" she asked when I was done.

"I'm assuming Felix," I said with a frown. "Since they were having heated words earlier."

She narrowed her eyes. "Why haven't you made your move on Felix if you think he's the mastermind?" she asked.

"Because I know that Felix isn't in charge," I answered quickly.

"So why do you think he's the one pulling Henry's strings?"

I shrugged and thought about it. "I guess I don't." I sighed and leaned back on the bed. "Who do you think he's talking about then?"

"I have some theories." She leaned back beside me. "Until I find solid evidence, I'm keeping them up here." She tapped her head.

"Problems?" I asked and shifted to be closer to her.

"Someone has broken into my office a few times and gone through my files," she admitted.

I thought about what Felix had said after she'd left the bar earlier that day. "Felix says he has someone watching you. That as of right now he doesn't think you're getting in his way."

To my surprise, she smiled. "I keep my real data on my phone not in my office or files now that I know someone has been breaking in."

"Smart," I admitted.

"I have a few tricks up my sleeve. Besides..." She reached over and brushed her fingers through my hair. "I have a secret weapon." I arched my eyebrows in question. "You," she said and then leaned over and kissed me.

Chapter Eighteen

---

*"When we have graciously endured every adversity, we
become like a shining diamond."*
–Lailah Gifty Akita

Rayne

I practically glided into my office the next morning. My body was still buzzed from its multiple releases the night before thanks to Jameson. We'd stayed awake all night together, talking about the case, about our lives, and, sometimes, not talking at all.

I'd never felt so much for someone so quickly before. There were times I felt as if he was already a part of me. Like he could understand everything I didn't say out loud.

The only other person in life I felt that instant connection with was Aria. She was my soul sister. What did that make Jameson?

When I stepped into my office, I pretended not to notice the few things that had moved. To help me keep track of whenever someone went through my files, I had cleaned most of the clutter from my desk.

I logged into my computer and opened the camera app that I'd installed the day before. The small hidden camera in my office wasn't technically authorized. I hadn't even told Randy about it. Not that I thought he was the one going through my stuff.

I sat back as I watched Abe Sterling enter my office using a set of keys at one in the morning and start going through my files. Where had he gotten a set of keys from?

Glancing out my door, I pulled up the schedule and matched Abe's work times with each time someone had messed with my files.

There were a few discrepancies in the schedule, but then again, most of us came and went when we wanted.

I began to wonder why a man who had been a police officer at the precinct for over three years would hinder my investigations.

I pulled up his information in our system and scanned his work details and history. He'd been reprimanded a few years back but nothing more. After hitting a roadblock, I changed to his social media pages.

For the next few hours, I scanned every post, video, and photo. I would have missed it had Nadia Monroe not been fresh on my mind, but when I saw her in the background of one of Abe's photos, I froze on it.

Once again switching gears, I pulled up Nadia's social media posts and arrest records.

By the time I headed to Randy's office, I was positive the two were either romantically involved or at least hanging out in the same circles. Which meant Abe was in tight with the Reapers.

When I got to Abe's empty desk, I sat down and pretended to make a phone call. No one in the office even glanced in my direction as I pretended to look for a pen in his desk drawers.

Feeling frustrated upon not finding anything that stood out, I continued to Randy's office.

"Got a sec?" I asked, poking my head in his office. I was slightly surprised when I realized he wasn't alone.

A very attractive black woman sat across from Randy. The pair appeared to be waiting for me, which was very odd.

"Good, you're here. I was just going to send for you. Have a seat." Randy motioned to the empty chair.

I shut the door and sat next to the woman. I remembered seeing her before but couldn't put my finger on where.

"This is DEA Supervisory Special Agent, Jasmine Thompson. Jameson is one of hers," Randy said with a nod. "She's here on official business."

I nodded my understanding. "How can I help?"

"We're getting ready to make our next move and I just wanted both of you to know that it might get a little messy," Jasmine said, glancing between us.

"How messy?" I asked.

Jasmine leaned back in her chair. "Enough that you, Officer Rayne, may have to make some spur-of-the-moment decisions. Think you can do that?"

"Yes ma'am," I said quickly.

The woman's eyes moved over my face for a few seconds. "I can understand what he sees in you. After talking to your father, I know you'll do what you must. My advice, when the time comes, is to stand your ground. No matter what."

I nodded again in understanding, but I wondered silently if she meant about the job or about Jameson.

If Jameson was almost finished with his job, would he leave Gemsville after or stay like he'd hinted?

"What's your timeline?" Randy asked, as if sensing the question in my head.

The woman shrugged slightly and turned back towards him. "It's not up to me to make this move. I'm just here doing the warning." She stood up.

"Thanks." Randy stood up and shook the woman's hand.

After she left, I turned to him. "She could have called instead of coming down here," I suggested.

"There were... other reasons she did this in person," Randy said, sitting back down.

"Such as?" I asked, sitting down again as well.

"Honestly, I think she just wanted to meet you," Randy said, running his eyes over me. "From the sound of it, you've made quite an impression."

What had Jameson told his SSA about me? I ran that question through my head for a moment.

"Someone's been breaking into my office," I said, changing the subject suddenly.

Randy's eyebrows rose. "Any idea..." he started, but I set my phone down on his desk with the frozen image of Abe standing at my desk on it. "Son of a..." Randy finished. His eyes moved from my phone to the door.

"You can't say or do anything." I broke into his thoughts. "Not yet."

"This is my house," he added.

"And it's the long game I'm looking at," I said, leaning forward. "I need to know why."

Randy was quiet for a moment before he nodded

slowly. "It's your game." He handed my phone back to me. "What do you need?"

"Information," I said, tucking my phone back into my pocket. "Everything you have on Abe."

Randy nodded and turned to his computer.

For the next half hour, we ran through Abe Sterling's background. He'd joined the precinct three years before. Even though his family was well established in the area, for a few years after he'd graduated high school he'd worked odd jobs, including at the junkyard and an auto parts store. Then he'd attended the academy and become a low-level beat cop.

He'd worked the night shift for the first year and switched partners a few times. He had been partnered with Quincy over the last few months.

"That's one I never trusted." Randy frowned.

"Who? Quincy?" I asked. When he nodded, I chuckled. "That's because you don't trust anyone I've dated."

"True," he agreed. "This Jameson, I'd like some time with him again."

My smile slipped. "Don't go there," I warned. "We tried to steer clear of one another. It didn't work out."

Randy laid his hand over mine. "It's my job to go there. Still, the man's background came back clean."

"You ran him?" I asked. I shouldn't have been surprised.

"I run every man who looks at you," Randy joked. He turned slightly to me after shutting down his computer screen. "There's nothing here. No answers. What's your plan?"

I cocked my head and thought. "Not sure yet," I admitted after a moment. "Whatever it is, I'll try to keep you in the loop."

Randy nodded. "Your mother would love to have you

over for dinner, but to be honest, the last round of chemo has her too tired. Since Carolyn had to go back to Florida last week, I think your mother is feeling lonely now."

"I was going to stop by after work today," I told him. "I have some lotion that Aria wanted her to try that I need to drop off."

I left his office and headed down the street for another sandwich. Suddenly, I was in a foul mood. I needed to know Abe's game. Was he working with someone or was he just trying to wiggle his way into my case work? I doubted that.

I didn't see Abe as the astute kind. I doubted the guy could find his car in a crowded parking lot, let alone solve a murder.

I stood in line at the sandwich shop and, instead of looking down at my phone like everyone else was doing while they waited, I glanced around the place. I doubted the old black-and-white tiles had ever been changed out. Many of them were worn through so you could see the cement floor underneath. The countertops were just as worn. Still, they had purchased new refrigeration cabinets to house all their meats and cheeses. And everyone in town knew that their bread was made fresh daily.

The couple that owned the shop, Hillary and Steve Klein, were old friends of Randy's and Edith's. They attended the same church and Hillary was probably Edith's closest friend, which is why I frequented the shop as much as I could.

I was raised to know the importance of supporting small local businesses and friends. When Jackson Pennington had moved into town, everything had changed. The way he threw his money around caused some smaller businesses, those ma and pa places, to go under.

While I waited for my Reuben on rye, I glanced up to

see Wyatt Taylor having a heated conversation with Clara in the back corner.

When I saw Wyatt grab Clara's arm, I marched across the shop and stood at the edge of the table.

"You might want to carefully consider your next move," I told Wyatt in a low voice. His hand instantly dropped from Clara's arm as his eyes narrowed.

"Stay out of this, Rayne," Wyatt hissed.

"Make me," I said, feeling like an empowered child.

How many times had I wanted to tell both of those boys off? Hell, what I wanted to do was shove my fist through their perfect noses. Instead, I crossed my arms over my chest slowly as he glared up at me for a few seconds.

"This is over," he told Clara. He jerked his chair out and stormed out of the shop.

"Thanks for that," Clara said with a sigh. "I knew the Taylors had a temper, I had just hoped Wyatt was different."

Had Wyatt just found out about Clara and Quincy? There were rumors the two had been seen several times around the office. It was bound to get back to Wyatt sooner or later.

Nodding my reply to her, I turned as I heard my name called and walked over to grab my sandwich.

Normally, I would have eaten there, in the shop, but suddenly I was in an even fouler mood, so I took my drink and food to the park to eat alone.

I didn't want to be around anyone at the moment.

I found an empty park bench by the little pond full of ducks and sat under a large oak tree and downed my sandwich.

I was so deeply invested in running through suspects and plots that I hadn't heard anyone approach me.

"How can you eat when it's so hot out?"

I turned to see Faye Baker sitting down on the other end of the bench. She was wearing a black ball cap, gray sweat shorts, and a blue tank top with running shoes. Obviously, she'd been out for a run.

"How can you run in this heat?" I shrugged and took another bite.

She sighed and leaned back a little. "Evie was about to break things off with Declan."

I set my sandwich down and turned towards her. "You know this firsthand?" I asked slowly.

Faye nodded slowly. "She told me about an hour before..." She pulled something out of her short pockets. "She wanted you to have this." Before she handed me the small piece of paper, she glanced around. "I think it's why she was killed. For the record, I don't think Declan killed her. I could get in a lot of trouble for talking to you," she said, still glancing around.

I took a moment and looked around. I'd picked this spot because it was secluded. From here, I couldn't see anyone else and, thanks to the large oak tree, no one could see us.

"I think we're okay for now," I said, taking the note from her fingers, noticing that they shook slightly.

"I know you care. I mean, about who did that to Evie. I know you'll get to the bottom of who killed her. I hope this helps." Before I could say anything else, she jumped up and took off running towards the walking bridge.

I waited a few heartbeats before opening the note.

"You have rats in your house and the king rat is more powerful than you think. Aim high, Detective Rayne. Thanks for sticking up for me. -Evie P.S. I swear on my son's life that it wasn't Declan that attacked me."

Shit. Why in the hell was I just now getting this? I

remembered Evelyn telling me about rats. Why had I just now remembered that? She'd warned me someone in my house was dirty. Abe. Who else?

For the rest of my break, I ran names through my head.

Since Abe's current partner was Quincy, and I knew he'd been poking his nose in my business already, he was top of my list. Who else? Shit.

"*Aim high.*"

What did that mean? Was she saying that someone high up in the precinct was corrupt or was she talking about Henry Taylor?

By the time I walked back into my office, my head ached and I was too hot to finish my food. I downed the rest of my iced tea and sat at my desk until I cooled off.

I poured over the details of Evelyn's case. Hitting a wall, I turned back to Sharon Taylor's murder case. The image of both women's lifeless bodies flashed through my mind. The contrast between the cases. The similarities. Everything was a stark reminder of the brutality that had robbed them both of their lives.

With a heavy sigh, I pulled up the autopsy report, the words blurring together as I read through the gruesome details. Sharon had been stabbed multiple times, the wounds inflicted with a precision that spoke of cold-blooded intent. Each gory detail was etched into my memory, a constant reminder of the horrors that lurked just beneath the surface of our seemingly peaceful town.

I traced my finger along the lines of the report, my mind racing as I tried to make sense of the evidence before me. Every detail mattered—from the angle of the wounds to the type of weapon used—and I was determined to leave no stone unturned in my quest for justice.

But as I delved deeper into the report, a sense of frustration began to gnaw at the edges of my mind. Despite my best efforts, there were still too many unanswered questions, too many loose ends that refused to be tied.

With a frustrated growl, I pushed back from my computer, rubbing my tired eyes as I tried to shake off the feeling of defeat. Sharon Taylor's murder was a puzzle with too many missing pieces, and I felt as if I was running out of time to put them together.

But I was stubborn and refused to give up. With renewed determination, I grabbed a cold soda and sat back down. Squaring my shoulders, I dove back into the case file, ready to fight for justice with every ounce of strength I had.

As I once again sifted through the details of Sharon Taylor's autopsy report, my mind couldn't help but scan through the list of suspects.

At the top of that list was Henry Taylor, Sharon's husband, whose motives were as murky as the waters of the bayou. Henry's tumultuous relationship with Sharon was no secret, marked by years of infidelity and betrayal. Could his rage have boiled over into violence, leading him to lash out in a fit of jealousy or rage?

Everyone in town knew of the Taylor men's violent tendencies. They were bullies, each and every one of them. Today's little scene at the sandwich shop was proof of that.

Next on the list were Wyatt and Beau, whose troubled pasts had left them with more than a few skeletons in their closets. Both men had their fair share of run-ins with the law, and their volatile tempers made them prime suspects in Sharon's murder. But were they really capable of such a heinous act, or were they simply victims of circumstance?

And then there was Faye, Henry's mistress, whose tangled web of lies and deceit had ensnared us all. Faye's connection to Henry was undeniable, but her true motives remained shrouded in mystery. Had she played a role in Sharon's murder, or was she simply a pawn in a much larger game?

As I pondered the tangled web of relationships and secrets that surrounded Sharon Taylor's death. I remembered the encounter with Faye at the park.

"She...wanted you to have this. I think it's why she was killed." Faye had looked scared.

Evelyn, Evie, had been brutally run down in the alley a block behind her work. Why?

I took out the note and scanned over the simple handwriting. Was this really from Evelyn? It sounded like her. The use of the word *rat*, which she'd used in the alley that day I'd gone to the bar to talk to Faye.

As I re-read Evelyn's final words, a chill ran down my spine.

Could her death be connected to Sharon's murder or was it simply a tragic coincidence? With each passing moment, the list of suspects grew longer, and the truth seemed further out of my reach.

I worked on both cases, going over every note I had until my eyes blurred. My headache grew with each moment I stared at the computer screen. I decided to clock out an hour before I normally would have and head over to drop off the lotion to Edith.

Since it was still boiling hot out, I pushed my Jeep's AC to the limit while I drove across town.

I walked into the house and called out that I was there. I instantly knew something was off when I didn't get a response.

Stepping into the enclosed sunroom, I gasped when I saw Edith on the floor, her body lying in a small heap. Dropping down beside her, I felt for a pulse with shaky fingers.

She was pale, the whitest white I'd ever seen. Her wig had fallen away and was lying on the floor next to her. A cup of tea had tipped over and, as I knelt beside her, I felt how cold the spilled liquid was. Which meant she'd been like this for a while.

"Please," I said out loud, my voice a whisper in the room. "Not her," I said as I searched desperately for any sign of life.

Chapter Nineteen

"Diamonds are forever—my youth is not."
–Jill St. John

Jameson

In the previous week and a half, I had made more than a dozen drops or pickups. Each one, I told myself, got me one step closer to the top. There was no doubt that Felix and Ben now trusted me. Completely.

I'd gone to the Nest two more times. Declan was now acting stir crazy and had obviously been told about Evelyn's death. The last time I saw the man, he'd been so strung out he could barely stand.

Still, Ben had acted as if it was the most natural thing on the planet.

We'd gone deep into the bayou once more to gather two more bags of cash. Every time, Ben handed candy to the little boy with the haunting eyes, who thanked him and handed over the cash as if he had no clue what he held, that so much money could have been his ticket out of the mud hole.

Felix had requested that I cut my hours back at the gym to accommodate all the running around. I'd been compensated with a crisp wad of bills to make up for the loss of income.

After each run, I'd checked in with Jasmine, who was sticking close to town and working her own angle. It wasn't the first time she'd stepped in and done her own thing, and I knew that whatever happened next, she'd be there to see things through.

I also knew there were a few dozen agents nearby who were ready to storm in when I gave the final word. It was a sign that I was getting closer to the end of the game.

I missed Rayne. I wanted to spend all of my days and nights with her. Years if possible.

We talked as often as we could on my secure line. Sent a few coded text messages back and forth.

Since that night a few weeks back, we hadn't had time to hold one another again.

I'd never felt lonely before. Never really thought about how empty and dark my nights were. Now, when I lay in bed alone, it was all I could think of. I missed her warmth, her softness, her laughter.

I had never loved a woman before now. Hell, I hadn't thought it was possible for me. It had never seemed to be in the cards for my life. Now I was dreaming. Which was dangerous.

Often, when I should have been focused on work, I was thinking of our future together. I couldn't afford to let my guard down.

In the previous two days, I had avoided replying to Rayne's messages. I needed to push her away until I could give her all of my attention. Our future depended on it.

Tonight's run, a pickup from another shady motel

outside of some other little town along the old highway, was only shitty due to the summer rainstorm pelting my face as I drove on the old road.

I hadn't been out to the motel before and, honestly, hadn't even known of its existence. I was pretty sure I had crossed a few county lines by the time I stopped in front of the dive.

The sign was half lit and the no-vacancy light was the brightest thing in the evening sky, except for the occasional bolt of lightning off in the distance.

I stepped under the torn awning and knocked on the door to room 212 and waited.

"Yeah?" someone said from inside.

"I hear there's a full moon tonight," I said, using the code words.

The door flew open, and seconds later I stumbled back as two large dark figures rushed me. I didn't even get a chance to ball my fists before the first blow to the side of my left temple had me seeing stars.

Half dazed, I was dragged into the room and tossed on the floor. Steel-toed boots kicked my sides, shoulders, head. I heard screaming. Felt my skin tear. Tasted blood.

Then, nothing.

When I woke, sunlight was streaming through torn blinds, hitting me directly in the one eye that I'd forced open.

"Shit." I coughed and rolled over. The bag of drugs I'd brought with me to hand over for the cash was gone. Along with my wallet, motorcycle boots, and jacket. Both of my guns and my knife were gone as well. I'd wager they'd taken off with my bike too.

"Shit." I groaned and wobbled as I hung out on my

hands and knees. Droplets of blood fell from my mouth onto the matted carpet.

I'd let my guard down and it had cost me.

I wiped my mouth with my shirt sleeve and moved to stand up. Out of the corner of my eye, I saw a dark figure sitting in the chair across the room and stilled. My entire bruised body went on guard.

Until I saw the kid's eyes staring blankly back at me and realized his throat had been slashed. He'd bled out all over his football jersey.

"Shit." I sat down on the carpet, staring at the dead kid.

No doubt, the high school jock had been the one I was supposed to meet.

I closed my eyes and assessed how badly hurt I was. Not as bad as the kid, I thought quickly.

Bruised ribs, black eye, bloody nose. I reached up and touched it—not broken at least. Fat lip. I ran my tongue over each tooth, thankful that none of them wiggled.

I hadn't even gotten a hit in. I hadn't seen either man's face. Hadn't heard any names or seen anything other than darkness.

Was this a set up? Had Felix and Ben been the ones to jump me? The two men in the room had been roughly their size. Big. Full of muscles. Steel-toed bike boots. Still, something told me it wasn't them.

It could be another test though. To see how I'd handle waking up in a motel room with a dead kid.

Looking around, I saw a pair of dirty white sneakers. They were a little small, but I pulled them on. Whatever happened next, I wasn't going to deal with it barefooted.

I walked over to the window and glanced out. Yup, my Harley was MIA. Shit.

They'd taken everything I had, including my phone.

Could I chance making a call on the motel's phone? I glanced at the thing sitting on the nightstand and knew better.

From what I could tell, the only thing leading me to the scene was a few drops of my dried blood on the already dirty carpet. I'd wager there was a hell of a lot of DNA on the damned thing.

I glanced down at the dirty white shoes and doubted they'd be missed. The kid was wearing what appeared to be a brand-new pair of Air Jordans. Expensive. Why hadn't they taken those?

Using my shirt sleeve, I opened the door. I pulled my hoody over my head, and stepped outside, making sure no one was watching.

Quickly, I stepped into the alley and walked down a side road. I didn't see so much as a car or another person for almost an hour. I stopped at an old gas station that had probably closed twenty years before and used the pay phone, which surprisingly worked, to call the emergency number.

Jasmine answered on the second ring.

"What's wrong?" she said, sounding worried.

Half an hour later, a car pulled up to the back of the gas station and I slid into the passenger seat.

"There's a fresh pair of clothes." Jasmine nodded to the back seat. "We done here?" she asked me.

I rolled to the back seat, prepared to change out of my ruined clothes.

"No," I answered. "I don't think it was Felix or Ben." I'd thought about it while waiting. "Not their style," I mumbled as I switched the ruined clothes for the clean ones.

"Are you sure you don't need medical help?" she asked as she drove.

"I'm sure," I assured her and winced as I moved wrong.

"Shit, they fucked you up good," she said, glancing in the mirror.

"Yeah," I agreed.

"The kid?" she asked solemnly.

I shrugged. "You made the call?"

"Yeah, the manager will check on the room. When he calls it in, our team will go in quietly," Jasmine answered.

"Rayne?" I asked.

"Not her jurisdiction," Jasmine said. "We're two counties away."

"Right." I groaned. "Still, I'd like her to be clued in."

Jasmine nodded. "Have you thought about what you're going to tell Felix?"

I closed my eyes and laid my head back after finishing changing. "Not yet. I want a shower and sleep first."

"We could get you the cash," Jasmine offered.

"Then what happens when word gets out that I was jumped? My bike gone? They'd question where I'd gotten the cash."

"Right." Jasmine sighed. "I'll drop you off just outside of town. You can walk the rest of the way."

"Thanks." I closed my eyes until I felt the car stop.

"Your stop." She turned to look at me. "Here's a backup phone." I took it and pocketed it. "If you get spooked, you know where to meet me. Safe house," she said as I climbed out.

Since the cabin was no longer safe, we'd changed locations. There was a house a few blocks away that she had rented under her alias.

She had presented herself in town as a business investor named Jasmine Rice who was looking to invest in a few properties around town.

After five minutes of walking, a familiar truck pulled up next to me and I groaned as Ben stared back at me.

"What in the hell?" He jumped out of the truck and helped me into the passenger seat. "Don't tell me Mason did this to you?"

"Mason?" I blinked a few times and shook my head. "The kid?"

Ben's eyes narrowed. "Yeah, the kid who was supposed to pay you for the drop."

I shook my head again. "Two big guys, bigger than Felix." I wiped my lip. "They jumped me before I could blink. Slashed the kid's throat, stole everything, even my fucking bike."

"Shit," Ben said, hitting the steering wheel. "Mason is dead?"

I nodded and rested my head back. Okay, so not Ben and Felix, I thought.

"You okay?" Ben asked as the truck started moving.

"Bruised. Pissed about my bike," I said. "Pissed they got the jump on me," I added.

"Did you see their faces?" Ben asked.

I shook my head without opening my eyes.

"Two big guys?" Ben asked again. I nodded again and groaned a little with pain.

Ben was quiet.

"Know 'em?" I asked, cracking my eye open.

"Yeah," Ben said with a sigh. "I have a clue who." He glanced at me, his eyes running up and down me. "Killed the kid?" he asked, and I nodded.

"Slashed his throat." I motioned. I wanted to add that it pissed me off, but I knew it wouldn't matter to Ben.

"We'll get them back," Ben said.

"Who?" I asked.

Ben's eyes narrowed. "You're in no shape. We've got you on this one."

"Who?" I asked again. "It's personal."

Ben shook his head. "You're sitting this one out." He stopped at my place. "Get some rest. Take a few days to heal. Let me know if you need... anything."

I nodded. I was feeling nauseous, so I climbed out of the truck and headed upstairs.

I stumbled into my loft apartment, each step sending waves of pain radiating through my bruised ribs. The taste of blood lingered on my lips, and I could feel the sting of a fresh cut on my cheek. I reached up to touch the tender skin around my eye, wincing as I felt the telltale swelling beneath my fingertips.

With a sigh of relief, I made my way to the bathroom. I stripped off my fresh clothes, which were now stained with blood, and stepped into the hot spray of the shower. The water cascaded over me, washing away the grime and blood that clung to my skin, but no amount of scrubbing could erase the memories of the beating I had endured or the image of the dead teen.

I downed a couple of aspirin and drank what felt like a gallon of water and then pulled on a pair of shorts. Exhausted and sore, I collapsed onto the bed, the soft mattress offering little comfort to my aching body. I closed my eyes, hoping to find some respite in sleep, but my mind refused to quiet, replaying the events of the night over and over again. The empty look in the high school kid's eyes. Knowing the pain that would come to his family with today's sad news.

Finally, exhaustion overtook me, pulling me into a fitful sleep plagued by nightmares of violence and death.

When I awoke, the sunlight streaming through the

windows cast a warm glow over the room. I blinked away the remnants of sleep, my eyes slowly focusing on the figure standing at the foot of my bed.

"Rayne?" I croaked, my voice rough from disuse.

She smiled softly, her eyes filled with concern as she approached me. "Jasmine called me. How are you feeling?"

I winced as I shifted, the pain in my ribs flaring to life once more. "Could be worse," I muttered, forcing myself into a sitting position.

Rayne nodded, her expression sympathetic as she reached for the first aid kit on my bedside table. Had she set that there? How had she gotten into my place? How long had I been out?

"Let me help you with those cuts," she said, her voice gentle as she began to bandage the wounds on my face. "Want to tell me about it?"

As she worked, I filled her in on the events of the previous night—the ambush in the hotel room, the discovery of the dead high school student.

Rayne listened intently, her brow furrowed in concentration as she processed the information. "Sounds like you stumbled onto something," she said finally, her voice tinged with concern.

I nodded, a knot forming in my stomach as I realized just how deeply I had unwittingly waded into danger.

"Ben seemed to know who jumped me," I added. "He claims they'll pay them back."

She was quiet for a moment. "I'll keep my eyes out for the Reaper's retribution."

I leaned back on the headboard. "I didn't know what to tell them, how I'd gotten out of this," I mumbled. "Shit, I fucked up." I took her hand in mine. "I dropped my guard."

She frowned at me. "Why?"

My eyes locked with hers. "You know why."

She closed her eyes for a moment, then leaned in and brushed her lips gently over mine.

"You rest here," she said, "I'll make you something to eat."

I nodded gratefully, sinking back onto the pillows as Rayne disappeared into the kitchen.

I glanced at my windows, only now afraid that she'd be seen in my apartment. Then I realized I didn't give a fuck. It was the middle of the day, and Ben had just told me to take time off.

I'd wager every member of the Reapers was elsewhere, plotting to pay back whoever had jumped me. The last thing they'd do was watch my place.

The scent of sizzling bacon and frying eggs soon filled the air, and my stomach rumbled in anticipation.

Minutes later, Rayne returned with a plate piled high with eggs and bacon, setting it down on the bedside table with a soft thud. "It's all you had. It's almost seven at night, but you get breakfast for dinner," she said, her smile warm as she handed me a fork.

"Since it's the first thing I'll eat today, it's perfect," I said, digging into the food eagerly, the familiar taste of home-cooked comfort easing some of the tension that had settled in my bones. Rayne watched me eat, her expression thoughtful.

As I finished the last of my meal, Rayne reached out to take my plate, her touch gentle against my bruised skin. "You should get some more rest," she said softly, her eyes lingering on mine.

I nodded, suddenly overcome by a wave of exhaustion. "Thanks," I murmured, my voice barely above a whisper.

"I've missed you," I added, pulling her down with me. "Stay with me for a while?"

"For a while," she agreed as she rested her head against my arm.

With her by my side, her long soft hair brushing against my cheek, I fell almost instantly into a deep sleep. Her sexy scent filled my dreams.

When I woke in darkness, the bed was empty and cold and every part of me ached.

Chapter Twenty

"Better a diamond with a flaw
than a pebble without."
–Confucius

Rayne

"I don't give a damn, Richard," I practically yelled into my phone. "I want that report in my inbox in ten minutes or I'm going to haul my butt over and kick your skinny ass myself." I slammed the phone down without waiting for a response.

I paced the floor of my office until I heard the chime of the incoming email.

For the next hour, I read and re-read the autopsy and forensic reports on Mason John Williamson. The seventeen-year-old Madison High School student and football star had been found at the County Road Thirteen Motel with his throat slashed.

Mason had a few juvie priors, mostly for drugs. His

father, Judge Williamson, had no doubt spent a lot of money to brush most of his juvenile offenses under the rug.

Madison County was in an uproar. There were no clues at the scene aside from some tire tracks in the parking lot. Those were from a car, not a Harley, so wouldn't lead to Jameson.

It was two days since the kid's death and Jameson getting jumped, and I'd just now gotten my hands on the crime scene reports. I'd spent the last two days worrying whether he'd left anything at the scene that pointed to him being there.

I'd also been keeping an eye out for the Reaper's payback. If I knew exactly who had jumped Jameson and killed Mason, I seriously wondered if I'd enact my own payback or just do my job.

The Reapers were bad news but, so far, they hadn't stooped to murdering any high school kids. At least not that I knew about.

When someone knocked on my door, I waved them in without glancing up from the screen.

"Got a minute?" Sabrina asked, stepping into my office and shutting the door behind her.

I groaned and flipped off my screen. "How did you get in here?"

She smiled as she sat down across from me. "I'm dating someone with a badge."

I narrowed my eyes at her. "The hell you are."

She laughed. "Well, we've gone out on a dozen dates in the past month." She shrugged. "I think it'll stick."

"Who?" I asked, still looking at her through narrowed eyes.

She rolled her eyes and, when I didn't waver, she threw her hands up, and said, "Owen."

I thought about it for a second. Owen was one of the good ones. Naive, young, and stupid in a lot of ways, but good to the core. No wonder he'd let her go at the Taylors that morning.

Not wanting advice on my own love life, I let it go and nodded. "Okay, you can date him."

Sabrina laughed. "Gee, thanks for your approval."

"What do you want?" I leaned back in my chair.

Sabrina sobered. "The Madison County High School kid's murder. Know anything?"

I shook my head. "You?"

She tilted her head slightly as her eyes ran over my face. "You're lying."

I mimicked her move. "So are you," I said just as firmly.

"Rayne, we can help each other."

"Why do you think that?" I asked, crossing my arms over my chest.

She was silent for a moment. "Mason was a small-time dealer. Pot and roids mainly. He sold to most every football player around. He owed money."

"To?" I asked. So far, she'd given me more info than any of the reports from the local PD had on the kid.

"Local gang. Word on the street was that he owed them so much, they'd stopped selling to him and had moved on to threats," Sabrina added.

Which is why he'd gone to the Reapers for the deal, I thought. Trying to get more drugs to sell in order to pay his debts back.

"Okay," I nodded. "Thanks for the info."

"No." Sabrina laughed. "Now it's your turn."

I thought about what I'd found out and wondered what the blowback would be if Sabrina reported on it.

"Mason's throat was cut from ear to ear with an unknown weapon. His death was quick."

Sabrina's eyes narrowed. "Everyone knows this. What do you know?" She stretched the words out.

I sighed. "Whoever killed him stole everything except a brand-new pair of Air Jordans worth eight grand."

Sabrina jerked slightly. "Okay." She wrote something down in the little notebook she always carried around. "So our murderer doesn't know about sports fashion. What else did the murderer steal?"

"Cash," I said. "Drugs."

"What kind?"

"Roids. Pot," I answered. "Like you said."

"So, you think it was his old suppliers?"

I shrugged. "What's the word on the street?"

"Word is that it's his new suppliers." She leaned closer. "The Reapers. Declan, namely."

My eyebrows shot up. "Has he been seen?"

She shook her head quickly. "No, but he's built up quite the list of sins in his absence. Sort of like the boogieman. He's being blamed for everything from theft to toothaches." She leaned back. "Are you looking into the case?"

I lied and shook my head. "Out of my jurisdiction."

She sighed and glanced around my office. "I don't suppose you have any updates on Sharon's murder or Evelyn's hit-and-run?"

I thought about keeping quiet for a moment. These cases were closer to home. There was information I didn't want out there in the world. No use spooking the locals.

"I believe the two are connected," I said, surprising Sabrina and myself.

"You do?" She leaned forward. "Why?"

I took a deep breath. "For now, that's all I have." I stood

up. "You can see yourself out." I motioned towards my closed door.

"Rayne," she whined. "You can't say something like that and expect me to leave." She took my arm. "Give me something more."

I shook my head. "Report it," I said, "just like that. What I said." I locked eyes with her and she stilled.

"You're using me?" She gasped slightly. "Seriously?"

I smiled. "Have a good day. I'll make sure to root for you and Owen." I opened my door and motioned for her to leave.

"I hate you," she whispered with a slight smile as she passed by, then she stopped suddenly. "I'm glad your mom is okay. She scared us all. She's home now?"

I felt my heart sink as I nodded. "We hired a full-time nurse to watch her. The last round took everything she had left out of her."

Sabrina touched my arm. "I'm praying for her."

I nodded, fighting back the fear and worry I always felt when remembering finding Edith on the floor. Waiting to feel the weak pulse under my fingertips through my own rapidly beating heartbeat. Hearing her raspy breathing as I waited for the ambulance.

Randy and I had sat up all night by her hospital bed, wondering if each breath she took would be her last. Just as the sunlight broke in the hospital room's windows, she'd woken up and we knew she was out of the woods.

That was the worst fear I'd felt in my life. Until Jasmine had called me that next morning and told me that Jameson had been jumped.

I didn't know how much more my heart could take at this point.

I watched Sabrina leave. I wanted to leave the two of

them to their own demise. Sabrina's relationships never worked out. She was too much like me. Stubborn. She poked her nose into too many parts of a person's life. There were no secrets around either of us. We were both strong-headed women not afraid to speak our minds.

Then I thought of Jameson and smiled. Maybe Owen was like Jameson and liked that about Sabrina?

"Got a second?" Randy asked, walking towards me.

"Sure," I said.

"Let's go for a ride."

I locked my office and fell in step with him. It wasn't often Randy asked me to go for a ride so as we walked out, several people watched with curiosity.

Randy drove in silence and the second we hit the county road, I knew where he was heading. Our favorite fishing spot.

Shit. This had to be bad news.

We only went up there nowadays when things got worse than worse.

"Mom?" I asked softly.

"She's good," he answered quietly. "This isn't about her."

I nodded, understanding he wouldn't say anything more until we were sitting on the old pier. We'd spent a summer building the thing when I was in junior high.

When we climbed out of his car, he surprised me by pulling his fishing poles from the trunk. "No live bait, but we'll make do." He handed me the tackle box.

We walked side by side down the trail we'd forged over the years until we stepped out into the clearing where our lake sat.

When we were each seated on the pier, fishing poles in hand and our first lines cast, he finally spoke.

"I'm retiring." He blurted it out, much like you would bad news, quickly and loudly.

"It's about damn time." I laughed. "God, I thought you were dying."

He glanced sideways at me and then shook his head. "Damn it, girl, you are the best of us."

I laughed again and nudged his shoulder. "When's the big day?"

He took a deep breath. "Soon. No one knows but you and Edith. After the other day, well, I need to be with her."

I nodded. "Agreed."

We sat there in quiet, the bugs buzzing over the top of the water, the fish not biting, the late summer wind barely blowing the treetops.

"I have someone in mind to fill my shoes," Randy broke into the silence.

"Not me," I said quickly.

Randy chuckled. "No, not you."

"Who?"

Randy glanced at me. "I'm hoping he'll want to stick around after he's done cleaning up our town."

"Jameson," I whispered.

"I'll appoint him until there's an official election. But everyone knows, once you get your foot in the door, you stick. I glanced at his file, and he's more than qualified. Hell, he's far more qualified than I was when I took over. About the same age too." Randy used the back of his hand to wipe a bead of sweat from his brow. "I forgot my hat," he mumbled.

That couldn't be right. Randy couldn't have taken over as chief of police when he'd been Jameson's age.

She thought about it and then groaned. "I'm old."

Randy laughed and wrapped an arm around her. "Not yet. Besides, you'll always be our little girl." He hugged her.

"I'm glad you're retiring." I sighed against his chest. Then, before he could answer, my line tugged and I pulled in the first fish of the evening.

Later, when we walked into the house loaded down with six cleaned fish, Edith and her new in-home nurse, Nelly, were sitting at the kitchen table having tea.

Nelly was a middle-aged black woman who had worked at the hospital for almost a decade before deciding to start in-home services. She had a daughter a few years younger than I was who was in college in Georgia to become a nurse.

The woman's husband was a deacon at the church Randy and Edith went to. Both of my parents had known Nelly and her family as long as anyone else in town. They liked her, trusted her, and knew she was a perfect fit to watch over Edith until her chemotherapy was finished in three weeks.

"This is a surprise," Edith said when I walked over and kissed her cheek.

"We caught six fish. I caught four of them," I said, "which means he's going to cook them up for us." I motioned towards Randy, who chuckled.

"That's the rules," he said, setting down the cooler with the fish inside and then walking over to place a kiss on Edith's cheek. "How are you?" he asked her as he looked towards Nelly.

"Good," both Edith and Nelly said at the same time.

"Talk to me about work," Edith said, turning to me.

While Randy cooked, I filled Edith in on every single boring detail of my life since I'd seen her last.

Since I couldn't say much with Nelly there, I stuck to the basics. We had all agreed not to talk about Jameson with

Nelly around. Not that we didn't trust her, but there was a code that cop families went by—don't share secretive information with outsiders.

As much as Randy and Edith trusted Nelly, she wasn't part of the family.

We ate grilled fish, rice, and grilled vegetables and chatted about the coming cool season. Nelly filled us in on her daughter's school and the boy she'd met at the hospital.

By the time I left that evening, I desperately wanted to swing by Jameson's place. I wanted to stay with him that night. To fall asleep in his arms and make sure he was okay.

Seeing the cuts and bruises on his body had pained me. Knowing what had happened to him pissed me off. I used the anger to fuel my investigation into Mason's murder.

I had details the cops in Madison County didn't—that two large men had jumped Jameson. That Jameson was in the room. The time frame of his arrival. Knowing that whoever jumped him and killed the boy had taken off with his motorcycle, wallet, phone, guns, the drug money, and drugs.

Knowing this, I had tracked Jameson's phone to a dumpster behind a bar in Madison County. I planned on staking out the bar that weekend. I would have gone sooner, but the place was only open on Friday and Saturday nights. I wanted to see if there were two very large men hanging about.

Crawling into bed that night alone, I stared at my last message to Jameson. He still hadn't replied.

"How are you doing? Bruises healed? I miss you."

My last three texts had gone unanswered. Was he avoiding me for a reason?

He'd told me he'd dropped his guard because of me.

The guilt of that weighed heavy and had kept me up at night. I could have cost him his life.

Was he trying to pull away because he was afraid or because he'd come to his senses?

So much doubt plagued me, and by morning I was in a piss-poor mood. Deciding to face my fears head-on, I drove into town to Jameson's building. I would grab a coffee and pastry at the bakery downstairs before I marched my ass up those stairs and gave the man I loved a piece of my mind.

Seeing Jameson sitting at the corner booth had me pausing and swallowing all my anger.

His head was bent over, a cup of coffee gripped in his hands tightly. He looked bruised, lost, tired, miserable.

When he finally glanced up at me, his eyes widened slightly and locked with mine. I could tell instantly that everything I'd questioned had been wrong.

He'd probably spent the last few days sleeping and trying to recover from the beating he'd taken.

I motioned with my head towards the counter and ordered my food and coffee. When I sat in front of him, putting a plate of pastries between us, he smiled up at me.

"Hey," he said softly.

"Hey," I said and sipped my coffee. "You look like shit."

He chuckled, then winced. "Bruised," he mumbled.

"More like broken," I told him. "You should have gone to the ER."

He shook his head. "Too many questions."

"About that. What's the story going around." I nodded towards him. "What are you telling everyone that happened?"

"I laid my bike down in the rain the other night. Which is why my bike is MIA," he said with a sigh.

"Smart." The story would fly. He looked like a man

who'd gone down on a wet road. "I found your phone," I said.

He frowned at me. "Where?"

"The last time it pinged off a tower it was at a bar not far from the motel. I'm going to check it out Friday."

"No," he said firmly.

I arched my brows. "I thought we'd established how this works." I motioned between us.

He sighed. "Yeah, right. Please don't go."

I smiled. "Wanna come with?"

He thought about it and then nodded. "Hell yeah."

"We can call it our first official date," I added with a smile.

He chuckled in return. "I'd like that."

Chapter Twenty-One

"Diamonds may be precious,
but friendship is priceless."
–Unknown

Jameson

The idea of Rayne confronting the two burly men who had ambushed me sent a shiver down my spine. I refused to be caught off guard by them again, and I'd sooner face hell and the devil himself than allow Rayne to step directly into harm's way.

Tonight could end up being very bad for me. I knew there was a chance of word getting back that I'd been seen with Rayne. Hell, at this point, I was taking a huge gamble. The image of the kid staring back at me pissed me off enough that I was willing to chance everything.

While she drove us out of town and headed into Madison County towards the Gator Hole Bar, where my phone had last pinged, I kept trying to convince her to let me go into the bar alone first and look around. Of course, she was having none of it, and by the time she parked in the bar's parking lot, we'd just finished our very first argument.

Seeing Rayne climb out of her Jeep and slam her door somehow oddly settled me. Just knowing there was that much fight in her calmed my nerves slightly.

Seeing the real anger in her eyes, I pulled her into my arms.

"Hey," I said softly, kissing the top of her head. I felt her tense in my arms and then instantly soften. "Sorry," I murmured. "I don't want to see anything happen to you. I'm not sure I could survive it."

She relaxed even more and sighed against my chest. "I'm stronger than I look. I do have two black belts."

I remembered her telling me she'd spent most of her youth in karate and tae kwon do.

I nodded. "I have no doubt you can handle yourself. These guys, however, are really big and, well, if they bested me with one blow, I'm afraid what could happen if we both let our guard down."

She pulled back and looked up at me. Her eyes searched my face. I ran my gaze over her beauty, knowing every feature, even in the dimly lit parking lot. "Then we don't let our guard down." She glanced around the empty lot.

"Right." I brushed my lips quickly across hers, and then, stepping back, I took her hand in mine.

I followed Rayne through the parking lot, both of our senses on high alert as we approached the Gator Hole. The place, a ramshackle hut nestled against the shore of a bayou, looked like it had seen better days. String lights cast a dim glow over the outdoor seating area that surrounded the entire building.

Most of the walls had sliding glass doors on them that all sat open, allowing the warm summer breeze to blow through the entire building.

About two dozen patrons were lounging at picnic tables outside, sipping beers as they were enveloped in the humid Louisiana night.

"Definitely not what I expected," I muttered under my breath, scanning the crowd for any sign of the two men who had jumped me.

"Yeah, now I know why it's not on the travel guide for this area," she murmured.

As we made our way towards the bar area, a feeling of unease settled over me. In all my years undercover I'd only been bested once before and it had been in a fight ten to one. I'd hobbled away from that fight with more than one broken bone.

The air thickened with the scent of sweat, stale beer, and swamp. There was a banjo playing somewhere and the noise grew louder as we made our way towards the bar. The sound filled the outdoor space, and the twangy melody that reverberated through my bones.

Rayne glanced at me, her eyes reflecting the flickering lights overhead. "You sure about this?" she asked, her voice low but determined.

I nodded, my jaw set with resolve. "Yeah, we've come this far," I replied, trying to sound more confident than I felt. My concern for her safety somehow had my fears doubling.

The busty redhead behind the bar eyed us with suspicion as we leaned against the old wood countertop. To be honest, I couldn't blame her. We were outsiders in a place where locals obviously ruled. She seemed to regard us as if we were a puzzle as we approached.

"Can I help you two?" she asked, her voice laced with a thick Southern drawl I'd been faking for over a year.

"We're looking for a couple of guys," Rayne said, her tone steady. "Big, mean-looking fellas. They jumped my man last week and took off with his ride. You know anyone like that around here?"

The redhead's eyes narrowed slightly, but she shook her head. "Can't say I do," she said, her tone guarded. "If you ain't buying a drink, you'd best move on."

I exchanged a glance with Rayne, and we both knew what that meant. We were on our own in this place, with no one to watch our backs but each other.

"Beer," I said, slapping a twenty down on the bar.

With a nod, the redhead cracked open two cold bottles with the bottle opener on her belt buckle and set them down in front of us. The twenty disappeared into her jean shorts pocket, and she turned away without getting me any change back.

We made our way deeper into the dimly lit area and found two chairs to sit down in. The sound of laughter and conversation was barely audible over the loud banjo music. We scanned the faces around us for any sign of the men. So far, no one seemed to fit the description.

We hardly spoke as we focused on watching everyone who was watching us. It was very obvious tensions were high now that we were there.

But as the minutes stretched into hours, it became increasingly clear that finding those two men wouldn't be easy.

"I doubt they're going to show," she said under her breath. "I think we made our point. Most likely, word has spread that we're looking for them. This could really mess things up. Us being here. Together."

"Right," I agreed.

After two hours of listening to the music and sipping warm beer, Rayne and I made our way out of the Gator Hole. Somehow, the night air felt heavier than before, suffused with tension and the promise of danger. We had come up empty-handed, and I could feel the frustration gnawing at the edges of my resolve.

But before we could even reach the parking lot, a pair of shadows emerged from the darkness, blocking our path. My hand instinctively went to the holster at my waist where my backup weapon sat, but I forced myself to stay calm while my senses remained on high alert.

I was right. The two men were huge and easily loomed over us, casting a menacing shadow in the dim light. They were the same ones who had jumped me a few days back, I was instantly sure of it. I could see that they recognized me when both of their faces twisted into smirks of triumph.

"Well, well, well," one of them drawled, his voice dripping with malice. "Looks like we found ourselves a couple of marks. This one's come back for another whooping."

Rayne stepped forward, her stance defiant. "We're not looking for trouble," she said, her voice steady despite the danger that lurked. "But if you want to start something, I'll wager that we'll finish it."

The men exchanged a glance, a silent communication passing between them. Then, without warning, they burst out laughing.

"Go on home to your daddy, little girl," one of them said.

"Where's my bike?" I asked in a firm tone. Both men's smiles turned harder.

"It's ours now. Along with everything else that punk owed us."

"So you killed Mason Williamson because he owed you money?" Rayne asked as she lifted her chin.

I watched as both men went on high alert.

"You're that little cop girl from Gemsville, ain't you?" one of them asked. "Your daddy runs things over there."

"We didn't do shit to no one," the other said when Rayne didn't reply.

We were losing them. If I didn't do something quickly to turn the conversation around, we'd walk away empty-handed.

Stepping forward, I said, "I don't give a shit about anything but getting my bike back," I said, trying to veer the conversation away from the fact that I had made the drop and now I was here with a cop.

"Like we said, it was payment." Then, without warning, both men lunged forward, their fists swinging in a flurry of blows right at Rayne.

I reacted instinctively, knocking Rayne out of the way from the first fist. The blow landed on my left shoulder and bounced off. Then I was busy ducking and weaving as I fought to keep both men at bay. Rayne was right beside me, her movements fluid and precise as she landed blow after blow on one of the attackers, which almost seemed to bounce off the heavy-set man. Thankfully, she was quick and easily ducked whenever the guy reached for her.

Despite my best efforts, I knew I was losing. The men were bigger, stronger, and seemed to be fueled by a rage that knew no bounds.

I took blow after blow on my already bruised body and felt winded and unprepared. I was too concerned about Rayne's safety to care about my own.

Hearing her grunt when the man landed a hit, I felt a

surge of adrenaline coursing through my veins, dulling the pain and sharpening my focus.

Just as I laid out the one man that I'd been fighting, red and blue lights lit up the parking lot and suddenly we were surrounded by Madison County police. My heart sank as I realized what this meant—we were caught in the middle of a mess we hadn't anticipated.

Did Rayne's authority run to this county? Shit. As with all the times before when I'd ended up in situations like this, my cover was too deep to break. Even now.

"Hands where I can see them!" a voice boomed over a megaphone, cutting through the chaos of the fight, while light blinded us all. Rayne and I exchanged a glance, both knowing that we needed to comply.

"Shit," the last big guy who was still standing said under his breath. Then he kicked his buddy in the ribs. "Wake up, Earl," he said as he slowly lifted his hands.

Slowly, Rayne and I raised our hands.

I knew that if word of me and Rayne getting arrested got back to the Reapers, it could be the end of my mission.

As the officers closed in on us, their weapons drawn and their faces grim, I couldn't help but wonder how we had ended up in this mess. All we had wanted was to find answers, to bring justice to those who deserved it. To a high school kid who had gotten involved with the wrong people.

"I'm police," Rayne said. "I can show you my—"

"Don't matter," the officer said. "I know who you are. You're in my county now." The man yanked Rayne's arms behind her. "You can't just come into my home and make a mess." He glanced over at the still-conscious man. "Bobby, get Earl and head on home."

This was bad, really bad. We were just trying to do our jobs, but now it looked like we were the ones in trouble and the two real crooks were going to walk free. Rayne's eyes met mine and we knew we were in it deep.

As the officers took us into custody, I made a silent vow to myself—we would get through this, no matter what. Even if it meant the end of my assignment, we'd come out of whatever hillbilly, bullshit, crooked-cop crap we'd just stepped in. Together.

Several hours later, and after a few new bruises were given to me by my arresting officers, I walked out of the station with Rayne.

"You okay?" she asked, eyeing me.

"Yup," I said, holding in a groan. I nodded to where Randy Cordova stood leaning against his car, watching us.

"It looks like you two stepped in it pretty bad this time," Randy said, running his eyes over me. "Anything broken?" he asked.

I shook my head. "My pride."

"I'm guessing those were Sheriff Dupont's sons that jumped us?" Rayne groaned.

Randy nodded. "Yup. How about I take you two to breakfast?" He motioned towards his car. "I'm afraid your Jeep got towed. They'll hold it until Monday," he told Rayne. "Probably charge you an extra couple hundred to get it out, just because you're mine." He wrapped his arm around Rayne for a moment. "Next time you come out here, give me a heads up."

Rayne sighed and held onto her father. "Yeah, I thought we could slip under the radar. I had no clue it was the Dupont brothers that jumped Jameson. I haven't seen them in years. They've gotten a lot bigger. I guess I should have known."

As we climbed into Randy's car, the early morning sun cast long shadows across the empty streets of the small town. It appeared that every cop in this county wanted to use me as a punching bag. I could honestly say I was going to be happy to leave the town behind us.

Relief washed over me as I breathed in the fresh air. I climbed in the car, grateful for Randy's timely intervention.

"Thanks for bailing us out," I said.

Randy started up the car and glanced in the mirror at me. "No problem at all," he replied, his voice gruff but friendly. "This will be a bitch to keep quiet though. You might have to rearrange a few things. There's no keeping this from the Reapers. Several of them are from Madison County."

"Yeah." I nodded. "It will probably move up my time-line." I sighed, too tired to focus on what it meant beyond the moment.

As we headed out of town, I noticed that everyone was just beginning to stir awake, the quiet hum of morning traffic filling the air.

On the outskirts of the little town, we pulled over to a gas station that had a small diner.

The place was a quaint little place with its neon sign flickering invitingly in the early morning fog. As we stepped inside, the smell of sizzling bacon and freshly brewed coffee enveloped us, making my stomach growl in anticipation.

Much like at the bar the night before, when we walked in, everyone turned to watch us.

"Clayton folks don't get along much with Gemsville folks," Randy said under his breath. "Still, they won't mess with me." He smiled as he led us to a booth in the corner. As I sat down, I tried not to groan as pain shot through my ribs. What I needed was an ice pack, a few aspirin, and sleep.

Randy wasted no time in getting down to business after ordering his coffee.

"So, what the hell happened back there?" he asked, his brow furrowed with concern. "All I heard was that you two got into some trouble with the sheriff's boys."

I exchanged a glance with Rayne, knowing that there was no point in hiding the truth from our friend.

"Bobby and Earl Dupont jumped us," I replied, my voice grim. "We were just leaving the bar."

"They're running a drug ring in their father's county," Rayne said, her voice low but determined. "And it appears they've been selling stolen vehicles on the side. They're the ones who jumped..." She stopped and looked at me. I nodded, assuring her that she could tell Randy everything.

After she quickly ran through what had happened to me the other night in the hotel, Randy's eyes widened in disbelief, and his jaw slacked with shock. "Damn," he muttered under his breath. "That's some serious shit."

I nodded, my thoughts racing as I tried to make sense of everything that had happened in the past few days. "We need to figure out our next move," I said, my voice determined. "I have a feeling those two aren't going to stop. And when word of last night gets to the Reapers, my cover will be blown."

Rayne took my hand under the table. "We'll deal with what comes next," she said to me.

We ordered food and ate in silence after a group of people came and sat in the booth beside ours.

I wanted to spend more time with Rayne, but when Randy stopped in the parking lot a few blocks from my place, I knew we wouldn't have time. Besides, I had to get back to work and assess the damage last night had caused.

"We'll talk," I told Rayne and slid out of the car. "Thanks again," I said to Randy.

The moment I stepped through my door, I knew just how deep of shit I was in.

Felix lounged on my sofa, sipping a cup of coffee.

"I heard you and that pretty little detective went and had yourselves some fun last night," Felix said, glancing me up and down.

I took one step into the room and then Ben appeared out of nowhere behind me.

"I told her that I'd been jumped after crashing my bike. She told me she had a lead on my shit and was trying to help me get my phone back," I said, trying to relax.

Felix's eyes narrowed. "Funny thing," he said, setting his cup down on my coffee table. "I thought we were your family?"

"You are," I said, taking another step. I was still armed but there was no way I'd pull a gun on Felix. Not yet. He was trying to make a point. I fucked up and I knew it.

"Then why the fuck are you running to some cop for help?" Felix's voice rose.

"I didn't run. She offered and, well"—I smiled—"I was horny."

Felix's eyes narrowed. "That may have played a month ago." He stood slowly. "You cut us. Cut us deep." He nodded to Ben, who had moved behind me.

Ben grabbed my arms and held them. I knew what was coming, so I relaxed into the first of Felix's blows. To be honest, the Dupont brothers and the cops who had locked me up had hit harder.

It was obvious that Felix was going easy on me.

When I was kneeling on the ground, gasping for air,

Felix hovering over me, he added, "Cut your family out again and we might just cut back," Felix warned as he yanked my hair. "You'll have your shit back, including your bike, by nightfall. If you need a fuck, use Izzy or one of our other girls." He dropped his hold on my hair and walked out.

"Clean yourself up. We have a job to do," Ben said once Felix was gone.

I glanced up at Ben. "For real?"

Ben's eyes narrowed. "Since it appears you're healed enough from getting jumped, Felix wants us to take a drive."

I stood up and nodded. "I need a shower," I said motioning towards my bathroom.

Ben nodded. "I'll head downstairs and grab us some sandwiches and coffee."

"Thanks," I said, disappearing into my bathroom.

Shit. What in the hell did I just get away with? More importantly, what was I heading into?

Was Ben taking me out to get rid of me? Was this some ruse to lower my guard? Did they suspect me?

I was getting so tired of playing this game. It had over a year and I was no closer to finding out who was pulling Felix's strings than I had when I'd first come to town.

I itched to send a text to Rayne or Jasmine. Instead, I showered and changed, and when Ben knocked on my door, I left with him.

I sat back in his truck while he downed a bagel sandwich and sipped coffee. I even filled him in on spending the night in jail.

Since he and Felix already knew what had happened, I figured I'd stick to the story that Rayne had offered to help me find all my stuff that had been swiped. Which was true.

Hopefully, they wouldn't read anything more into the

situation other than an ex-lover trying to help me out of a bind.

I was surprised when we drove straight up to the Taylor house and parked next to a shiny, souped-up, cherry red Mustang.

"Looks like someone's enjoying his new income." Ben chuckled as he got out of the car.

New income? I glanced at the house. So, Henry Taylor was new to the business. Not the head of it.

"Want me to wait here?" I asked.

"Not this time," Ben said, motioning for me to follow him.

We stood on the front porch and waited for the door to open.

Seeing Wyatt Taylor grinning back at us after he opened the door slightly surprised me, but not as much as seeing who was standing behind him. My entire world shifted.

Chapter Twenty-Two

"I have always felt a gift diamond shines so much better than one you buy for yourself!"
–Mae West

Rayne

At Randy's request, I took the rest of the day off. I spent most of those first hours at home in bed, after I'd showered the dried blood and dirt off.

I woke sometime before dinnertime, made myself some macaroni and cheese, and ate it on the sofa catching up on my shows. I kept checking my phone, looking for messages from Jameson.

Somehow, I felt like a fool for trying to get his stuff back and peg the death of Mason on his attackers. Had I known they were the Dupont brothers, I would have never tried to look for them.

The Dupont family was untouchable in Madison County. Everyone in all of Louisiana knew that. Even if their father hadn't become sheriff, the family had run the county for decades.

Just before I crawled into bed, I sent a text to Jameson, knowing he wouldn't respond before morning.

To my surprise, he replied quickly.

"I finished that last chapter in the book I was reading."

I frowned down at the message and just as I was going to respond, asking him what he was talking about, my heart sank.

Last chapter. He was about to make his move. Which meant he was closing his case.

"Good," I responded. "I'm glad you enjoyed it. Will you be starting the next book soon?"

This response took a little longer.

"I'm going to wait a while. Maybe watch a few movies or get lost in a show."

I smiled at that. I wanted to say more but knew we better not chance it.

"Night."

"Night." I fell asleep thinking about our future. Somehow, my rest wasn't as peaceful as I'd expected. My dreams were filled with dark shadows and time speeding by too fast as I tried to accomplish simple tasks.

I woke to my phone ringing. Seeing Randy and Edith's face on the screen, I sat up and answered as I glanced at the clock.

"What's wrong?" I said, after seeing that it was a quarter past five in the morning. "Mom?"

"Is at home resting peacefully," Randy said. "I need you in the office at six sharp."

"Okay." I settled back on my bed. I usually got to the office around eight.

"We've got a big meeting. All hands are needed on

deck." His voice sounded strained. I understood instantly. Jameson had either made his move in the night or was about to.

"I'll shower, get ready, and head in now," I said, standing up.

"See you then." He hung up.

As I walked into the precinct, my nerves were jangling. I wanted a large cup of coffee but figured I didn't need the caffeine. Randy was busy in his office on the phone and didn't even look up when I strolled by and headed straight to my own office.

Sure enough, by six o'clock sharp, every cop and employee on the payroll was in the office. More than a hundred people crowded into the bullpen.

Sherry's voice came on over the loudspeaker, which had only been used a half dozen times in the past five years.

"We need everyone to gather in the bullpen," Sherry said quickly. Then the speaker clicked off.

I stood up, took a deep breath, and stepped out of my office. If I hadn't looked around the room at every single person, I would have missed him. Jameson and a few other men I didn't know were standing in the hallway, dressed in black, and I froze in place.

"Thanks," Randy said, getting everyone's attention.

No one else in the room seemed to notice the extra dozen or so bodies circling the room.

"At approximately oh-nineteen hundred last night, Bobby and Earl Dupont's bodies were found floating in the Red River by some fishermen." Several people gasped. Those who didn't know who the brothers were remained silent. My heart practically stopped beating as my eyes moved to Jameson, who was staring straight ahead.

Was Jameson here because Randy believed he had something to do with their deaths?

"Both men had been stabbed to death, their faces slashed beyond recognition." Randy's eyes moved to me and my heart jumped for another reason.

Sharon Taylor.

Was Randy trying to tell me that the Dupont brothers' deaths were connected? Why hadn't I been called in on this sooner?

Most of the Red River ran through my district. Still, if they had been found in Madison County, then I wouldn't have been called.

So many questions ran through my head.

"Technically their bodies weren't found in our district, but we've been asked to lend a hand on this one. Rayne, you'll be taking the lead," Randy said to me, gaining my full attention again.

I nodded in acknowledgment.

"Why call us all in for that?" someone complained.

Randy held up his hand to stop all the voices. "Quiet," he said, and the room went silent again.

I glanced around and realized why. There were now more than a dozen new people surrounding our group. Randy had been stalling until Jameson and his men were in place. Which meant someone in the room was dirty. The rat. I glanced around quickly. My eyes landed on Abe a few feet away from me. To Quincy, whose desk I was standing by and who was less than five feet from me.

My entire body tensed, ready for whatever came next.

"As some of you may notice, there are a few extra faces in the room." Suddenly, everyone looked around and all at once noticed Jameson and his team.

"What is this?" someone asked.

"I was asked to allow these agents access to every employee's and officer's desk, locker, and computer." The room exploded with questions and people shouting. Once more Randy held up his hands and then shouted for everyone to be quiet. "They finished their search around one this morning." Randy nodded toward Jameson.

I turned and for a split second his eyes landed on me. Then he started to move forward, walking quickly right at me. My heart skipped. Sank.

I'd been looking at him and hadn't realized why he was heading towards me. I hadn't felt the strong arms wrap around my body and pull me back a step. The first thing I did feel was a weapon against my temple.

"This is bullshit," Quincy shouted.

It was then that I realized Jameson hadn't been watching me. His eyes had been on Quincy Ingram. My ex-boyfriend. The man I'd slept with more than a handful of times last year. Someone I'd let into my life was now holding a gun to my head so that he could, what? Escape being arrested? For what? Sharon Taylor and the Dupont brothers' deaths? Oh god. Did Quincy have anything to do with their murders or was this about something else? The drugs?

Jameson glanced over his shoulder as everyone else in the room screamed and rushed around.

Out of the corner of my eye, I watched as several agents grabbed Clara and slapped handcuffs on her. She screamed and fought back. Several more people were grabbed and handcuffed as they scattered, including Abe Sterling.

I closed my eyes for what felt like only a moment, but somehow there were only a handful of people left in the room with us. Quincy and I stood in the middle, the gun pressed tightly against my temple.

Jameson stood a few feet away, staring at us without moving. Randy stood to the left of us, frozen in fear. Two more agents stood off to the side. Everyone else had been ushered out of the room.

"You don't want to do this," I said to Quincy.

"Shut up, Rayne," Quincy hissed in my ear. "You don't know anything."

"I know everything," Jameson said smoothly. I could hear the fear behind his tone. "I know that you've been working with the Reapers. You, Abe, and a few others that you persuaded to join in your little side hustle. I know you killed Sharon Taylor, who was working with the FBI to rat you out about all the missing funds you and she had siphoned off to fund your little escapades. Her death killed their case since there was nothing linking the two of you together. Until we searched your computer and found photos. It seems like you were one of her favorite boy toys," Jameson said.

Quincy's arm jerked, and his hold on my arms tightened.

"You've got it wrong," Quincy screamed, his eyes moving around the room as more agents slowly crept in. "I didn't do this," Quincy whispered in my ear. "Sure, Sharon and I... had fun. But I had fun with lot of other women in town too. Including..." He jerked me slightly.

"At one point, sure, we had fun. Now you're holding a gun to my head." I tried to hide the fear in my voice. My palms were so sweaty I doubted I could ball my hands into a fist.

Suddenly Quincy grew quiet as Jameson moved closer. His voice was barely a low growl. "If you harm one hair on her head, I'll make sure you are shoved in the darkest hole imaginable and never come out again."

I felt Quincy jerk once and then I felt the gun disappear from my temple. "I didn't do this, Rayne." The sound of the gun firing knocked me sideways. My ears screamed and I couldn't hear any other sounds. I felt the blood splatter on my hair, and my shirt as I fell onto my hands and knees.

Then strong arms lifted me and carried me as muffled voices cried out. Someone was screaming.

"Rayne," Jameson said over and over.

"Sweetie." Randy's voice finally broke into my mind and suddenly I realized I was the one screaming.

"Daddy?" I cried and blinked the tears from my eyes. He was there, hovering over me, next to Jameson.

"We're here," Randy said softly. "You're okay."

"Do you have her?" Jameson asked Randy, who nodded.

"Go, do what you have to."

Jameson leaned down, an inch from my lips. "I love you," he said, then he pressed his lips to mine for a second before quickly disappearing.

I wanted to tell him I loved him too, but he was gone so quickly.

"What?" I asked Randy, blinking a few times. "What happened?"

"Quincy took his own life," Randy said, sitting next to me. I looked around and realized we were on the sofa in his office.

"Why?" I shook my head.

"The DEA has been working through the night. They've arrested Wyatt Taylor, his girlfriend, Clara, Abe, and Laura Kinney. Five dirty cops and employees under my watch." Randy shook his head.

I sat up slightly, feeling something sticky in my hair and running down my back. I didn't want to think what it was. A shiver raced over my body.

"I... can I shower?" I asked after a moment of composing myself and trying not to vomit.

"Yeah." Randy's eyes moved over me. "I thought we were going to lose you."

I watched tears fill his eyes. "I want to hug you right now, but..." I held up my hands and shivered again. "I'm trying not to think about what is on me."

Randy sighed. "Quincy was... for a while, I thought he was good for you."

"Me too," I said, taking his hand.

"Go shower in the locker room. I'll be here"—he shook his head—"dealing with things."

I walked very stiffly towards the locker room. I kept my eyes away from the bullpen as I passed through. The entire building was empty now.

Jameson rushed towards me. "Everything okay?"

"Shower," I said, holding in bile.

"Right. I'll find you a change of clothes." He turned to go.

"Don't bother. I have some in my locker." I rushed towards the locker rooms.

Inside, I tossed my clothes into the trash as I disrobed. When the lukewarm water hit me and I felt a chunk of something slide down my back, I leaned over and lost my stomach contents.

I don't know how long I stood under the water, unwilling to reach up and make sure there wasn't any more of Quincy in my hair or on my skin. I stood under the spray, my eyes closed, thankful that I hadn't witnessed what Quincy had done behind my back. I was shivering when I heard Jameson's voice.

"Are you okay?"

I opened my eyes, tears mixed with the shower water.

"I can't..." I said, shaking my head.

Suddenly, Jameson was there, holding me. My tears and the shower water soaked his black shirt.

"You're getting wet," I said into his chest.

"Let me help you," he said softly.

He pulled me back under the spray, took a handful of soap, and started washing my hair. His fingers brushed through my tangles, gently removing anything I'd missed or hadn't wanted to touch.

"I was so scared," Jameson said softly. "So afraid I'd lose you."

I watched his eyes move over to mine. "I love you too," I said with a weak smile.

"Shitty timing." He smiled down at me.

I nodded and swallowed. "What happened?"

After assessing that he'd gotten my hair clean, Jameson shut off the water and walked over to get me a towel.

Once I was wrapped in it and sitting on the bench next to my locker, he took my hand.

"I'm sorry, it looks like I'm going to be tied up here for a few hours," Jameson said to me. "Can I come over to your place after? Explain everything then?" He lifted my hand to his lips.

I nodded and watched him stand up, lean in, and kiss me, before heading out of the locker room.

I pulled on my spare jeans, shirt, and running shoes, then I ran a comb through my hair before heading back outside.

Randy was there, sitting right outside of the locker room, waiting for me. The hug he gave me had more tears rolling down my cheeks.

"We aren't going to tell your mother about this. She'd kill us both and make you retire with me," he said softly.

I laughed and agreed. "Right. I love you, Dad," I said during the hug.

"My girl." He sighed. "I'm sorry about... Quincy." I nodded and swallowed. "I know you two broke things off. Still..."

"Still." I sighed.

"Jameson, he's a good one. Down to the core." He smiled at me.

"Yeah." I smiled back. "I think he's the one." I glanced around and saw him talking to one of the other agents.

"I'm going to have a mess around here. Until then, you've still got lead on things. Until you're one hundred percent sure whether Quincy had anything to do with the deaths, I expect you to work the case," he said, and I smiled and lifted my chin slightly as I nodded. "That's my girl." He hugged me again. "Take the rest of the day." When I opened my mouth, he narrowed his eyes. "That's an order."

I chuckled. "I love you, Dad."

He smiled and leaned in to brush a kiss over my cheek. "Love you too, sweetie."

"I'll see you in a few hours," Jameson said to me. "Will you be at your place?"

I nodded. "I'll be there. I've been kicked out of here for the day."

"I'll fill you in then." He took my hand.

I nodded again and then reached up on my toes and kissed him. "Later."

Driving back home, I was in a daze. I tried to stop what had just happened from running through my mind.

When I got home, I took another very long hot shower, scrubbing my hair and body until my skin was red and my hair was squeaky clean.

I dressed in yoga pants and waited for Jameson to arrive.

I ate a handful of saltine crackers, afraid that if I ate anything more, I'd lose it again. I sat in my living room in a daze.

My mother called and chatted with me like it was a normal day. She'd heard some of the basics about what had happened down at the station, but I knew that Dad would make sure that everyone kept the gory details from her.

I tried to act as if nothing bad had happened and when she asked if something was wrong, I faked having a headache and got off the phone. Then I continued to stare out my windows, waiting for Jameson to arrive. Hardly blinking. Hardly breathing. My mind raced.

Shortly before sunset, Jameson showed up with a bag of fast food from one of the chicken places between here and the police station. He looked tired and yet relieved to see me.

After I let him inside, he set the food down and wrapped his arms around me, holding me tight for the longest time.

"My god," he said, several times. "I thought... I've never been so afraid before."

I closed my eyes, melting into his hold. I wanted—needed—to feel like I'd survived for a reason. What I had with Jameson was far more than anything I'd experienced with Quincy. "Jameson, I need you. I need to feel alive," I said, looking deep into his eyes. "I need to know this is real." I shook my head as my throat closed. "Please."

His kiss was the answer to everything I'd needed to know since the events of that morning. My mind instantly settled and was free of all the worry, the fears I'd been wrestling with endlessly for hours.

When he lifted me up in his arms and carried me back to the bedroom, I knew that my words, my simple *I love you,* weren't enough to express how I felt for him. It could never be enough.

As we slowly peeled off our clothes and came together, there was no doubt that what was between us was the real deal. Jameson was part of my soul. He would always have my heart.

I felt him move inside me as I desperately held onto him, wrapped my body around his, and those actions said more than words ever could. Here, lying together in the darkness, this was the strongest love that we could show one another.

Later, when we were still, his arms wrapped around me, my head resting on his shoulder while he stroked my hair, he whispered those words again.

"I love you." He shifted to look down at me. "I've never said those words before."

"I love you." I smiled up at him, his face barely visible in the darkness. "I haven't said them either."

Then, to my shock, my stomach growled loudly, and we laughed together.

Chapter Twenty-Three

"The soul is placed in the body like a rough diamond, and
must be polished,
or the luster of it will never appear."
–Daniel Defoe

Jameson

While we sat in Rayne's bed, eating cold grilled chicken and Tater Tots, I filled Rayne in on everything that had transpired since I'd seen her the morning before.

I'd been going nonstop since then. Seeing Quincy standing behind Wyatt in his police officer's uniform had set the last wheels in motion.

Suddenly, everything made sense. The reason the Reapers had become so powerful, so untouchable, was that they'd had inside help.

They had known exactly where not to be and when and where they were safe to make drops. Quincy, along with a few others in the station, had paved the way for them to successfully run their operations in and around town without fear of being caught.

When Ben dropped me off back at my place after the massive drug pickup from the Taylor home, I called Jasmine and filled her in.

After the short call, we decided to make our move. Then we got word about the Dupont brothers having been found floating in the river, cut up in a very similar way to Mayor Taylor. Since Ben had been with me during those hours, we looked into Felix's whereabouts. He'd been at the Bayou Bar, surrounded by most of the other Reapers. All except one.

Declan.

Jasmine took a team out to the Nest, where Declan was taken into custody, and after checking the footage of all those cameras we'd hidden around the building after my first visit to the spot, we confirmed that Declan had left for four hours during the time the brothers had been killed. Declan had had just enough time to make it to Madison County, commit the murders, and get back.

Some of the footage had gone black for some reason during the night, but it was enough evidence to make our next move against the Reapers. All of them. I knew that Declan didn't do anything without Felix saying so and my guess was that Quincy was the head honcho behind the scenes. The man pulling all the strings.

I wondered if he'd gotten close to Rayne for the same reason Felix wanted me to get close to her. To keep her off their scent. It made me sick to know she'd been used so much.

By early afternoon, more than four dozen agents had descended on the town. After getting Declan into custody, we'd gathered Wyatt Taylor before heading out to grab every last Reaper. We'd gotten most of them while they were tucked safely in their beds.

I even found my bike in Felix's garage and guessed he was going to return it to me later that night like he'd promised. Had Declan delivered it to him after disposing of the brothers?

In order to arrest so many at once, we needed to keep the element of surprise. Thankfully, we ran into problems only two times. One of the Reapers tried to outgun us and ended up with a bullet in his leg, thanks to Jasmine. The other tried to take off on foot and was caught easily by the dogs.

The rest, to my surprise, had gone in peacefully. At Jasmine's orders, I had remained in the background until every single Reaper was in custody.

Shortly after one in the morning, Jasmine had me take a team to the station. After calling Randy and clueing him in on the move, he cleared the building out under the guise of some sort of emergency with the sprinkler system. We started searching Quincy's desk, locker, and device first, which led us to all the others under his control.

By four o'clock in the morning, we had what we needed. To be honest, the handful of people involved in the scheme hadn't even tried to hide their involvement. No doubt they believed no one would suspect them or search their offices.

Clara Mangrum had been the biggest surprise. She hadn't been involved in the Reapers' drug ring but instead had embezzled almost fifty thousand dollars in funds from the department itself. I'd wager it was a little more since some of the bail money she stole was probably in cash, which couldn't be tracked the way the pile of checks she'd taken could be.

Some of the checks tied her to the mayor's office, evidence that we were handing over to the State Attorney General's Office to further their investigation.

We had boxes and boxes of evidence that would be used to charge everyone arrested.

By the time I walked into Rayne's house, I was beyond tired and starving. I knew that it would be days, maybe weeks, before we closed out everything on the case. Still, at least for now, we had everyone in custody, and I was looking forward to spending my free time with Rayne.

I'd already put in a request for an extended amount of time off and was seriously questioning whether I ever wanted to go undercover again. I was over it. I knew what I did was important. Getting to the heart of evil saved lives. I had no doubt about that.

Still, for the first time in my life, I wanted a life of my own. Being able to see Rayne in my future was the driving force. Especially after that morning.

What she did was just as important. Still, part of me wanted to ask her to quit. To do something, anything, less dangerous.

Then, logic hit me over the head.

You couldn't walk into a movie theater or a mall without fearing violence these days.

She'd had an ex-lover hold a gun to her head at her workplace. I knew the statistics about violence against women done at the hands of someone who supposedly cared for them. Most women, most people for that matter, weren't as lucky as Rayne to walk away from those kinds of situations.

When I was done filling her in, we were back lying in each other's arms. Rayne was tight up against my side.

"You've been busy," she said with a yawn. "You must be exhausted."

"I am, but being here with you makes it all worth it," I admitted. I pulled her closer and just held on. She smelled so good. Felt so good. This was right.

Falling asleep next to Rayne was the first time in years that I felt completely relaxed and in control of my future. Waking with her wrapped around me had other things filling my mind.

As I slowly blinked my eyes open, the soft morning light filtered through the curtains. I couldn't help but feel a sense of peace wash over me. This is where I belonged. Where we belonged. Together.

Somehow, the events of the previous day seemed like a distant memory now, replaced by the warmth of Rayne's presence beside me.

Stretching lazily, I rolled over to find Rayne already awake, her eyes fixed on me with a soft smile playing at her lips. "Morning," she greeted, her voice husky with sleep.

"Morning," I replied, returning her smile as I leaned in to press a gentle kiss to her lips. The weight of her against me felt like home, grounding me in a way I hadn't known I needed.

I wanted to spend the day with her here, in bed, but knew that in less than half an hour, my phone would be going off with calls demanding my presence.

"I have to go back in. You?" I asked.

She nodded. "Most likely we'll have meetings to discuss what happened. For now, we're keeping"—she paused and took a deep breath—"certain details from my mother."

I nodded, understanding. "Breakfast?"

"Shower first." I saw her shiver and wondered just how

many showers it would take for the memory of yesterday to be washed away.

"I'll cook," I offered.

She smiled. "I'd like that. Make yourself at home. I think you can find your way around my kitchen easily enough."

I brushed my lips across hers. "I love you," I said, then added. "If I say it too much, let me know."

She chuckled. "I don't think it's possible to hear it too much when I feel the same way."

With a contented sigh, I rolled out of bed and made my way to the kitchen. A few minutes later, after easily finding what I needed, I made the coffee, and the smell was like a siren's call. As I started to prepare breakfast, I could hear the sounds of Rayne in the shower.

I easily found eggs, bacon, and the fixings for cinnamon toast. Her pans hung over the island and by the time the aroma of sizzling bacon filled the air, she came out fully dressed for the day. Her hair was still wet and tied in a long braid.

We carried our plates out to the back deck to enjoy our food out there, the morning sun casting a warm glow over everything it touched.

Sitting side by side, we ate in companionable silence, the only sound the gentle rustle of leaves in the breeze. But as we finished our meal, the weight of the conversation we needed to have hung heavy between us.

"So," Rayne began, her voice soft but determined. "What happens now?"

I paused, the question lingering in the air like a delicate promise, and looked into Rayne's eyes.

"Whatever it is, we'll do it together. I've asked for time

off. I'll extend it as long as I can until we come up with what's next for us." I reached out to take her hand in mine.

With a smile, Rayne squeezed my hand, her eyes shining with unspoken emotion. "My dad's about to retire. He actually thought you'd make a great replacement."

I was surprised and a little shocked at first. But then I really thought about it. That could work. Couldn't it?

Then her words played over in my head. Most of the time when Rayne talked about Randy, she called him by his name. However, just now, she'd called him Dad, and she'd done so yesterday as well. I wondered if she realized that.

"Maybe I'll have a chat with him about it," I suggested.

Just then my phone started ringing, and I spoke with the Jasmine for the next few minutes.

"I've got to head in," I said after hanging up.

"Me too," Rayne said as we carried our dishes back inside.

"I'll clean this up later," I offered.

"Don't bother. I have a little time now. I'm due to be in around eight." She glanced at her watch.

"Dinner?" I asked.

"I'm supposed to go over to my folks' place. I'd love for you to meet my mother," she suggested.

"What time?" I asked, feeling nervous suddenly. I'd never met a woman's parents before and, even though I'd had several encounters with Randy, suddenly the thought of meeting Rayne's mother made me anxious.

"Six. We can ride together if you're here a little before then."

I walked over to her, wrapped my arms around her, and held on. "I'll be here at five thirty. If it's okay with you, I'd like to move a few of my things here. I need to clear out of the apartment they had me in. We're using it as our base now."

She smiled. "Yes, you can move in with me."

I chuckled. "Another first," I said as I brushed my lips across hers. "See you this evening."

Jasmine and the team had set up camp, so to speak, in my old apartment. When I walked in, it was like walking into an office building instead of the place I'd called home for over a year.

The atmosphere was tense, the air heavy with the weight of the events of the day before. Jasmine was there, her brow furrowed in concentration as her fingers flew across the keyboard.

"Morning," I greeted several other agents, most of which I had never met, as I made my way over to the desk she had set up. She looked up, a weary smile gracing her lips as she acknowledged my presence.

"Morning," she replied, her tone tinged with exhaustion. "We've got a lot of work to do today."

I nodded, my gaze drifting to the other DEA officers scattered throughout the room, each one buried in their own mountain of paperwork from the boxes of material we'd gathered. We had made a lot of arrests yesterday, taking down the entire Reaper gang in one fell swoop, along with Wyatt Taylor. But there was still so much to do, so much evidence to compile and process.

And then there was Quincy's death to contend with. The fact that he had shot himself still weighed heavily on my mind, a grim reminder of the darkness that lurked beneath the surface.

I was worried how Rayne would handle being back in the station where it had happened, but to be honest, I'd seen a huge change in her from when I'd arrived the night before to this morning.

Our task for the next few days was to not only find proof that Quincy was the head of the Reaper's drug organization but to make sure no one else in town was involved.

So far, we had come up empty-handed. His bank account wasn't that of someone who shuffled thousands of dollars around like play money.

As I settled in at my desk, I booted up Quincy's files that had been stored on his home and office computers. My fingers flew across the keyboard as I searched for any shred of evidence that might prove he was the head of the drug ring. But as I sifted through the files, photos, and reports he'd worked on, my heart sank. There was nothing here, no incriminating documents, no hidden files on his computer that showed he was in charge. No trace of large amounts of money being moved around.

It was as if Quincy had been careful to cover his tracks, leaving us with nothing to go on.

What we did have on him was his presence at the Taylor's residence, and the massive drug pickup I'd gone on with Ben the other day.

Quincy had bossed Wyatt Taylor around as if he'd been in charge. The man even barked at Ben for bringing me inside for the deal, which indicated that Quincy had been present the other times I'd been at the Taylor place.

Frustration bubbled up inside me, and I slammed my fist down on the desk, the sound echoing through the quiet office. We were running out of time and, without proof, we were fighting a losing battle.

I glanced over at Jasmine, who waved me over to her desk. I made my way over to her. She looked up as I approached, her expression serious as she gestured for me to take a seat.

"I've been going through Quincy's files, trying to find anything that shows he was the head of the drug organization," she said, her voice low.

I nodded, my stomach churning with unease. "Me too. Did you find something?"

"I think I did," she replied, her eyes flicking to the computer screen in front of her. "There's a series of encrypted files here, buried deep in his hard drive. I've been trying to crack them, but it's slow going."

My heart leaped in my chest as I leaned in closer, studying the screen intently. "Do you think they could contain evidence of Quincy's involvement?"

"It's possible," Jasmine admitted, typing furiously. "But it's going to take some time to decrypt them. We're going to need all the help we can get."

I glanced around the office, my mind racing as I considered our options. We couldn't afford to waste any more time, not with the charges against each of the Reapers and Wyatt looming on the horizon.

"How about calling in reinforcements," I suggested. "And in the meantime, I'll see what else I can dig up on Quincy's connections. I know a team went through his place last night, after..." I took a deep breath. "I'm going to head over there myself and see if I can find anything."

Jasmine nodded, her expression determined as she turned back to her computer. "Got it. Keep me posted."

Half an hour later, I stood outside Quincy's modest residence, the midday sun beating down on me. Fall was in the air. I could see the leaves changing with each cooler night we had, even though the days were still so very hot and humid.

I pushed open the front door and stepped inside. The air was heavy since the air conditioning unit had been shut off sometime in the night.

The house was small, cramped, with furniture that looked like it had seen better days. Not at all what I'd expected for the head of a massive drug cartel.

As I made my way through the rooms, I couldn't help but feel a pang of sadness for the man who had once lived here but was now gone in such a tragic way.

If he'd remained alive, we'd have all the answers we needed. So far, everyone in custody was talking to us. They had been booked into the federal prison a few counties over. Each of their interview transcripts were sent over as they were being held.

I began my search in the living room, rifling through drawers and cabinets. I knew the place had already been searched but something told me I could find what they couldn't. Aside from a few unpaid bills and a collection of dusty knick-knacks, though, there was nothing of interest to be found.

Frustration gnawed at the edges of my mind as I moved on to the bedroom, my footsteps echoing in the empty silence of the house. It was there, amidst a clutter of old clothes and discarded magazines, that I spotted it: a framed photograph that had tipped over and had fallen into the rest of the mess.

My heart skipped a beat as I picked up the photograph, my fingers trembling slightly as I studied the image of Quincy and Rayne smiling together. It was from when they had still been dating, long before everything had fallen apart. Before she'd found him cheating on her. Stupid idiot.

But as I turned the photograph over, my breath caught in my throat. Tucked behind the picture was a piece of paper, yellowed with age and creased from being folded too many times.

With trembling hands, I unfolded the paper to find a ledger. I began to read. It appeared that Quincy was in deep with a large sports gambling collector. So deep, I cringed at the numbers on each line.

Each time a payment was made, there was a date beside the amount with the new balance underneath.

Several other letters from a debt collector were behind that, all of them demanding payment for an outstanding debt owed to a local sports bookie. My eyes widened as I read on, my mind racing with the implications of what I was seeing.

Quincy was in serious debt, far more than I had ever realized. And if he was willing to go to such lengths to hide it, who knew what else he was capable of?

I'd wager every payment date coincided with a money drop or a drug deal. Still, this didn't prove he was in charge. After all, the amount I'd seen on the pool table at the Nest could have cleared most of this debt away. There wasn't any proof of payments to any of the Reapers on the sheet either.

Had his debt been the reason he'd started the drug ring in the first place? We'd already found proof that when Felix and Ben were first arrested years back, Quincy had been the arresting officer.

As I was about to put the paper in my pocket and replace the photograph, I tensed as I heard footsteps approaching. I instinctively reached for the gun at my waist. But as the figure stepped into the room, I relaxed slightly when I recognized Rayne's familiar silhouette.

"What are you doing here?" Rayne's voice was sharp with concern as she took in the scene before her. "And what's that you're holding?"

"I came here for the same reason as you. To search for evidence," I admitted, holding up the ledger for her to see. "I think Quincy may have been involved in more than we realized."

Rayne's eyes widened as she read through the ledger, comprehension dawning on her face. "Sports gambling," she murmured, her brow furrowing in thought. "That could explain a lot. This is a lot of debt."

I nodded. "I think Quincy's debts may have driven him," I said grimly. "And if he was willing to resort to criminal activity to pay off those debts, who knows what else he might have been involved in?"

Rayne's expression hardened with determination as she met my gaze. "We need to find out everything we can about Quincy's connections," she said firmly. "If he was involved in the deaths of Mayor Taylor and the Dupont brothers, we need to know." I nodded in agreement. "I'm here to look for evidence to tie him to the stabbings." She glanced around. "It appears your guys already tossed the place."

I realized suddenly that, even though we both wanted to prove Quincy's guilt, we would have easily overlooked any evidence tying Quincy to the mayor's death or that of the Dupont brothers. Since we had Declan in custody and were almost positive that he was the one who had killed the brothers, did that mean we believed he'd killed the mayor as well? Why? Had he been told to do so by Quincy or Felix?

"I can help you look?" I suggested.

I watched her bite her bottom lip for a second, then shrug. "I suppose you're probably higher up than I am in the whole law enforcement scene. I don't really know the rules, but I can't see that it would hurt anything."

I smiled. "Trust me, if we do find anything, it will benefit both our cases."

"Right." She glanced around. "Where do we start?"

Rayne and I decided to conduct our search methodically by going room by room. We combed through every room for any shred of evidence that might tie him to the murders of Mayor Taylor and the Dupont brothers.

We started back in the living room, pulling apart cushions and rifling through drawers in search of anything out of the ordinary. But aside from a few old newspapers and a pile of unpaid bills, there was nothing to suggest Quincy's involvement in anything more sinister than a messy personal life.

Frustration ate at me as we moved on to the kitchen, opening cabinets and peering into closets in search of hidden clues.

I watched Rayne bag a few kitchen knives and realized she was still looking for the murder weapon. It wasn't as easy as finding someone who owned a particular gun. This was a knife. Everyone had knives. I had one in my boot or strapped to my leg most days.

Once again, our efforts yielded little more than dust and disappointment and a dozen or so steak knives.

"We're missing something," Rayne murmured, her brow furrowed in concentration as she surveyed the room. "Quincy was smart, too smart to leave anything incriminating lying around."

I nodded in agreement, my mind racing with possibilities. "We need to think like Quincy," I said, my voice low with determination. "If he was involved in these murders, he would have taken steps to cover his tracks."

With renewed purpose, we continued our search, scouring every inch of the house for any sign of Quincy's involvement. But as the hours passed and the sun began to sink below the horizon, it became increasingly clear that our efforts were in vain.

"I don't understand," Rayne said, her voice tinged with frustration as we stood in the empty living room, surrounded by the remnants of our fruitless search. "There has to be something here, something we're missing. Why else would he have..." She broke off.

I understood what she was saying. He'd been caught, but as a police officer, he knew that he could probably get away with a slap on the wrist and a few years behind bars for the drug charges. But murder, well, that changed everything. The only reason we could think of for the man killing himself was that he was tied to something darker. Something that would have assured he'd be locked up for life.

I sighed heavily, running a hand through my hair in frustration. "I don't know," I admitted, feeling a sense of defeat settling over me. "But we can't give up. We have to keep looking, keep digging, until we find the truth."

Rayne nodded in agreement, her eyes shining with determination. "Wherever the proof is, I won't stop until I have answers," she said firmly.

"*We* won't stop," I corrected, taking her hand in mine. "We're in this together. Until justice is served and we have all the answers."

Chapter Twenty-Four

"True friends are like diamonds—bright, beautiful, valuable, and always in style."
–Nicole Richie

Rayne

There were a lot of really good reasons why I enjoyed Jameson staying with me at my place. The best reason was the sex we managed to slip in during a shower once we got home from work.

I'd never had sex that made my legs wobble and honestly fear that I'd fall on the slick tile and hurt myself. Thankfully, Jameson was there to hold me up.

We'd just managed to get dressed when there was a knock on my door.

"I'll get it," I told Jameson, who was trying to find a clean shirt in the boxes of his things a few other agents had delivered.

I held in a groan after opening the door to Sabrina.

"What in the living hell, Rayne," she said, her arms crossed over her chest.

I rolled my eyes. "I'm not answering any—" I started as I tried to shut the door.

Sabrina pushed the door open and rushed to hug me. "I just heard everything," she said into my hair. "Are you okay?"

I tensed for a second and then relaxed. "Off the record?"

She jerked slightly. "For this, yes. I know you and Randy are trying to keep it from getting back to Edith." She leaned back and looked me in the eyes. "I promise you right now that I won't print a word of what happened inside the bullpen."

I saw the truth in her eyes and nodded. "Come on in. We have some time before we need to head over there for dinner."

"We?" Sabrina's eyes arched.

Just then, Jameson stepped into the room, thankfully fully dressed.

"Sabrina, meet DEA Narcotics Investigator Special Agent Caleb Jameson Morales. Jameson, Reporter for the *Gemsville Herald*, Sabrina DeRouen, an old friend who has agreed that what we say next is off the record."

"You were in the Reapers." Sabrina pointed at Jameson, who smiled and nodded.

"Undercover," he said smoothly.

Sabrina's eyes moved between us as Jameson stepped up and wrapped his arm around me.

"You two are a thing?" she asked.

"Yes," we both answered at the same time.

Sabrina walked over and sat down on one of my chairs,

and we followed and sat on the sofa together. "Did Quincy really hold you at gunpoint and then kill himself?"

I nodded, feeling the tight knot in my gut.

"How did you hear?" I asked.

"I have my resources," she countered. "The DEA"—she motioned towards Jameson—"you really think that he was in charge of the Reapers? The head of some drug ring?" Jameson shrugged. Sabrina turned to me. "And you think he killed Sharon, Bobby, and Earl?" I shrugged. "What about Evelyn?" she asked.

I shrugged again. "We're still working the case. Looking for proof."

Sabrina remained quiet for a moment. "Quincy and Evelyn did have some history. Not any that might cause him to run her down in the alley though."

"They did?" I asked with a slight frown.

Sabrina's eyes turned to me. "Sure. I mean, he dated a lot. Went through more than a handful of women before and after you."

I shrugged. "I didn't pay too much attention. I suppose I've had my share of flings around town too."

"I'd wager none of them held a gun to your temple," Sabrina said softly. "Are you okay?"

I nodded as I swallowed. "I'm... dealing. The station is making me see a counselor, standard procedure and all. I start next week.

"What now? The entire Reaper gang is locked up for how long?" she asked.

"Until they are each individually charged," Jameson answered. "In a federal court."

Sabrina nodded. "And Wyatt Taylor too?" Jameson nodded. "I heard you had Declan in custody as well?"

"These facts you can report on. My father will be making a statement tomorrow morning," I added.

"I know, he's doing a press release at six tomorrow. I'm scheduled to be there, along with half the reporters in the country." She sighed and leaned back. "That just means no one will pay attention to a small-town reporter."

"What if I could get you a one-on-one with the arresting officer?" Jameson said.

Both Sabrina and I looked at him.

"Jameson," I warned him, and he turned his eyes toward me.

"It's my call. Tomorrow's press release has vague details. I can give more. In time."

Sabrina sat forward. "Seriously?"

Jameson nodded and stood up. "Tomorrow. I'll meet you at the bakery under my apartment in town around eleven. For now"—he took my hand and helped me stand up—"we have dinner plans we don't want to be late for."

As we pulled up to my parents' house, I couldn't help but feel a mix of eagerness and apprehension swirling in my stomach. Dinner with my family was always special, but tonight felt different because this was the first time Jameson was with me. My entire body tingled with an undercurrent of excitement and tension.

Randy greeted us at the door with a warm smile, his eyes tired but welcoming as he ushered us inside. The familiar scent of home-cooked food wafted through the air, mingling with the soft murmur of conversation as we settled around the dining room table.

"Evening." Randy shook Jameson's hand and came in for a hug.

"Dad." I smiled and hugged him back.

"It's taken you twenty-three years to call me that and

really mean it," he said over my head. "She called us Mom and Dad for a few years when she was younger, then watched a movie where an adopted daughter called her parents by their first names and started doing that." He rolled his eyes. "We just sort of went with it. Calls me Dad or Daddy every now and then, but I could always tell it didn't come from here." He touched his heart. "Now..." he smiled.

In my head they would always be Mom and Dad, even if I called them Randy and Edith.

"It helps to keep things professional when we work together," I added as I laughed. "How's Mom?" I asked, looking around.

"Tired. Her last chemo session is tomorrow," he added with a smile. "Then we get to heal and see how things went before her next surgery."

"She'll have a follow-up, reconstruction from her double mastectomy, once she's strong enough," I told Jameson, who nodded.

We stepped into the dining room where Edith was propped up in a chair. The silver wig that Aria had given her could have fooled anyone. Even I almost forgot it wasn't her own hair as I leaned in and brushed a kiss on her cheek.

"Mom, this is Jameson," I said and stood back as Jameson shook my mother's hand.

"Mrs. Cordova, it's a pleasure," Jameson said smoothly.

"Please, call me Edith." My mother motioned for us to sit. "Randy will set the table while we chat."

We were halfway through the pot roast meal when Randy finally broached the topic of his retirement. I felt a surge of mixed emotions wash over me.

"I've been thinking about retiring," he said, his voice tinged with weariness. "And I think you'd be the perfect person to take over as chief of police. I've already broached the subject with your SSA." He chuckled. "She was surprisingly optimistic about the move."

The words hung in the air between us, heavy with implication. I glanced at Jameson, a flicker of surprise and pride dancing in my chest as I realized the magnitude of the offer my father was extending to him.

"I... I don't know what to say," Jameson said, his eyes searching mine. "I'd be honored, but I haven't quite figured out what's going to happen after I close this case. Can we take a while to figure things out?" He took my hand in his.

I squeezed his hand reassuringly, offering him a supportive smile. "Take your time and think about it," Dad said with a smile. "But know that whatever decision you make, we will support you both."

"Thanks, Dad," I said, feeling my heart swell with love.

As we continued our meal, the conversation turned to lighter topics, and soon we found ourselves reminiscing about my parents' past. Dad chuckled as he recounted the story of how he and Mom had first met at a local diner, their eyes meeting over a spilled cup of coffee.

"It was love at first sight," Dad said, his voice tinged with affection as he glanced at my mother. "I knew from the moment I saw her that she was the one."

Mom blushed at his words, her eyes sparkling with fondness as she reached for his hand with her frail one. "Oh, Randy, you're too sweet," she said, her voice soft with emotion. "I knew from that first moment that you were the man I wanted to spend the rest of my life with too."

As I listened to all of my parents' stories, which I knew by heart, I couldn't help but feel a sense of warmth and nostalgia wash over me. Despite the challenges they had faced over the years, my parents' love for each other had only grown stronger with time, a testament to the enduring power of true love.

Even after they'd found out they couldn't have any more children after their one and only child had died as a baby, they'd claimed they'd never given up hope. Shortly after little Randy Jr's death, Randy had found me, and their lives had gained a new purpose.

As the last rays of sunlight dipped below the horizon, casting a warm glow over the backyard, we all fell into a comfortable silence, content to bask in the peacefulness of the moment. And as I looked around at my family, bathed in the soft light of the setting sun, I felt an overwhelming sense of gratitude wash over me.

In that moment, surrounded by the people I loved most in the world, I knew that no matter what the future held, we would face it together, with love, laughter, and unwavering support. We watched the stars begin to twinkle like diamonds in the darkening sky and I hoped there would be many more nights like this to come. My eyes moved to my mom and her frail state, and I sent up a silent prayer.

Please, if there is a god somewhere up in that star-filled sky, please don't take my mother.

The next morning, before the sun even rose, there was a pounding on my door.

Jameson groaned and then jerked awake, instantly on guard.

"I know you're in there, Rayne." Aria's angry voice echoed in the darkness. "Jameson, I know you're in there. The two of you get your naked butts up and come tell me why in the hell I'm just finding out what happened on the news."

"Shit," we both said at the same time.

"She was out of town. I should have texted or called her." I groaned, pulling on a bathrobe.

"Hurry up," Aria called out. "I don't give a damn if you're naked. I'm still going to kick both of your—"

I swung the door open to a very angry-looking Aria, who after one look at me and Jameson, narrowed her eyes and stormed past us into the house.

"I just drove over eight hours. Eight fucking hours." She turned towards us as her voice rose. "Why did I have to hear what happened, what really happened to you in the bullpen, from Sabrina? Sabrina!" She practically screamed it as she crossed her arms over her chest.

Instead of answering her, I walked into her arms and held her stiff body.

"I'm sorry," I whispered. "Everything has been so... crazy." When Aria didn't budge, I sighed. "Fine," I leaned back and looked my best friend in the eyes. "I'm officially using my do-over card."

Aria's eyes narrowed slightly, then she held out her hand. I rolled my eyes and walked over to the kitchen junk drawer. After a few moments of looking around for it, I pulled out the tattered card and placed it in Aria's hand.

"Done." Aria took the card and shoved it in her pocket, then she balled her fist and gave me a Charlie horse on my arm. "Do-over transaction is complete." She glanced over at Jameson with a frown. "You, unfortunately, don't have a do-over card. You're DEA?"

Jameson nodded. "Deep undercover," Jameson added firmly. "Need-to-know basis."

"I'm her best friend." She pointed towards me. "Trust me when I say it was a need-to-know basis."

"Duly noted. I'll keep that in mind for the future," Jameson said with a grin. "We good?"

Aria ran her eyes up and down. "Is your real name Jameson?"

"Caleb Jameson Morales. I'm originally from the Chicago area. Only kid of Boris and Molly Morales. Joined the DEA fresh out of a tour in the marines. Took my first undercover assignment when I was a baby at twenty-two. Took down one of the largest drug lords in LA within my first year. I just turned thirty..." He glanced at his watch. "Well, actually, I will turn thirty in two days." He smiled.

"Seriously?" I asked, then I turned to Aria. "You've gotten more out of him in five minutes that I have since I met him," I joked.

Aria smiled and then nodded. "Okay, good. One last very important question."

"Shoot," Jameson said.

"Do you love my best friend?" Aria asked with all sincerity.

"With all my being," Jameson responded, causing Aria to squeal.

"Good." She rushed towards us and hugged us both. "Now, I'm going to make us all some pancakes. After the two of you shower. You smell like hot steamy sex." She laughed as she disappeared into my kitchen. "Breakfast is in ten minutes everyone," she called out. "So no shower sex."

I laughed and took Jameson's hand and pulled him into the bedroom. "Sorry, we're sort of a package deal."

"It's okay. I like her. Remember, we spent our first unofficial date together?" He leaned down and brushed his lips against mine.

"Right." I sighed and melted against him.

"A lot can happen in ten minutes," he said as he walked me backwards towards the bathroom.

As we walked into the kitchen, the smell of pancakes

greeted us, and my stomach rumbled with anticipation. Aria stood at the stove, flipping pancakes with practiced ease, a look of concentration on her face. I couldn't help but smile as I watched her, grateful for her presence after her long drive home.

"Just in time," she greeted us, her voice cheerful despite the early hour. "Coffee?" she said, holding up a mug. "I didn't know how Jameson liked his, so it's black." She motioned towards the other cup.

I walked over and took the mug from her.

"Jameson likes it black," he said from behind me. "Thanks." He walked over and took the cup and took a sip.

"Sit, I'm almost done," Aria said. We sat down and soon Aria joined us, carrying a plate piled high with pancakes, syrup dripping down the sides. "Breakfast is served," she announced, setting the plate down on the table before flopping into a seat beside me.

We dug into the pancakes eagerly, savoring the delicious meal and the comfort of each other's company. As we ate, Jameson filled Aria in on the latest developments in the case, detailing the arrests of the Reaper gang members and the shocking death of Quincy.

"It's been a crazy few days," he admitted, running a hand through his hair before taking my hand in his. "But we're all okay and, better yet, we're making progress. Hopefully, we'll have everything wrapped up soon."

"Everything?" Aria frowned. "As in, you're leaving?"

"No, I'm sticking," Jameson assured her.

"For how long?" Aria asked.

He glanced at me and smiled. "For as long as Rayne wants me."

I nodded. I wanted to say forever, but I didn't want to spook him or myself.

For now, I pushed those thoughts aside, focusing instead on the warmth of the sun streaming through the window and the laughter of my friends as we enjoyed our breakfast together. On this moment, surrounded by love and friendship.

Halfway through the day, after I'd spilled my third cup of coffee down my shirt, I was ready to call it quits. I had stubbed my toes on Quincy's desk earlier and had closed a door on my little finger at one point.

Today was shaping up to be jinxed. I'd had a handful of days like this before and knew it was better for me to call it quits early.

I knocked on Randy's door, and when he glanced up I told him I was heading out to visit mom

"Everything all right?" he asked.

"It's a jinx day."

He smiled. "You used to have those when you were young. I didn't know they followed you into adulthood."

"Neither did I. I'm going to bring her some lunch."

He nodded. "She'd like the visit. She just got home from her chemo session. It sounds like everything went well."

I stopped by Mom's favorite diner and ordered food to go. While I was waiting, I watched a young family eating at a table and couldn't help but smile.

I'd never thought that I wanted kids, never even imagined being lucky enough to find someone to have them with. Jameson made me dream about things I'd never wanted before.

I was too busy daydreaming to see Isabella Sinclair leaning against my Jeep waiting for me as I stepped outside. When she saw me heading her way, she stood up straight and stormed towards me.

"You bitch," she said before trying to slap me.

"Easy," I said, setting the food down in my Jeep as I easily dodged the blow. "I'd hate to have to arrest you for striking an officer."

"Bullshit," Izzy said. "You did this. You locked them all up."

"I didn't do anything," I said calmly, releasing Izzy's arm. "I'm sure you've heard by now it was the DEA that did all the arresting."

Izzy's eyes narrowed. "What about Nadia? Did you lock her up too?"

I frowned. "No, she wasn't on the arrest list."

"She's missing," Izzy threw back at me. "I haven't seen her since the night everyone else got hauled in. If I ever see that no-good, lying son of a bitch Jameson again, I'll—"

"Careful. Remember, I am a police officer," I warned.

"Scratch his eyes out," Izzy finished. "No wonder he wasn't interested in me. The two of you were made for each other," she spat. "Stay out of my way." She stormed down the sidewalk.

All things considered, I figured I got off easy. Still, knowing that Nadia was MIA unsettled me. I drove by her place and knocked on the door. Her car was parked in front of the one-car garage. When she didn't answer, I glanced in the window. Seconds later, I busted the door in and dialed 911, then started CPR on Nadia.

Chapter Twenty-Five

"Angels are like diamonds. They can't be made, you have to find them. Each one is unique."
–Jaclyn Smith

Jameson

I got the call while I was out grabbing lunch. Hearing Rayne's voice instantly excited me. Then her words sank in.

"Nadia just OD'd." Her voice was a little shaky. "I was able to bring her back, briefly. The EMTs are still working on her."

"Where are you?" I asked after hearing the weariness in her tone.

She was quiet for a moment as if she was thinking. "210 Cardinal Street."

"I'll be right there," I said, glancing around as I drove down the side streets. When I pulled up in front of the small house and parked next to Rayne's Jeep, the ambulance was just pulling away, sirens blaring.

Seeing the look on Rayne's face, I rushed to engulf her in my arms.

"It looks as if she'd been on a drug binge since the arrests," Rayne said into my chest. "Her place is a disaster."

I glanced over her head into the open door and could see the mess. I'd witnessed drug binges before. There was junk food trash, soda cans, needles, and drugs lying everywhere. Yeah, Nadia had locked herself away for at least a few days.

"Why'd you come here?" I asked, curious.

"Izzy visited me. She's pissed. Upset about you. Hurt about the arrests. She blames me." She sighed and leaned back. "Something she said nagged me enough to stop by. I had just picked up lunch to take to my mother. She finished her last chemo round and I wanted to celebrate with her. Besides, today is a jinx day." She shook her head. "I'll explain what that means later. Anyway, it nagged me. Izzy said that Nadia hadn't been around since the arrest. She thought we'd hauled her in too. Only..."

"We didn't," I supplied. "There was no evidence Nadia or Izzy were anything but entertainment to the Reapers."

Rayne nodded. "So I stopped by." She motioned with her head. "When she didn't answer, I looked in the window and saw her. I had to bust the door down. She was blue and barely breathing. While I was on with 911, she stopped breathing."

"You got here just in time," I said with a smile. "Sounds like whatever jinx you had paid off."

She closed her eyes. "I've been certified in CPR since I was fifteen. This is the first time I've ever had to use it. My brain just sort of... clicked into gear. I was afraid I'd forget the counts. Breaths versus compressions. I didn't." She smiled slightly.

I held onto her as a patrol car pulled up with Owen and his new partner, Simon, who had replaced Abe. "We heard," Owen said, walking up and hugging Rayne. "You okay?"

To be honest, I wasn't normally a jealous man. The easy way Rayne and Owen acted around one another was like how siblings are together. But for a split second, jealousy reared its awful head and I had to focus on squashing it.

"Yes, but I'm taking off the rest of the day." She glanced around. "Maybe you could..."—she nodded towards Nadia's place—"finish things here?"

Owen nodded and then eyed me. "Owen Morrison," he said, holding out his hand towards mine. "I've heard you are DEA."

"Jameson Morales," I replied and shook the officer's hand. I knew who the man was. I'd run every officer in the county. Owen, as far as I could tell, was not only clean but a decent man.

"You and Rayne?" Owen asked. I nodded, wondering if there was history between them that I didn't know about. "I'm dating Sabrina," he added with a smile. "Rayne, she's like a sister," Owen supplied. "One that is obviously shaken. Take her home." Owen hugged Rayne again. "I heard your mom just rang the bell at the clinic." He smiled. "Go celebrate with her."

"Thanks," Rayne said. I took her hand and started leading her towards the cars, but she stopped and threw over her shoulder, "You're shaping up to be a decent cop."

Owen laughed. "It was touch and go there for a while, wasn't it?"

Rayne smiled and then nodded.

"Want to leave your car here?" I asked.

She shook her head. "I'm good to drive."

"I just picked up my lunch. How about I follow you and we can celebrate Edith's victory together?"

"I think she'd like that."

When we pulled up to her parents' house, I parked beside her Jeep in their long driveway. I knew that it was a significant day and Rayne would easily push the horror of what had just happened, what she'd just had to do to save a woman's life, to the back of her mind for her mother.

We found her mother sitting in the sunroom we'd sat in the night before after dinner. The woman's eyes were shining with relief and yet I could easily see the exhaustion. She looked tired but happy, her strength evident despite the toll of her cancer treatment. Nelly, the in-home nurse, stood up as we entered.

"Jameson, Rayne, this is a pleasant surprise," Edith said, receiving Rayne's hug and kiss.

"I brought you your favorite," Rayne said, holding up the bag with the food in it.

"I figured I'd tag along," I added quickly.

"Lucky me." Edith chuckled. "Come, sit, we'll eat out here." She motioned to the chairs.

"I'll just go have my lunch inside while you three have a little visit," Nelly said, and disappeared.

I couldn't help but admire Rayne's mother's strength. Despite everything she had been through, she remained steadfast and hopeful, a true inspiration to us all. I'd never seen her smile waver, which had me thinking about my own mother.

Every year, no matter where I was, she'd call me on my birthday. That was tomorrow, but maybe once we left here I'd call her early.

As if Edith read my mind, she asked.

"Rayne tells me it's your birthday tomorrow?" Edith asked.

"I turn thirty," I said with a slight grin.

Edith chuckled. "It's just a number. You'll blink and it doubles." She sighed. "You mentioned last night that your family is still in Chicago?"

"My folks are. They divorced when I was younger. Somehow, after that, they became closer than when they were married." I smiled.

"When was the last time you visited them?" she asked.

"Mom," Rayne groaned after taking a bite of food and swallowing it. "You're digging too far."

"Am I?" Edith asked me.

"No, it's fine," I answered with a smile. "A little over a year ago, before I took this assignment, I went home for a few weeks while everything was getting set up here."

"Do you plan on going back soon?" she asked as she took a sip of her drink.

"To visit." I nodded and glanced at Rayne. "For now, I've moved my things into Rayne's place and plan on sticking here until I figure out our next move."

Edith smiled and nodded. "Now, Rayne, talk to me about the fall festival."

Rayne groaned and then looked at me. "We spend almost two days making pies and cakes."

"Don't like baking?" I asked her.

She shrugged. "I like spending time with Edith," she said, reaching over and taking her mother's hand.

"I love baking," I told Edith. "Maybe this year I can help?"

"We could use the extra hands." Edith laughed. "Now that I have a full stomach, I'm going to go lie down."

I stood up quickly and helped Edith up. When she was gone, Rayne turned to me.

"How about we take a walk?" She motioned to the back door. "There's a lake not far from here."

I stood up and took her hand, and she led me outside.

As Rayne and I walked along a wide dirt pathway that led to the lake, the crisp autumn air filled my lungs. It was invigorating and refreshing. When we reached the water, the golden sunlight danced on its surface, casting a warm glow over everything it touched.

"So, what do you think?" Rayne asked, breaking the comfortable silence between us.

I glanced at her, a soft smile playing on her lips, her eyes sparkling with anticipation. "About what?"

"Our future," she replied, her voice filled with a quiet determination. "Our dreams, our goals. Where do you see us in five years?"

I pondered her question for a moment as the sounds of birds and bugs zipping around us echoed against the stillness of the lake. "Well, I've always dreamed of making a real difference in the world," I began, my words slow and thoughtful. "And working as an undercover DEA agent has given me a taste of that. But my wants have changed recently. I wanted to take down the big players, the ones who think they're above the law. I sacrificed everything to achieve that goal."

"Now?" she asked.

"I don't want to sacrifice anymore," I admitted. "Not when there's something really important that I don't think I could ever give up." I brought her hand to my lips and brushed a kiss across her knuckles.

Rayne smiled, her hand finding mine as we continued to walk. "So, this isn't just temporary?" she asked softly.

"No." I smiled back. "What about you? What are your dreams?"

"To keep serving my town. The people I care about here." She glanced around. "Maybe a little of that." She motioned across the field and trees to where her parents' house sat.

"A family?" I asked.

She nodded. "You?"

"I've never allowed myself to dream of having one before," I admitted.

"Now?" she asked, her voice a whisper.

I turned to her and wrapped my arms around her. "Now, I can't stop thinking about it."

"Me either. Ever since I found out I was adopted, I had always told myself that I wouldn't have a family of my own. That all changed recently and now I want one. With you."

I brushed my lips across hers.

"Is this happening too fast?" she asked softly against my mouth.

"No, this is right. Can't you feel it deep in your bones?" I asked, feeling the warmth that she caused spread throughout me.

She nodded. "From the first moment I saw you."

I couldn't help but smile at her words, feeling a sense of peace wash over me. We continued our walk by the lake until I had to go back to work. Rayne returned home.

We spent the following day, my birthday, which happened to fall on a Saturday, in bed the entire day. To be honest, I couldn't have asked for a better way to spend the day. We ate cold cereal in bed while watching movies in between bouts of lovemaking.

It was the perfect day.

After that, the days flew by and less than two weeks

after we'd made all those arrests, our cases against every person we'd hauled in were closed out. The rest of the team, including Jasmine, headed out of town to their next mission. I, however, remained in Gemsville and officially put in my notice to the DEA.

I hadn't yet agreed to take Randy's position, but Randy and I talked about it whenever we hung out with Rayne's parents.

The days before the fall festival finally came, and both Rayne and I were back over at her parents' place helping Edith bake.

Edith had finally gained most of her energy back and could stand or move around for more than ten minutes at a time. Rayne had even confided in me that her mother's hair was growing back and was more than just peach fuzz under her wig.

Nadia had been checked into a facility in Lafayette, and I'd run into Izzy a handful of times and successfully avoided talking to her. I could tell that she was angry at me and figured she'd get over it soon enough. After all, rumors were going around that she had started dating someone new, now that the Reapers weren't taking up all of her time.

Felix and the rest of the gang had officially been charged and were all awaiting trial dates. Declan was being charged with the same drug trafficking crimes as the rest of them since there wasn't proof that he'd killed anyone.

Rayne worked diligently to find proof tying him to the murders, often with me helping out. I had to admit, I was growing extremely frustrated at the lack of clues.

Still, since Quincy's death, Rayne had been making a point to spend more time with her family and I was really keen on it. I liked Randy and Edith. A lot.

The four of us were currently standing in their kitchen

focused on our tasks as we baked. I had had no clue that every year Edith was in charge of baking all the pies for the pie-eating contest as well as most of the cakes for something called a cakewalk.

As we worked together in the kitchen, the scent of freshly baked pies and cakes filled the air, mingling with the warmth of the oven and our laughter.

Rayne and her mother were busy rolling out dough and cutting it into perfect circles for the pie crusts, their hands moving with practiced ease. Randy stood at the counter, his apron stained with flour as he mixed together the filling for the pies, his expression one of focused concentration.

I watched them all with a sense of awe, amazed by their dedication and skill. It was clear that baking was more than just a hobby for them—it was a labor of love, a way to bring joy to those around them.

As I joined in, helping to shape the dough and fill the pies, a sense of belonging washed over me. These people, this family, had welcomed me into their home with open arms, accepting me as one of their own.

Suddenly, I knew I was exactly where I was meant to be. With Rayne by my side and her family surrounding us, I felt more at home than I ever had before.

By the time we pulled the last pie out of the oven, I'd made up my mind to ask Rayne to marry me. Now I just needed the perfect time and place.

Every man was told that women loved big grandiose gestures. Is that what Rayne would want too?

I wanted something intimate, personal, something to encompass all of those quiet moments we shared, the stolen glances and tender touches, since the moment we'd met.

While we sat down at the kitchen table to let the pies cool and to frost the rest of the cakes, I plotted.

The fair started the next evening. I'd seen them haul all the rides into town a few days back and set them up at the county fairgrounds.

Shit, I needed a ring. I frowned as I finished frosting a chocolate cake. There were a few jewelry stores in town. I could stop by one of them in the morning and pick out a ring.

I glanced over at Rayne's ringless fingers while she was frosting another cake. What size ring did she wear? What kind of ring would she like?

"You're distracted," Edith said to me, breaking me out of the questions that circled my mind.

I glanced over at her and then thought of another very important step. I had to ask Randy first. Right? Wasn't that important to ask her father for her hand before asking Rayne?

"Just need some fresh air," I said, standing up.

"I'll go with you." Randy removed the apron he was wearing and set it down. Then he walked over and kissed Edith on the cheek. "We'll be back."

"Take your time. Rayne and I can finish the last three cakes," Edith said with a wink.

As Randy and I stepped outside, the cool fall evening air enveloped us, and I took a moment to collect my thoughts. This was it—I was going to ask Randy for his blessing to marry his daughter.

"There's something I wanted to talk to you about," I began, my voice steady despite the nerves that were threatening to overwhelm me.

Randy turned towards me. His expression was almost humorous. "Spit it out, son. I could tell you've been thinking about it for the last hour." He chuckled. "Right about the time you got as pale as a sheet."

Did he know? Crap. Did that mean Rayne knew? I glanced back towards the house, then took a deep breath, gathering my courage. "I love your daughter, more than anything in this world. And I want to spend the rest of my life making her happy. I want to ask her to marry me."

Randy's eyes softened, and he placed a hand on my shoulder. "Edith and I can see that you're a good man. And we know how much you care for Rayne. We knew this was coming, had talked about it for the past few days, and you have our blessing."

I felt like shouting with joy as relief flooded through me. Instead, I smiled like a stupid kid who had just won a prize. "Thank you. That means the world to me."

"Just know that if you hurt her, it won't be me you have to worry about," Randy joked. "I raised her to fight her own battles."

"I know it," I agreed.

"Besides, I'm pretty sure Edith would beat me to you." Randy laughed and slapped my shoulder.

We stood there for a moment, father and soon-to-be son-in-law, sharing a silent understanding. And as we headed back inside to join the women, I knew that I was one step closer to making Rayne my wife.

The next morning, I headed out to shop for a ring after Rayne went into the office. We were all set to head to the fair later that evening just before sunset.

As I looked around the first shop. I realized just how overwhelming it all was. There were too many rings to choose from. The diamonds had different cuts and shapes and sizes, and that didn't even include the ring itself. What type of metal did she want? With my head spinning I walked out of the store and suddenly got an idea.

I walked into Jazzed Up and was happily surprised to see Aria chatting with Sabrina.

"I need your help," I said eagerly. "Both of you."

The women looked at me with curiosity.

"What's wrong?" Aria asked.

"Nothing's wrong. I have..."—I glanced at my watch—"five hours to pick out an engagement ring for Rayne and figure out how in the hell I'm going to ask her to marry me tonight at the fair."

Both women rushed me as they cheered. I was hugged and then pushed out the door as they dragged me down the street. To my surprise, we walked into an old antique shop instead of a jewelry store.

"This is what she wants," Aria said, pointing to the glass case.

I looked down at a vintage yellow-gold ring with an oval diamond settled in the middle of more than two dozen smaller diamonds.

It was so perfectly Rayne that my heart leaped in my chest.

"This is hers," I said softly.

"Oh! You should ask her on the Ferris wheel," Sabrina added with a little jump.

"She loves that ride," Aria added as they both hugged me again.

Chapter Twenty-Six

"You are a diamond dear,
they can't break you."
–Unknown

Rayne

Sitting in my office scanning over the pages and pages of data I had on the cases I was still working, I wanted to throw something. Or better yet, hit something.

There was nothing here. Nothing that would tie Declan to any of the murders, including Evelyn's hit-and-run. Declan didn't even own a working vehicle, just a motorcycle.

From what I'd been told, when he'd found out about Evelyn's death, he'd been shattered. Word was, he'd spent a week binge drinking and doing as many drugs as he could.

Which was either a sign of a guilty conscience or a

grieving man. The fact was, I wanted him to be guilty. I wanted the man to be locked up.

Even if he wasn't guilty of running down and killing Evelyn, he still had her blood on his hands.

Through my mother, I'd learned that Evelyn's son had received a very large donation, enough to care for the child for the rest of his life.

At least Felix had done that for Evelyn. I stood up to pace for a moment.

Today the office was practically empty. Most of the officers were out at the fairground on parking and traffic duty. Only a handful remained in the office.

Since that day a few weeks back, I'd avoided the bullpen. Now, my eyes landed on Quincy's desk, which had gone untouched since the agents had taken away his computer and anything else they thought might hold clues.

Deciding to take one last look around, I slowly made my way over to his desk. My eyes avoided the spot where he'd taken his own life.

I don't know why I hadn't thought of it before, but when I saw a picture frame lying face down on his desk, I remembered Jameson telling me he had found the gambling ledger in a picture frame.

I picked it up and turned it over and saw the image of Quincy and me at the creek the previous summer. My heart sank.

I hadn't had feelings for him other than friendship since that day I'd caught him cheating almost a year ago, but that didn't mean I wanted him dead. Tears burned my eyes as I flipped it back over and removed the back.

There were three things stuck between the image of our smiling faces and the cardboard stand.

The first was a receipt from the county. Why was that

in there? The second was a handwritten note. I'd seen this handwriting before.

"*You're falling into his trap. He's going to pin everything on you. We are going to take the blame for everything. Meet me tonight behind the bar in the alley. I have the proof you asked for.*"

As I read the note, and then read it again, my heart practically beat out of my chest.

Evelyn. This was her handwriting. I remembered it from the note Faye had given me.

Did this mean that Quincy was the one who had run Evelyn over and killed her?

I set the paper down and unfolded the next sheet. It was a series of numbers, in Evelyn's handwriting.

Could this be the proof that Evelyn was talking about? Whatever they meant, there was one thing they proved— Quincy was not the mastermind. He was the fall guy.

I headed back to my office and stared at the numbers for a while before typing them into my computer system to see what came up.

The possibilities were endless. The first number was nine digits, the same as a social security number or a bank account number at the local bank. The next group was ten digits. A phone number?

I picked up my phone and tried it, allowing it to ring six times before I hung up.

The last number was only three digits long.

272.

After typing this into my search bar, I was slightly surprised when the address to the city and county building popped up at the top of the search.

If these numbers signaled a bank account or social security number, followed by a phone number, and then the address for the mayor's office, these could be just the clues that I needed.

Since I had time before the bank closed, I walked over there, figuring I'd see if they could give me any information.

I took photos of the notes with my phone, then locked them away in my desk drawer and headed out.

When I stepped into the bank, I was assaulted by a puff of frigid air and shivered. Most businesses had already turned their air conditioning units down to accommodate the cooler weather. Obviously, the bank wasn't one of them.

Glancing around, I realized I was in luck. Lisa Childs was working. The woman had graduated a few years before my class and was always nice to me. I walked over and knocked on her door.

"Rayne." She glanced up and smiled at me, then waved me inside. "What a pleasant surprise."

"Hi, Lisa," I said, stepping inside and shutting the door behind me. "Do you have a moment?"

"For you, I have a few." She chuckled and waved me to a seat across from her.

"I don't know if you can actually help me, but I figured I'd give it a shot." I pulled out my phone.

"Whatever it is, I'll give it a try," Lisa asked.

"Can you tell me if any of these numbers are bank accounts here at the bank?" I said, handing her my phone with the image of the note on it.

Lisa frowned down at the phone. "I can't give you names," she warned.

I shrugged. "Gotcha. If they are account numbers, I can get the proper papers to get more information. I just figured I'd try first."

Lisa nodded and then started typing into her computer.

She stilled after trying the first row. "This is an account

here." She took a deep breath, and I saw her eyes narrow. "I..." She slid the phone towards me as if it were suddenly poisonous. "Where did you get these?"

I tucked the phone back into my pocket and stood up. "Thanks, I'll see the judge first thing Monday morning to get the proper paperwork to get more details from you. I hope to see you at the fair this weekend."

Lisa's smile was slightly strained as she nodded at me. "See you there."

I turned and walked out. I glanced down the street and, to my surprise, I saw Jameson, Aria, and Sabrina walk out of the antique store.

The three of them looked so happy. I watched each of my close friends hug the man I loved before Jameson walked to his car and drove away. Aria and Sabrina strolled back to Jazzed Up and disappeared inside without seeing me.

What in the hell?

I was halfway to the salon when realization dawned on me.

The night before, Jameson had gone out on the back porch and talked with Randy for half an hour. When the men had come back in, they were very chummy. Now Jameson and two of my close friends were shopping.

I stopped just outside of the antique store and gasped. My ring!

I rushed through the doors and, to my surprise, the ring I had admired for the past ten years was gone.

"Mr. Lief," I said, getting the owner's attention. "Where is it?"

The man's eyes widened and then softened. "Sorry, girl, it's sold."

I glanced at the door and felt my heart jump in my

chest. There was only one person in the world who knew how I felt about that ring. Aria.

"Thanks," I said, and turned to rush down the sidewalk. When I strolled into Jazzed Up, Aria was combing through Sabrina's hair. The pair saw me and their faces turned blank.

"Spill," I said, crossing my arms over my chest.

Both women looked at one another and shook their heads slowly.

"Trust us," Aria said softly. "Just this once, don't go poking around."

My chin rose and I turned my attention to Sabrina. "Would you stop looking into why your two best friends were just seen walking out of a store with the man you love?"

"Aww." Sabrina smiled and then said sarcastically. "Am I one of your best friends?"

I rolled my eyes. "Talk."

"No, sorry, this time I can honestly say that this reporter has nothing to report." She held her hands up. "I'm just here to get my hair trimmed." She motioned towards Aria.

"And I'm just doing the trimming." Aria smiled and went back to combing through Sabrina's hair.

"My ring has been sold," I blurted out. This stopped Aria's movement.

"Ring?" she said after a slight pause. "What ring?"

"You know damned well what ring," I said firmly.

"Rayne." She drew my name out and then whined, "Don't do this. Please." She held up her hands in a begging gesture. "Just... turn around, walk out of here, and forget you saw anything. Please."

I sighed and, after taking a few deep breaths, I smiled. "I'm getting proposed to."

Both women smiled quickly, and I squealed like a freaking junior higher.

Then they were hugging me and doing a little crazy circle dance.

"You don't know anything," Aria said when we stopped. "If you love him, you'll forget this."

I nodded. "Right." I kept nodding. "Oh god. What am I going to say?"

They both laughed and then said in unison, "Yes."

"Sit." Aria shoved me into the chair. "Sorry, Sabrina, I'm going to have to postpone your trim. Rayne needs my help to look her best tonight."

"Oh god, he's asking me tonight?" I paled.

"Way to keep a secret." Sabrina elbowed Aria.

"Shut up," Aria said, spinning me around in the chair. "I think you could do with a few more highlights."

I left the salon two hours later. I only had an hour before I was supposed to help my folks and Jameson deliver the pies to the fairgrounds, so I went home and changed.

It took me almost half an hour to finally settle on the outfit—white cotton button-up shirt with a mustard-colored tank top underneath it, along with the flare jeans Aria and I had bought the last time we'd shopped together. I finished it off with ankle-high heeled boots. I even took time to curl my hair and apply a little more makeup than I normally wore.

Damn. I looked like a woman. Even smelled like one after I spritzed on some of the perfume that I'd gotten last Christmas from my mom.

When Jameson walked in, he did a double take and, without saying anything, he walked over and wrapped his arms around me and kissed me until I was breathless.

"You look, smell, and taste delicious," he purred next to my ear, which sent goose bumps traveling all over my body.

He was wearing his signature black T-shirt and a pair of those worn blue jeans I loved to see on him. We had yet to get his motorcycle back from evidence, but he still had on his worn steel-toed boots. God, he was everything I'd ever dreamed of.

"Your folks are pretty punctual people, aren't they?" he asked, trailing his mouth down my neck.

I laughed and pulled away from him. "My father is the chief of police. I was once two minutes late for curfew and he had three cop cars out looking for me," I joked.

Jameson groaned. "Okay, later," he promised, and he kissed me again. "Let's go."

For the next hour, we piled all of the baked goods into the back of my mother's minivan, which for some reason she'd never traded in.

When we arrived at the fairgrounds, there were more than a dozen people waiting to help unload all of the pies and cakes and cart them to the pie-eating-contest tables and the cakewalk tent.

The first night of the fall festival was when most of the main events took place. The following two days were when people enjoyed the hayrides, corn maze, carnival games, and all the blue-ribbon events, which involved cooking the best-tasting food or growing the biggest gourds. Not to mention the rodeo and animal contests, which all concluded the last evening of the fair.

After we finished helping unload everything, Jameson took my hand in his. "Do we have time to stroll around?"

I laughed. "I have never, nor would I ever, try to win a pie-eating contest or a cakewalk. We have the entire night to do whatever we want." I glanced up at the Ferris wheel. "Just as long as I get to ride that beast at least a dozen times." I laughed.

"Oh?" Jameson turned away and looked at the large wheel, which was already spinning slowly. "You like heights?"

"I love them, especially when you're strapped in. You can see everything from up there." I sighed. "What do you want to do first?"

"First, how about food? I skipped lunch."

"Corn dogs and funnel cake?" I suggested.

He shrugged. "Turkey legs and then later funnel cake?"

"Deal." I laughed and wrapped my arm in his as we strolled through the grounds.

I desperately tried to put the fact that Jameson was going to propose to me out of my head. We grabbed two turkey legs and a boat of French fries and then found a picnic table to sit at.

After we were done eating, we strolled through rows and rows of carnival games, winning a few and losing more. We enjoyed the hall of mirrors followed by a few of the smaller rides. We spent an hour laughing and having fun together, and I snapped more photos than I ever had at the fair. I even changed the background on my phone to the one I'd taken of us on the carousel.

"Next up is that bad boy," I said, pulling Jameson towards the Ferris wheel.

"Wait, let's do the corn maze first," he suggested. "If we ride the wheel first, you'll cheat and map it out in your head."

I laughed. "Fine, maze first, then the wheel, but I want some cotton candy." I motioned towards the stand.

With a massive bag of blue cotton candy in hand, we entered the corn maze hand in hand.

"Have you ever come to this fair with anyone else?" he asked when we were sufficiently lost in the corn.

"Besides Aria?" I shook my head. "This is the most fun I've had at this thing since I was a teen," I admitted.

"This is my first fair," he said.

I stopped and looked at him. "Shut up." I slapped him on the shoulder. "Really?"

"Yup." He smiled. "My parents weren't really the hands-on type. I spent most of my days hiding from them at the bike park. I got a BMX bike when I was eight and rode it until I bought my first hog at seventeen."

"I'm sorry," I said, taking his hand again. "We'll just have to make this weekend a full-blown fair extravaganza for you," I joked.

"What does that even mean?" He laughed.

"It means we will ride every ride, eat everything they have to offer, and have as much fun as possible." I tugged on his hand. "Now, let's figure a way out of here so we can get a caramel apple and ride the Ferris wheel and then ride the spinning cups and throw up everything we've just eaten."

Chapter Twenty-Seven

"Diamonds are intrinsically worthless,
except for the deep psychological need they fill."
–Nicky Oppenheimer De Beers

Jameson

The moment we sat down in one of the seats on the Ferris wheel, my entire body seemed to freeze up. My hands gripped the bar in front of me as the ride slowly groaned and swayed into motion.

"Isn't this the best?" Rayne sighed beside me. "Hey, are you okay?"

The sound of worry in her tone shook me out of the temporary stupor. I wasn't afraid of heights, as I believed she was thinking now. My fears sprouted from the fact that I was about to ask the most important question of my life.

"Yeah, sure," I said, forcing myself to relax. I wrapped my arm around her shoulders, pulling her closer to me, which had a calming effect.

"I love this, being able to look down on my town. On everyone I love." She sighed and rested her head against my shoulder. "They're like stars in the night sky." She motioned to the crowd below as we climbed higher. "Each and every person down there is mine. And I know that deep down they are all good people." She turned to me. "Every single one of them would give you the shirt off their backs. Their love for each other burns brighter than the stars, their kindness is stronger than diamonds." She laughed and I kissed her.

"Diamonds in the Louisiana mud," I said, feeling the same about the townspeople that I'd come to know and love.

"I like that. Diamonds in the mud." She smiled and then took a deep breath as she glanced over the crowd below us. "Oh look, there's Aria and Tobias," she said, pointing into the crowd below. The ride slowed and then stopped with us at the very top while they let someone else on the ride below us. Just then the couple below us looked up at us and we waved back down at them.

This was the time. Aria had asked if she could record the entire event from below and when Rayne spotted them, it was my time to act.

Trying not to fumble, I pulled the small jewelry box out of my pocket and held it out. I gripped it as tightly as I could, tighter than I had gripped the security bar in front of me moments ago.

"Rayne," I said softly, getting her attention. When she glanced over at me, I was holding the small jewelry box out in front of her.

Rayne gasped in surprise, and I watched a spark fill her eyes.

I hadn't planned on what to say. Not really. I figured when the moment came, I'd know the right words.

Opening my mouth, I let how I felt about her flow out of me.

"You are the most wonderful thing that has happened to me. You changed everything I've ever wanted in life with just one kiss. I can't imagine not being with you, or growing old without seeing your smile, hearing your laughter, being with you. I'll do my damnedest to make your life as joyous as you make mine. Marry me?" I said and waited, unable to breath until I knew her answer.

Slowly, she reached out, laid her hand on my cheek. "I've never loved anyone like you before. Yes," she said with a smile. "Yes, I'll marry you." She laughed as I pulled her close and kissed her until we were both breathless.

"What did you say?" came a loud voice from below.

We both looked down to see Aria with a small toy bullhorn up to her lips and a phone with its camera pointed at us in the other hand.

Laughing, Rayne yelled down, "YES!"

"Put the ring on it then," Aria said back into the speaker.

Rayne turned to me and smiled as she held her hand out. "Yes, put a ring on it."

My fingers shook as I pulled the ring out of the case and slid it smoothly on her finger.

"It fits," I said softly with relief.

"It was meant for me," she said with a chuckle. She hugged me again just as the ride started to move.

"I had some help." I motioned towards Aria, who still had her phone camera pointed at us.

"Yeah, I figured," she said just before we kissed again.

By the time we climbed off the ride, there were a handful of people waiting for us at the bottom, including Rayne's parents, which made me realize I hadn't told my parents of my plans. We were engulfed in hugs and well wishes for a while and chatted with everyone.

I'd talked to my parents on my birthday and even had a video chat with each of them to introduce Rayne. Still, I'd been so focused and nervous about asking her that I'd forgotten to tell my own family my plans.

When the crowd around us died down, I pulled her into a quiet place and kissed her.

"I should call my folks," I said.

She smiled and nodded. "Do that while I run to the bathroom." She motioned towards the porta-potties near the fenced area that blocked the parking lot from the event.

I watched her walk away and pulled out my phone. I knew that my mother would be horrified if I called my father first, so I punched in her number.

After about ten minutes, I hung up the phone with my dad. Both of my parents' excited voices were still echoing in my ears. I couldn't contain the grin that spread across my face. It felt surreal, almost dreamlike, to have that conversation with them, to share the news that Rayne and I were engaged. It was a moment I had been waiting for, one that filled me with a sense of joy and anticipation for the future.

But as I looked around the bustling fairground, my smile faltered. Rayne hadn't come back yet and since there weren't any lines at the toilets, I doubted she had gotten caught up waiting.

I walked over there and glanced around, but she was nowhere to be seen.

I spotted Aria and Tobias at the fish ring game a few feet away and walked over to ask if they'd seen her.

"No," Aria said with a frown. "She may have gone to check up on her mother at the cakewalk booth."

We quickly rushed over to the cakewalk booth. When Randy spotted us, he made his way over.

"What's wrong?" he asked.

"Rayne went to the bathroom and now I can't find her," I said, realizing how stupid I sounded. I was unable to hide the worry that laced my voice.

Randy glanced around and then nodded. "I'll ask my men. Someone is bound to have seen her." He pulled out his phone.

After talking to Owen for a bit, he asked the man to contact everyone else currently on shift over the radio and keep him posted if they spotted her.

"Let's set out and scan the fairgrounds for her," he suggested. "Show me where you saw her last." He turned to Edith. "Stay put. She may come back here when she can't find Jameson," he said calmly.

Panic began to set in when I heard the calmness of his tone towards his wife. I knew it was just an act to keep her from worrying, which oddly made me worry more. A tight knot formed in the pit of my stomach and, half an hour later, when no one had spotted her yet, that feeling doubled. I scanned the crowd, my eyes darting from one face to another, searching for her familiar features amidst the sea of people.

By this time Randy had convinced everyone he knew to look for her. Almost a hundred people were calling her name, searching every ride, every booth, every stall and parked car for her. Yes, Rayne's diamonds had heeded the call.

"Rayne?" I called out, my voice lost amidst the laughter and chatter of the other fairgoers.

With each passing minute, my worry grew, gnawing at the edges of my mind like a relentless predator. I weaved my way through the throngs of people, most of which were calling her name, scanning every inch of the grounds, my heart pounding in my chest, my footsteps quickening with each frantic step.

I called out to anyone who would listen and asked them if they'd seen Rayne, holding up the photo that I'd taken on my phone shortly after we'd gotten engaged to anyone who didn't know her. I described what she was wearing, told those that knew her to keep an eye out for her. But no one had seen her. It was as if she had vanished into thin air.

I checked the bathrooms for the third time, the food stalls, even the Ferris wheel where we had just shared such a special moment. But there was no sign of her anywhere.

My mind raced with all the worst-case scenarios, each one more terrifying than the last. Where could she be? Was she hurt, lost, or worse?

As I continued to search, my thoughts were consumed by her absence. Every shadow seemed to hold a whisper of her presence, every passing stranger a potential clue to her whereabouts.

But despite my efforts, she remained hidden, her absence casting a shadow over what should have been a joyous occasion. And as the minutes stretched into hours, I couldn't shake the sinking feeling that something was terribly wrong.

Her parents continued to call her cell phone while everyone else scanned the fairgrounds. Every officer on the force was called in to search. We'd ridden there together, and her Jeep was still parked in the same spot.

"Here," someone shouted. "I found her purse and her phone."

Sabrina rushed up to me, holding the bag Rayne had been carrying earlier. "I only found it because the phone was ringing," she said a little breathlessly. "I heard it over behind the toilets."

"Where?" I asked, and then followed Sabrina as we ran to the spot where she had found Rayne's bag and phone.

"There." She pointed to the muddy ground behind the toilets. There was a chain link fence behind the area, separating the parking lot from the row of porta-potties. Part of the fence was not connected, and the space was large enough for people to get through it.

"Fan out from here. Let's search the parking lots," I called out to the dozen or so people who had followed us there.

Spying Aria, I held up Rayne's phone. "Can you unlock it?"

Aria rushed over and punched in Rayne's four-digit code. I made note of the digits for future use. "I only know this because we made our codes up together. It's mine on my phone too," she said, handing me the phone.

"What are you looking for?" Sabrina asked as I opened the photo app.

"Anything," I said, grasping at straws.

I ran through all of the photos she'd taken of us in the past few hours. An image of us shortly after I'd proposed while we'd been at the top of the Ferris wheel. Another of us on the carousel before our engagement. Some of us with all the pies. One of Aria, Sabrina, and Rayne at the hair salon earlier today.

Then an odd image of a sheet of paper with numbers filled the screen and I frowned.

"What's this?" I asked Aria and Sabrina, who both frowned at the image and shook their heads.

"Not sure," they both said.

I sent a copy of the image to my own phone and scanned the images of us again.

I almost missed it, almost didn't see him, lurking there in the shadows. The first image that I saw of him, right there in the background, was when we were in the hall of mirrors. Rayne and I were smiling at duplicates images of ourselves, and he was in the background. It was the look on his face that caused me to pause.

Then I scanned the other images taken that evening and noticed him in at least four others that Rayne had taken of the night.

"You took a video of our proposal?" I turned to Aria. "Let me see it," I said, holding out my hand for her phone.

I watched as the video started and moved between the ground and far above. Aria's head was smashed up against mine as we watched the moments before Rayne had spotted her. In the video, the Ferris wheel had just stopped, and I'd just wrapped my arm around Rayne's shoulders.

Instead of focusing on the faraway images of us, I scanned the crowd below us. He was there, standing at the base of the wheel, watching, waiting.

"Shit," I growled and glanced around for Randy. Taking both phones with me, I sprinted across the grass to where Randy was standing.

"Do these numbers mean anything to you?" I asked a little breathless.

Randy took Rayne's phone and frowned down at them. "The last one is the number for the address to the city and county building." He flipped through the images. He instantly saw what I had. "Jackson Pennington," he said under his breath, then he glanced at me. "His office is in the city and county building."

I nodded. "What's his home address?"

"I'll drive," Randy said, taking off. "Aria, Tobias, please make sure that Edith gets home safe." He tossed the van keys to Aria.

As we entered the parking lot, Randy yelled at Owen, who was standing by his patrol car directing traffic as everyone left the event.

"We're taking this," Randy said, jumping into the driver's seat.

"Sure thing, boss," Owen said. "Did you find..." Owen's words were cut off as Randy shut the door and took off at full speed.

"That son of a bitch," Randy said as he drove through town. "If he lays one finger on my daughter..."

"I get a chance at him first," I warned.

"Why?" Randy said as we weaved around traffic.

"I'm guessing these numbers mean something to him. Guessing he found out she had them. Hell, maybe Rayne had even figured out what they meant. Somehow connected him to..." To what? I thought quickly. "The only thing left unsolved was the murders," I said, feeling a shiver race down my spine.

"Why in the hell would Jackson Pennington murder Sharon Taylor?" Randy asked, taking a corner at top speed.

I glanced down at Rayne's phone. "This could be a phone number?" I said, pulling out my phone and punching the digits in.

The phone rang. When someone answered, I could hear breathing, Rayne screaming, then a gun shot before the line went dead.

"Shit, that was her," I said, jerking the phone from my ear. I turned the Mobile Data Terminal screen towards me and punched the phone number in. It took a moment before the data came up. "It's his cell number all right." I looked down at the phone and swiped the screen to the photo before the image of the numbers. This image was a hand-written note. I read it out loud for Randy.

"You're falling into his trap. He's going to pin everything on you. We are going to take the blame for everything. Meet me tonight behind the bar in the alley. I have the proof you asked for."

"This must be from Evelyn. To..." I stilled as it hit me.

"Quincy," Randy finished for me as we slowed down.

Shit. I looked at the next image. "What's this?" I showed Randy the image of a receipt.

He frowned at it.

"That's an old-school receipt for an evidence locker and police file case that we used to give out. We haven't used those in years." I glanced up as he stopped the car and shut off the lights and siren as we paused at the end of a long driveway just out of sight of the house. "I doubt he's here," Randy said. "Jackson is too smart to bring her back here. We'll check." He glanced at me. "Tell me you're armed."

I nodded. "You take the left, I'll go right."

We climbed out of the patrol car and both darted in different directions.

I raced through the brush and trees, keeping out of sight of the house until I could approach it without the possibility of being seen. I glanced in a few dark windows, feeling defeated.

Randy was right. There wasn't a car in the driveway or in the detached carport area.

"What now?" Randy asked after we looked in a few more windows. "The place is empty."

I thought. "Think you can find the locker or file that this goes to?" I asked, holding up Rayne's phone.

We rushed back to the car. When we pulled into the

station, Owen was there waiting with everyone else that was on duty.

"This way." Randy ran through the office and headed towards the evidence locker. He used his keys to unlock the doors and gate and then glanced down at Rayne's phone again.

"Nine thousand thirty-two. Shit." He closed his eyes. "Storage room." He turned and darted down the hallway. "We moved them a few years back. Anything older than ten thousand went back here." He opened another locked door and flipped on the lights. Rows and rows of file cabinets and stacked boxes on shelving filled the massive area.

It took him less than five minutes to find the box marked nine thousand thirty and when he pulled out the thick file marked thirty-two, I held my breath.

"It's an old arrest report for a teenager named Jack Wheeler. He was caught skinning a dog alive. They found several other skinned animals at his residence after an investigation. I don't remember this case. I think I'd just taken the chief job." Randy turned the page and we both gasped. There, in black and white, was an old image of a very young Jackson Pennington. "The Wheeler place is just outside of town on the bayou," Randy added, pointing to the address on the report. "Let's go."

This time more than half a dozen cop cars followed Randy and I out of town. We headed down a dirt road. When we came to a downed tree across the road, we parked.

"How would he get through this?" I asked as I climbed out and glanced around.

"There." Someone shined a flashlight on a large black SUV.

"That's his," Randy said, walking over to it.

"Four-wheeler tracks," someone else shouted.

"Block his car in," I called out as we all shot through the brush, following the tracks.

We made our way through the woods. It seemed to take us forever to hack our way through the thick brush and stay on the tracks.

When we spotted the lights from the cabin, we all stopped and gathered around the four-wheeler. Randy took the keys and pocketed them, then motioned to his men. Three of them headed to the right, three to the left. I went with Randy straight down the middle, directly towards the cabin's doors.

Everything was quiet. The moment we stepped up onto the porch, the steps made a loud creaking sound under our weight. Then I realized the lights coming from inside the cabin weren't candlelight. Dark smoke was streaming out from under the door and cracked windows.

I heard Rayne cough from somewhere inside the burning building and sprang into action.

Without thinking, I busted through the old wood door with Randy right on my heels. Flames licked at us and surrounded Rayne, who sat in the middle of the room, tied to a chair. There was blood trickling down her lip and from above her left eye, and her clothes were torn in places. The flames, thankfully, hadn't reached her yet.

"My god," I said, rushing to her. I knelt in front of her and cut the ropes with the knife that I kept in my boot.

"It was Jackson Pennington," Rayne said with a cough towards Randy as I gathered her up.

"Yeah," Randy said behind us, shielding himself from the growing flames. "Where is he?"

"He took off out back shortly before you got here, after he set the fire," she said with another cough. I lifted her gently into my arms and the three of us sprinted out of the flames onto the porch and into the dark night.

"I broke free and shot him in the leg before he overpowered me again. He knocked me out. I could have been out for a long time." She held onto me. "He was bleeding pretty badly. I doubt he could have gotten far on foot."

Just then another shot rang out, and Randy fell beside us. I fell to the ground, shielding Rayne's body with my own as more shots rang out in the night.

"Dad!" Rayne cried out, trying to push me off her so she could crawl to her father, who lay motionless a few feet from us. I could hear the fire behind us grow, consuming the old cabin, as the night suddenly grew oddly quiet.

"Clear!" someone shouted.

"Over here." Another shout.

"We've got him."

"Dad!" I let Rayne crawl to her father and moved over to his side. Blood trickled out of his left leg just above his knee.

"Damn it," Randy hissed.

"Officer down," I called out. "Get an ambulance out here."

"One's already on the way," Randy said with a sigh. "My boys called it in when we left." He coughed as he cupped Rayne's face. "I love you. If I don't make it through this, take good care of your ma." Then he passed out while Rayne cried.

Chapter Twenty-Eight

Rayne

My father was in surgery for six hours. Almost every minute of that time I sat holding my mother's hand in mine while Jameson held my other hand. Tears blocked my vision as people came and went in the waiting room at the hospital.

When someone, a nurse or EMT, tried to look at my own cuts, I pushed them away.

Only after the first hour did I finally let Jameson clean the dried blood from me. A jacket was placed over my shoulders. Someone handed hot coffee to me and to my mother.

Shortly after the sunlight started streaming into the windows behind us, the doctor came out to talk to us.

"The bullet grazed his femoral artery. He had a lot of tissue damage that took a while to patch up. He may walk with a limp from here out and will need a lot of physical therapy. Possibly another surgery in his future to help that process."

"Can we see him?" I asked.

"One at a time. He's still groggy but has been asking about you," the doctor said to Rayne.

"Go." My mother hugged me. "Go see him first. I'll come in after and stay with him."

I wanted to argue but knew better after seeing the determined look in her eyes. I wobbled slightly when I stood since I'd been sitting for so long. Jameson was there to steady me.

"We'll be right here," he said softly.

I touched his hand and then followed the nurse back to the recovery room where my dad was hooked up to many loud machines. His leg was bandaged and rested on a stack of pillows. There were tubes sticking out of his arms and his skin was so pale. His eyes were closed but when I moved closer, they slid open.

"You're okay?" he asked softly. I nodded and sat down next to him.

"You?" I asked, my voice cracking slightly.

"I've been better," he said with a weak smile. "First time getting shot. I think I'll make it my last."

His attempt at humor had tears flooding my eyes. I rested my forehead against his chest and felt his hand lift to brush my hair.

"I love you, Daddy," I said into his chest.

"I love you too, sweetie." He sighed and closed his eyes.

I watched him sleep for a while before going back out and letting Mom have her turn. An hour later, he was wheeled into a private room. After breakfast, the room started flooding with well-wishers and flower deliveries. My diamonds in the mud, as Jameson had described them.

Jameson tried to convince me to head home to shower, change, and get some sleep shortly before lunch.

"Go," my mother urged. "We'll be here."

"What about you?" I asked her.

"I'll get some rest while your father does." She smiled at me. I hugged her and then let Jameson lead me away. I was too tired to argue at that point.

As Jameson and I returned home, exhaustion weighed heavily on my shoulders. The events of the night had left us both drained. As I stepped through the familiar threshold, the weight of worry for my father still hung over me like a dark cloud.

"Shower first and then food?" Jameson suggested.

I followed him through the house to the bathroom and let him strip my ruined clothes from me. How long ago had it been when I'd dressed so carefully, getting ready for the special night that was supposed to be the most magical one in my life?

We showered and Jameson carefully washed away the dried blood still caked on my skin. When he shut off the shower, I stood still as he dried me off and helped me into a pair of soft sweatpants and a tank top. After he pulled on a pair of boxers, he combed through my hair, gently untangling it as he went. Then we made our way to the kitchen, and I sat at the bar while he heated up some leftover spaghetti. We were both too tired to prepare a proper meal.

The silence between us was heavy with unspoken

thoughts, questions, and worries, but the simple act of being together gave me a sense of solace.

As we ate, the weariness of the night finally caught up with me, and I struggled to keep my eyes open.

Jameson seemed to notice, and he lifted me in his arms and retreated to the bedroom. The softness of the bed was so welcoming as he lay me down and, after he pulled me into his arms, I fell into a deep sleep.

I woke sometime later with a jolt in the quiet darkness. The memories of the night mixed with other nightmares played just out of my conscious reach, hidden somewhere deep in my mind.

The rhythmic sound of Jameson's breathing filled the room, a soothing lullaby after the chaos of the night.

As I lay awake in the darkness, the memories of my ordeal with Jackson threatened to engulf me once again. The fear and helplessness I had felt during those long moments of captivity still lingered, haunting the edges of my consciousness like a persistent shadow.

Beside me, Jameson slept peacefully, his steady heart-beat against my ear a comforting presence in the stillness of the night. I reached out to him, seeking solace in his warmth and strength. His hand found mine, offering silent reassurance in the darkness.

"Jameson," I whispered, my voice barely audible in the quiet room.

He stirred beside me, sensing the unease in my tone. "What's wrong?" he asked, his voice laced with concern.

"I... I can't stop thinking about what happened. I have so many questions." The words tumbled out in a rush. "I keep replaying it in my mind, wondering if I could have done anything differently. Asking myself why. Why did he come after me? Why Jackson?"

Jameson shifted, then the light flickered on beside the bed and he pulled me closer, wrapping his arms around me in a protective embrace. "It's a lot to explain," he murmured, his voice soft. "Those numbers on your phone, the note, the receipt." He ran his hands through my hair. "They all lead to proof that Jackson Pennington used to be called Jack Wheeler, a kid who at the age of thirteen was already skinning live animals." I tensed as Jameson stopped.

"Skinning?" I asked.

He nodded. "The receipt was for an old police report."

"Sharon Taylor. The Dupont brothers," I said softly.

"I'd wager a whole lot more, now that we know where to look." He shifted slightly. "Someone like that doesn't just stop once they've started."

"The bank account," I said. "It must belong to him."

"What bank account?" Jameson asked.

"The numbers. The first one is a bank account. The second—"

"Jackson's cell number. I called it and heard fighting and a gunshot," Jameson said.

"I'd just woken up as he was dragging me into the cabin. The phone distracted him long enough for me to make my move. I pulled my gun out. He must not have known I carry one when I am off duty. After a brief struggle, I managed to shoot him in the leg." I turned to look up at him. "I don't even know if he is alive still."

Jameson shook his head. "Owen shot him through the heart when he aimed your weapon at him, after he shot your dad."

"Good," I said, meaning it.

"Owen texted me what they found. They spent the time while your dad was in surgery tossing his place. They believe the cabin held most of the clues, but they did manage to find evidence to pin all the embezzling on him instead of Sharon Taylor. They had proof he was blackmailing more than a dozen city workers, including several cops."

"Quincy?" I asked, feeling my heart drop.

Jameson nodded.

"They also tied his car to Evelyn's hit-and-run. Apparently, Declan and Evelyn had gone over to Jackson's place one night for a"—he cleared his throat—"threesome of sorts, and Evelyn had found proof of his involvement with the Reapers."

"He was the head of the snake," I said. Suddenly everything fell into place. The four-wheeler he'd used to take me to the cabin, that had been the motorcycle sound the Bobbys had heard. I'd been surprised at how close the cabin was to the Taylor's residence as we'd followed the ambulance carrying my dad out of there. Then I realized that the message Faye had given me from Evelyn made perfect sense now.

"You have rats in your house and the king rat is more powerful than you think. Aim high, Detective Rayne. Thanks for sticking up for me. -Evie P.S. I swear on my son's life that it wasn't Declan that attacked me."

"I failed her. I failed Quincy," I said, tears welling in my eyes as I leaned into his embrace, grateful for his comforting presence.

"You couldn't have known," he said, stroking my hair.

I knew that what he was saying was the truth. Still, guilt weighed heavy on my heart.

"I know," I whispered, my voice choked with emotion.

"There was enough evidence to prove that Jackson was blackmailing Henry Taylor. Which is why they used his place for the meetups after Sharon's death. Henry didn't like it much, but he had his own debts to pay off," Jameson explained. "I'm sure the list of Jackson's victims is very long. We'll get through this together." Jameson kissed the top of my head, his words a promise. "I won't let anything like that ever happen to you again."

"I know it's probably late, but I'd like to head back in to see my dad," I said, shifting away.

"Sure. We can bring your mom some dinner," he suggested as we dressed.

Half an hour later, we walked into my dad's hospital room, a bouquet of flowers from the gift shop downstairs in Jameson's hands and a bag with a box of chicken, mashed potatoes, and corn on the cob in mine.

"Dinner?" I asked after seeing my dad sitting up and smiling at my mom. "You're looking better," I said, glancing at Mom. She looked rested.

"I feel better," Dad said with a chuckle. "We got him."

"We did?" Jameson asked as he set the flowers down.

"Yup," Dad said with a grin.

"Owen and the guys just left," Mom added.

"Tell me," I said, putting the food down on the table in front of Dad. "Tell me everything."

While we ate, my dad filled us in on what Owen had found at Jackson Pennington's residence. Jameson was right, Sharon Taylor hadn't been his first human victim.

"There were more than a hundred images of five other young women, most likely runaways, who had fallen victim to him. The images were found on a private computer in a locked room inside his house. All of the images had been taken in the cabin."

I shivered at this. The same cabin he'd taken me to. I would have, no doubt, been his next victim if not for Jameson's timely phone call and the fact that I'd had a gun on me. Jackson had probably been in a lot pain and had wanted to go for help, so he'd decided to burn the entire place down instead of his usual MO.

"They will start excavating around the cabin after the cadaver dogs arrive in the morning," my dad added. "There were emails from Sharon Taylor to Jackson from a private email address where she accused him of the crimes the attorney general was accusing her of. She threatened that once she found the proof, she would turn it all in."

"So he killed her. Sufficiently shutting the case down," Jameson said.

"What about the brothers?" I asked.

My dad shrugged. "We haven't tied them to Jackson yet. We have, however, tied him to several large drug rings dating as far back as ten years. He bounced around in LA for a while, then Vegas."

"That's what brought me here," Jameson said. "I followed his trail here," he said to the room.

"We are now officially under the assumption that Jackson was the head of the Reapers, correct?" I asked.

My dad nodded slowly. "There is a ton of proof that he organized everything. From the get-go, Jackson was the founder of the Reapers, as far as the drug empire went. The property out on the bayou, the Nest as you called it, was paid for with cash. The same amount of cash was removed from that bank account number you found, Rayne, at the same time. Lisa, at the bank, was one of Jackson's victims. Shortly after you left the bank, she made a call to Jackson and told him about your little visit."

I shivered at this news. I doubt I'd ever be able to look the woman in the eyes again.

"The encrypted files on Quincy's computers were full of data he was compiling. From what we can tell, he was trying to stockpile enough proof to make a move on the man himself, even though he was a victim and deep in the business himself. I believed he was trying to get out. Before..." Jameson sighed.

"Jackson knew how to point all the blame on others," my dad said.

"Yes, and he would have reason to clear the brothers off his competition list. They attacked me and made a very public spectacle of murder. I'm wagering Jackson hadn't approved of that, and he would have felt it his right to remove them as obstacles," Jameson said, getting everyone's attention. "One thing about living and working with the Reapers for over a year, I understand the code they lived by. No killing. At least not by us." He closed his eyes. "We were to pick up and drop off only. Drugs. Money. Guns. Sometimes all at the same time."

"From where?" I asked.

Jameson's eyes moved to mine. "Several places. Some in other counties." He tilted his head. "The old man and the young boy. There's one more loose end I have to check on." He snapped his fingers, then pulled out his cell phone and stepped out of the room.

"What happens now?" I asked my dad as Mom cleared up the fast-food mess.

"Now, I retire," he said. "This moves my timeline up a little." He motioned to his leg as I took his hand. "Think you can convince your fiancé to step in for me?"

I smiled. With all the horrors that had happened in the past hours, I'd almost forgotten the good thing. I looked down at my finger. At the ring I'd dreamed of for years. The man I'd wished for had slid it onto my finger at one of my favorite places.

"Yeah, I think my fiancé will be happy to step up," I said, just before Jameson came back inside.

"Rayne." Jameson's tone had my smile dropping. He walked over and took my hands in his. "I..." He glanced at my parents.

"What it is?" my mother asked.

"I don't know how to say this but, during my time with the Reapers, one of our drop-off points was deep in the bayou. There was this man." He shook his head. "I thought he was old. Ancient. There was this little kid with him that would run around and do his bidding. During the bust, the kid was put into the foster care system. His DNA was taken to see if there were any living relatives because the old man died of a heart attack shortly after we took him into custody."

"It's standard procedure in the county now," my mother added. "We were firm advocates of the law passing." She reached over and laid a hand on my shoulder. "Because of Rayne."

"They found a match. A sister," Jameson said, and I felt my heart stop. "You."

My hearing and vision temporarily ceased.

"He's eight years old, severely malnourished, lacking any education, and completely alone."

"We'll take him," my parents said at the same time.

I turned to them. Love flooded their eyes for a boy they hadn't met yet. My brother.

"I figured," Jameson said. "He's on his way here. Should be here sometime tomorrow. I've requested that he be put into our custody for the time being. Until you're back on your feet or we make an even bigger decision than setting a wedding date," he said with a grin.

I wrapped my arms around him and held on. "I have a brother," I said and felt tears sting my eyes.

Epilogue

Rayne

I couldn't remember the last time I was this nervous. Wiping my sweaty palms on my jeans, I shifted in the chair and glanced over at my parents, who looked just as nervous as I felt.

The only one in the room who appeared calm was Jameson, who was glancing down at his phone.

"They just pulled up outside." He looked up at me. There, deep behind his eyes, I could see his fears. He felt just like I felt.

Taking his hand, I walked over and stood just outside my dad's hospital room and waited for the elevators to open.

When they finally slid open, a thin woman stood there holding the hand of a very small boy who appeared no older than six. My heart broke a little at seeing the boy's bones through his skin.

When they started walking towards us, he looked up from the ground and spotted us. His eyes moved to Jameson.

"I know'd you," he said in a thick Cajun accent as he pointed to Jameson.

"Yes, I know you too," Jameson said, kneeling in front of the boy. Then he held out a piece of candy and the boy smiled and quickly took it and tucked it in his pocket.

"Hi," I said, getting the kid's attention. I knelt beside Jameson until I was eye to eye with my brother. We had the same eyes. The same mouth. The kid's hair was a little curlier than mine, but it was the same color. "I'm Rayne. You must be Benjamin?"

"Benji," he corrected.

I nodded. "Benji, I'm your sister."

"Yeah." The kid looked down at his feet.

"Did your pa ever talk about me?" I asked.

The kid shook his head. "No, but my ma did. Before..."

We'd been filled in on how the kid's mother, my biological mother, had died shortly before Jameson had taken his first trip out to the bayou and met Benji for the first time. She had died of natural causes. Word was, since my biological parents, didn't believe in real medicine or even coming out of the swamp, she had died from a simple infection.

"She called you Heather," Benji said. I felt my heart drop in my chest. My name was Heather Dupuis. "I like Rayne better. Can I change my name too?"

I smiled. "If you want to."

He seemed to think about it for a moment. "Maybe later. When I know'd who I am." I smiled at that. "They told me I'm going to stay'd with you." The kid looked at Jameson.

"If that's okay with you?" he answered. "Rayne's parents, the ones who found her and cared for her, would like to have you stay with them. Would you like to meet them?"

Benji shrugged and I held out my hand for his. He hesitated and then took it and we walked into the room.

"What happened to you?" Benji asked my father.

"A bad man shot me," Dad answered with a grin.

Benji frowned. "Did you get the bad man?"

"We did." Dad laughed.

"You a cop?" Benji asked, looking at all of us.

"We are," Jameson said proudly.

"You too?" Benji looked up at me.

"I am." I smiled.

"Then I'd be one too. Someday." Benji smiled. "Just as long as I can eat candy."

We all laughed.

Also by Jill Sanders

The Pride Series

Finding Pride

Discovering Pride

Returning Pride

Lasting Pride

Serving Pride

Red Hot Christmas

My Sweet Valentine

Return To Me

Rescue Me

A Pride Christmas

The Secret Series

Secret Seduction

Secret Pleasure

Secret Guardian

Secret Passions

Secret Identity

Secret Sauce

Secret Obsession

Secret Desire

Secret Charm

Secret Santa

The West Series

Loving Lauren

Taming Alex

Holding Haley

Missy's Moment

Breaking Travis

Roping Ryan

Wild Bride

Corey's Catch

Tessa's Turn

Saving Trace

Christmas Holly

Maggie's Match

The Grayton Series

Last Resort

Someday Beach

Rip Current

In Too Deep

Swept Away

High Tide

Sunset Dreams

Lucky Series

Unlucky In Love

Sweet Resolve

Best of Luck

A Little Luck

Christmas Wish

Silver Cove Series

Silver Lining

French Kiss

Happy Accident

Hidden Charm

A Silver Cove Christmas

Sweet Surrender

Second Chances

Dancing on Air

Entangled Series – Paranormal Romance

The Awakening

The Beckoning

The Ascension

The Presence

The Calling

The Chosen

The Beyond

The Void

Haven, Montana Series

Closer to You

Never Let Go

Holding On

Coming Home

The Hard Way

Never Again

Pride Oregon Series

A Dash of Love

My Kind of Love

Season of Love

Tis the Season

Dare to Love

Where I Belong

Because of Love

A Thing Called Love

First Comes Love

Someone to Love

Fools in Love

FindingLove

Christmas Joy

Always My Love

Forever My Love

Searching for Love

Wildflowers Series

Summer Nights

Summer Heat

Summer Secrets

Summer Fling

Summer's End

Summer Wish

Summer Breeze

Summer Ride

Distracted Series

Wake Me

Tame Me

Save Me

Dare Me

Stand Alone Books

Twisted Rock

Hope Harbor

Raven Falls

Angel Bluff

Day Break

Diamonds in the Mud

For a complete list of books:

http://JillSanders.com

About the Author

Jill Sanders is a New York Times, USA Today, and international bestselling author of Sweet Contemporary Romance, Romantic Suspense, Western Romance, and Paranormal Romance novels. With over 90 books in eleven series, translations into several different languages, and audiobooks there's plenty to choose from. Look for Jill's bestselling stories wherever romance books are sold or visit her at jillsanders.com

Jill comes from a large family with six siblings, including an identical twin. She was raised in the Pacific Northwest and later relocated to Colorado for college and a successful IT career before discovering her talent for writing sweet and sexy page-turners. After Colorado, she decided to move south, living in Texas and now making her home along the Emerald Coast of Florida. You will find that the settings of several of her series are inspired by her time spent living in these areas. She has two sons and off-set the testosterone in her house by adopting three furry little ladies that provide her company while she's locked in her writing cave. She enjoys heading to the beach, hiking, swimming, wine-tasting, and pickleball with her husband, and of course writing. If you have read any of her books, you may also notice that there is a love of food, especially sweets! She has been blamed for a few added pounds by her assistant, editor, and fans... donuts or pie anyone?

facebook.com/JillSandersBooks

x.com/JillMSanders

amazon.com/Jill-Sanders/e/B009M2NFD6?tag=jillm-com-20

bookbub.com/authors/jill-sanders

instagram.com/jillsandersauthor

tiktok.com/@jillsandersauthor

www.ingramcontent.com/pod-product-compliance
Lightning Source LLC
Chambersburg PA
CBHW021236190726
48289CB00005B/1356